Testimony

Novels by Felicia Mason

For the Love of You
Body and Soul
Seduction
Rhapsody
Foolish Heart
Forbidden Heart
Testimony

In memory of Rev. Melvin Carroll Meade
uncle, friend

Felicia Mason

Testimony

KENSINGTON PUBLISHING CORP.
http://www.kensingtonbooks.com

DAFINA BOOKS are published by

Kensington Publishing Corp.
850 Third Avenue
New York, NY 10022

Copyright © 2002 by Felicia L. Mason

All Kensington titles, imprints and distributed lines are available at special quantity discounts for bulk purchases for sales promotion, premiums, fund-raising, educational or institutional use.

Special book excerpts or customized printings can also be created to fit specific needs. For details, write or phone the office of the Kensington Special Sales Manager: Kensington Publishing Corp., 850 Third Avenue, New York, NY 10022. Attn. Special Sales Department. Phone: 1-800-221-2647.

Dafina Books and the D logo Reg. U.S. Pat. & TM Off.

Library of Congress Card Catalogue Number: 2001095357
ISBN 0-7582-0059-5

First Printing: June 2002
10 9 8 7 6 5 4 3 2 1

Printed in the United States of America

ACKNOWLEDGMENTS

Through the years, I have been blessed to have had the opportunity to sing under the direction of some very talented musicians. Whether student directors, church choir directors or industry professionals, each taught me a life lesson and nutured my love of music. Thank you: Elizabeth Kinnett, Mark Montini, Jeffrey LaValley, Dr. Curtis R. Lewis, Edwin, Walter and Tramaine Hawkins, John Guyton, Jr., Sylstea Sledge, Everett Strong, and Thomas Dudley.

No book is written in a vacuum. From answering questions to reading portions or all of the manuscript, several people assisted as I wrote this story. They are Tracy Dunham, Esq.; Michelle Fronheiser; Dr. Lee Tobin McClain; and James R. Ford, minister of music at Sixth Mount Zion Baptist Temple. My editor, Karen Thomas, believed it could be done. Paula Barnes kept the encouragement coming all the way to "The End." And finally, a depth of gratitude to my pastors at Zion Baptist Church, Dr. L.T. Daye, Sr. and Dr. L.T. Daye, Jr., and their wives, Sis. Daisy Daye and Sis. Toni Daye, who continue to encourage and support me in all of my writings.

PART
ONE

ENSEMBLE

1

Let every thing that hath breath praise the Lord.

—Psalms 150:6

"We're already behind schedule, Roger. This isn't a good way to launch this tour."

Roger McKenzie stared straight ahead, his own mind unsettled as he tried to ignore the negative words coming from the man whose job it was to keep them all motivated. Roger would be the last person ever to voice the fears he had had about this trip. But there was little he could do about it at this point. He'd signed contracts, made agreements, committed the group's time and talent. People were expecting the Voices of Triumphant Praise to teach classes, perform concerts, and live up to the hype Roger generated on the choir's behalf.

"Vincent, it's going to be all right," Roger said, giving his friend the assurance he himself so desperately needed. "God's grace is sufficient."

Roger had leveraged so much to make this tour happen: time, money, and personal relationships. His total concentration had been on the benefits of getting this particular message out when those around him said it couldn't be done. He, however, answered to a higher authority. And the word from on high had been to go forth.

The Reverend Vincent Hedgepeth nodded. "I believe and trust in grace, Roger. But I also know that—"

Roger held up a hand, staving off the flow of negative energy from the man everyone in the choir called Reverend Vince.

"If you want to leave now, you can," Roger said. "I'm going forward and so is the tour."

With that, Roger, founder and director of the Voices of Triumphant Praise Gospel Choir, got up and made his way past five rows of seats where choir members sprawled on their tour bus. Some slept; others read. Krista, arms raised, unraveled large green rollers from her hair. Roger smiled at her and she winked up at him.

"I didn't have time to do this before we left," she said.

"You missed one," Roger said, lifting a strand of hair and guiding her hand to the curler.

"Thanks."

He continued on his way. These people were his family, his way of life. They depended on him, looked up to him. And on this, their latest tour, he would be able to give back to all of them the joy they'd given him. And maybe, just maybe, they'd make a mark on the world. That, above all else, was what he hoped and what he wanted.

Roger had big dreams for this choir. With their latest CD, *Spread the Word,* he hoped the word would be spread about the choir as well as the love of God. Roger lived and breathed gospel music. He loved singing, directing, and writing the music. It was all he'd ever wanted to do.

He stopped at a small dining area on the custom-made bus and reached into a bag of pretzels on the table. They'd gotten the bus fully outfitted from a country-and-western singer who'd upgraded to a newer model. Getting the stench of cigarettes out of the vehicle had been harder than overhauling its engine. The bus had been a blessing though, coming at a time when he'd maxed out his credit cards trying to get the choir and their equipment from engagement to engagement every weekend in rented vans and cars.

The Voices of Triumphant Praise had been riding in high style for the past couple of years. And they'd actually outgrown the confines of the bus. All of their sound equipment and the musicians' instruments traveled behind in a white panel truck driven by their sound technician. The money earned from this tour would allow them to get the truck painted and detailed with the choir's logo and contact number.

But all of that was yet to come. Right now, Roger's worries stemmed from another direction.

"Whazzup, Roger?"

He paused, leaning against the built-in shelving. "Not much. You guys all right back here?"

Glenna nodded, then jerked her head toward a seating area beyond the two restrooms. "Georgie and Tyrone have some issues. I'm worried about them."

Roger's gaze took in the couple: his cousin Tyrone in jeans and a Voices of Triumphant Praise sweatshirt, seated on the padded bench; and Georgie, standing above him. Georgie was always dressed up. While most of the choir and musicians had on jeans or sweats for the hours-long bus ride north, Georgie wore a cream-colored linen pantsuit and heels. She looked as if she were going out for afternoon tea. He couldn't hear all of their words, but the whispered intensity of the exchange wasn't lost on him.

"How long have they been at it?"

" 'Bout since we started," Glenna said. "I don't think Georgie wanted to come on this trip. Something's up with them."

Roger silenced the inner sigh that threatened to overcome his spirit. *Is every step a struggle, Lord?*

He didn't expect, nor did he receive, an answer to the entreaty.

Glancing at his watch, Roger estimated the time it would take them to get to their hotel and then the first engagement. They were supposed to open a festival at a community college in Northern Virginia.

"We gonna be late, ain't we?"

He nodded. They were an hour behind schedule. "I already called ahead though. They know we're running late. Instead of being first, we'll go on when we get there."

Glenna nodded and reached for the pretzel bag.

A moment later, the bus lurched hard to the right, then zigzagged across the road.

Glenna yelped as she scrambled for purchase. Roger fell across the table with an "Oomph!"

The big bus lurched hard to the right, sending them both tumbling over. Roger grabbed Glenna and tried to shield her from the snack foods and cups falling all around them.

Someone in the front cried out.

The bus shuddered, and then came to a complete halt.

Seconds ticked by and no one said a word; then chaos erupted.

"My leg, Roger. You're on my leg."

"Sweet Jesus, is everybody okay?"

"What happened?"

Roger helped Glenna up. He brushed off his clothes and hers.

"You all right?" he asked.

She nodded. "Just more shocked than hurt. Go check on the others. I'll see if Georgie and Tyrone are okay."

After inspecting Glenna once again, Roger turned his attention to the passengers in the front of the bus.

"Is everybody okay?" he said, quickly making his way down the aisle. "Anybody hurt?"

He did a visual check and a count of all the choir members: Krista sitting by herself, Danita and Ti'Nisha sharing a seat across from Quent and Lamont, Mary and Drake together, Margaret near the front, with Calvin and Reverend Vince.

The bus driver sat in his seat, scowling out the rearview mirror.

"What happened, Jerry?" Roger asked.

"We either blew a tire or I ran over something in the road."

"Where's Dwayne?" someone asked.

Just then they heard knocking from the middle of the bus.

"Everybody off!" Jerry and Roger said at the same time.

Grabbing purses and carry-on satchels, the choir members hustled off the bus, even as the banging and knocking grew louder. It sounded as if something in or on the bus was about to blow up at any moment.

"Hurry up, ya'll. I don't think this is the day the Lord is calling me home," Glenna said.

"I hear you, girl," Danita said. "Get a move on."

A couple of people chuckled at the exchange, but they all did move a little faster.

"Steer clear of the bus," Roger called. "And somebody check on the truck to make sure Marcus and Scottie are all right."

When everyone was off the bus, Roger and the bus driver investigated the noise. "It sounds like it's coming from here," Jerry said.

The knocking was louder.

"Hey, open the door!"

"It's Dwayne."

Roger and Jerry had to pry the bathroom door open. Dwayne stumbled out. "Man, what the heck happened? One minute I'm standing there taking care of business; the next minute I'm bouncing all over the place."

"You're also bleeding," Roger said.

"Where?" Dwayne said, touching his head. It was his arm that was bloody, though. "Oh, man. I must've cut myself on something."

"We'll get you to the hospital."

"Hospital? It's just a scratch, Roger. I'm all right. Just a little shaken up."

"I'd still like you to get looked at."

Dwayne waved his other arm. "My sister's a nurse. I'll clean it up and have her look at it tonight when we get to D.C. What happened?"

"I don't know," Roger said. "But everybody's outside."

"I'm gonna go check for damage," Jerry said.

Dwayne followed him while Roger did a quick inspection of the rest of the vehicle's interior.

"It's a tire," somebody called from outside.

A strip of black rubber on the road backed up the claim.

Glenna frowned at the folks who stood close to the road surface. "Y'all get back before somebody gets hit," she said, waving her hand at the oncoming vehicles.

Traffic was light, but there were still cars, vans, and trucks whizzing by. The panel truck pulled up behind them. Several people went over to Marcus and Scottie, who were getting out to see what had happened.

A moment later, the crunch of tires and flashing blue lights got everyone's attention. Calvin waved to get the cop's attention, as if the big purple-and-gold bus with *Voices of Triumphant Praise* painted on it hadn't already caught his eye.

The state trooper rolled up behind them and approached. One of the women handed Dwayne a moist towelette to wipe up some of the blood from the gouge on his arm.

"Howdy, folks," the trooper said. "What seems to be the problem?"

Everybody started talking at once. It took the trooper a few minutes to sort things out. With Jerry, he inspected the tire that had blown.

The choir had been blessed. Other than Dwayne's injury and a bump on the head from a falling carry-on, no one was the worse for wear. So, with no other damage to the bus or its passengers, and no clear evidence of any wrongdoing on Jerry's part, the trooper didn't cite the bus driver.

"I have a first-aid kit in the car," the trooper told Dwayne. "I'll get a bandage for you."

As the officer strode back to his vehicle, Krista and Danita checked him out. "He can give me a ticket any old day," Danita said.

"That's the truth, girl. Look at that walk."

"Ya'll need to quit," Glenna said, coming up next to them. She leaned forward with words just for their ears. "But the brother *is* fine."

The three women laughed together as they admired the view.

After handing Dwayne a bandage and shaking hands with Roger and Jerry, the trooper pointed out a place across the road where they could get some assistance. Roger pressed a *Spread the Word* CD into his hands, and the trooper waved good-bye.

"Well, the good news is that that place right over there," Jerry said, pointing across the way a bit, "should be able to get us up and running."

"And the bad news?" someone asked.

"The bad news," Roger answered. "Is that we don't know how long it'll take." *Or how much it's going to cost,* he thought.

Just less than two hours later, with the biggest injuries Dwayne's arm, a bump on the head someone suffered from the carry-on bag, and a charge on Roger's credit card, the choir was ready to get back on its way.

After prayer and cell phone calls to their motel and to the contact for their engagement that evening, the Voices of Triumphant Praise got back on their tour bus.

So far, things weren't going very well. The anxious and suspicious sort would have taken that as a sign.

"We almost didn't make it here tonight," Roger said several hours later. "We got a little banged up in an accident on the way. But by the glory and grace of God we stand before you tonight, a testimony to the goodness of the Lord."

The college-aged crowd buzzed as people carried on their conversations and milled about, mostly ignoring the acts on the stage in the student union hall. Impatient at the delays that marked what was supposed to be the kickoff of Campus Week at the community college in Northern Virginia, much of the audience had already walked out by the time the Voices of Triumphant Praise finally took the stage.

Standing before what should have been a packed room but was instead a rapidly thinning crowd, Roger lifted his right hand and snapped off a four-beat. The choir burst into song, their voices drowning out the irritated hum of the nonchalant audience.

A few people clapped along with the rhythm, but mostly the choir was ignored, much the way a lounge singer is ignored by bar patrons and customers engrossed in their own conversations and dramas.

As he directed, Roger kept glancing over his shoulder, hoping their message landed on willing and needful ears. From the corner of his eye he saw a flash. A strobe light went off on the far left side of the room and several people got up to go see what the attraction was.

Roger's brow creased. He turned back to the choir, but half of them were also trying to see what was happening across the room.

The drummer skipped a beat. Glenna missed a cue. From offstage he saw Georgie shake her head in disgust. Margaret's anxious, embarrassed gaze flickered between the waning audience and Roger. She shrugged, the motion a defeated gesture that summed up the night: The first day and engagement of the *Spread the Word* tour was a complete and total flop.

Roger himself felt defeated.

At their motel a few hours later, he remained in a foul mood. He'd gotten everyone checked in and to their assigned rooms. He'd originally planned a celebratory group dinner for their first night, but because it was so late, people just grabbed something to eat at the diner next to the motel or from KFC a few blocks down the street.

Roger and Reverend Vince shared a room this leg of the trip. Later on, Vincent would meet with some of his seminary buddies, and his wife planned to join them in Philadelphia. While Roger unpacked, Vince sat at the desk, his notebook and study Bible open to the first book of Corinthians.

"The Devil set a trap and we walked straight into it," Roger said, stomping from the suitcase to the closet.

"You sure it was the Devil? He gets blamed for a lot of stuff we put on ourselves." Vincent Hedgepeth, in his early fifties and graying a bit at the temples, liked to think of himself as Roger's older, wiser brother, though their relationship more often took the role of father to son. Since the Reverend Hedgepeth and his wife didn't have any children, Vincent didn't mind the father-figure role. Right now, though, Roger seemed to need more than a father; he needed a friend to offer an objective perspective.

"We were off tonight," Roger said. "The musicians were a half beat behind and acting like they were playing some other gig. Georgie had *attitude* written all over her face. And what was that off in that corner, a step show or something? Those college kids were the rudest bunch I've ever seen. We were an ineffective witness."

"We were three hours late," Vincent pointed out.

Roger reached for a vest in his bag, unfolded it, then threw it on his bed.

"I'm going to call a rehearsal." He reached for the phone on the desk near Vince, but Vince grabbed the receiver and held it away from him.

"And what's a rehearsal going to do? Between the late start and the accident, everybody's already tired and irritable. We had a rough day. A good night's rest is what everybody needs right now. Especially you. We'll start off fresh and right tomorrow morning with prayer and Bible study. I think Paul's letter to the church at Corinth about not focusing on God's plan is where we'll begin."

The not-so-subtle barb hit home.

"All right, Vincent. Just out with it. You've been itching for this fight. What's on your mind?"

Vincent pulled his reading glasses off and leaned back in the straight chair, folding his arms over the slight paunch at his waist. As spiritual adviser to the choir and to Roger, Vincent took his ministerial and counseling duties seriously. "I'm not trying to fight with you, Roger. You asked me to come on this trip to be a counselor. Well, I'm counseling now."

"I meant to the choir members."

"Hmm," Vincent said as he replaced the telephone receiver and pushed the phone out of the way. "So, you're saying you're so perfect you don't need any guidance?"

Roger sighed. Pinching the bridge of his nose, he closed his eyes.

"It *has* been a long day, Hedgepeth. And I still have music I need to go over. What's your sermon tonight?"

Facing Roger, Vincent braced his elbows on his thighs and steepled his hands. "It's not a sermon," he said. "I'm worried about you, Roger. You've been running yourself ragged for months now. It's like you're being chased by a demon the rest of us can't see, and you're making everybody in the group run right along with you."

Trying to ignore Vince, Roger unzipped the long leather bag that protected his keyboard. He pulled the stand out and quickly set it up.

"We got a late start this morning because you overslept," Vince said.

"I had a rough night the night before. I apologized to everyone. . . ."

"It's not about an apology, Roger. It's about listening to your body. At the rate you're going, you're gonna have a heart attack from stress. You're what, twenty-eight? Twenty-nine?"

"I'm thirty-one," Roger said.

"Well, I've got more than twenty years on you and I can see when somebody needs to slow it down. You push yourself and push yourself. When are you gonna rest?"

Roger sat on the edge of his bed as he wiped down the keyboard. "I don't have time to rest," he said. "I have goals. We have commitments. The choir—"

"The choir knows all of the music, has worked long and hard to make this tour happen, and everybody knows what's on the line. Riding people like a dictator isn't going to make them inclined to perform at their peak, particularly after the kind of day we've had. It makes them cranky. You can't *make* success happen, Roger."

Roger didn't believe that for a minute. But he also wasn't in the mood to listen to one of Vincent's sermons, either, not when he had a thousand things to do before his head could finally hit the pillow. That he was actually avoiding sleep was something he didn't want to face.

"Look," he said, snatching up the vest he'd tossed on the bed and hanging it in the closet. "We're gonna be on the road for seven days. Let's make the most of it. I don't want any more nights like this one at that college. We have a demanding schedule over the next week. I'll get some rest when this tour is over. We all will."

He reached in his briefcase and pulled out a roll of antacids. He rolled the wrapper down, popped three of the tablets in his mouth, then ripped the excess paper off and pocketed the remainder of the roll.

Vincent stared at him.

"What?" Roger said, looking around. "What?"

It had been a long time since Margaret let her hair down, literally and figuratively. This trip, though, was her opportunity to do that and some other things.

She shook her hair, letting the long wavy mass fly free; then she closed her eyes and massaged her scalp.

"Your hair's pretty," Glenna said. "I wish mine looked like that."

"I beg your pardon?"

Sharing a room with Glenna Anderson wasn't exactly how Margaret would have made room assignments. She really wanted to be in Roger McKenzie's room. But good little Christians didn't do that sort of thing. And Roger barely gave her the time of day. As long as she sang her parts and wore the right outfit to their singing engagements, Roger was happy. That he cared about precious little else besides his music pricked Margaret to the quick.

"I was talking about your hair," Glenna said, breaking into Margaret's thoughts.

Margaret stared at the other woman. Glenna's hair was cropped short with some sort of chemical that made it bone-straight. Today it was a mild auburn color. In the time since she'd first come to the choir, Glenna's hair had been everything from the red-pink of a boiled Maine lobster to the deep blue of twilight. Margaret had even had the misfortune of seeing a platinum-blonde version of Glenna, platinum with jade streaks. She sometimes wondered if Glenna and Dennis Rodman went to the same hairdresser.

"I . . ." Margaret realized she had nothing to say. She and Glenna had little in common, and the other woman's eyes sometimes seemed to probe too deeply.

Glenna took three dresses out of her garment bag and hung them in the closet. "I brought my own racks, so I'll leave these for you," she said.

"Racks?"

Glenna looked at her oddly, then reached into the closet, pulled out a hanger, and waved it in front of Margaret.

"Oh, you mean hangers. Well, you can use them. I always travel with my padded ones. I don't like to get creases in my clothing."

Glenna glanced at her own wire hangers, then looked back at Margaret. "We've never roomed together before," she said.

Margaret stared in the mirror at her eyebrows. She'd had them arched before leaving, but the left one didn't seem to align quite right. She reached for her purse, wondering if she'd dropped a pair of tweezers in there. "No, we haven't."

"I guess Roger just wanted to mix it up a little, huh?"

Or punish me, Margaret thought.

In the mirror, she watched Glenna return to her battered and nicked suitcase, an ancient and heavy piece of Samsonite. Somehow, Margaret doubted the ill-usage came from any extensive travel on Glenna's part. Then the thought struck her that maybe there were roaches in the other woman's bags.

Margaret clutched her stomach, suddenly imagining all manner of crawling, unpleasant things getting into her own expensive luggage. Her anxious gaze charted the distance between her bags and Glenna's.

It was too late to make a room change, unless she put it on her American Express, footing the cost of the tour's six nights herself. But that would make it seem as though she didn't want to room with Glenna, and that wasn't the impression she wanted to leave with the others, Roger in particular.

With another wary glance at Glenna and her suitcase, Margaret sighed.

It was going to be a long tour.

In their room, Tyrone and Georgie Thomas picked up the argument they'd started on the bus.

"You always take his side!"

Tyrone slammed his shaving kit onto the bathroom sink. "Georgie, you are acting like a six-year-old."

"How dare you! Let me tell you something, Tyrone Blackstone Thomas, I'm only here and with this godforsaken choir because I love *you.* Not Roger. Not his music. You! And lately I've gotten pretty sick of Roger being the third person in this marriage."

He froze. "What are you saying, Georgie?"

She looked at him, her lower lip trembling. Georgie folded one arm across her ample chest and covered her mouth with the other.

"I'm saying, Ty, that I feel neglected. All of your energy, your time, your focus goes to Roger and to Blackstone. What about me—Georgie—and our marriage?"

Tyrone took her hand and squeezed it. "God hasn't forsaken this choir, Georgie. We had an off night. But with everything that happened today—the late start, the accident—it just threw us off, that's all."

Georgie shook her head and stomped away.

"That's what I mean, Ty. Listen to you. I'm talking about us, me and you. And you're talking about the choir. Forget the choir for once, would you? *Can* you?"

He closed the distance between them. "You really feel like I've been neglecting you?"

Georgie spread her arms wide and pirouetted. Silky ribbons in soft peach flowed from her. "I spent fifty dollars on this nightgown and you haven't said a word."

Ty grinned. "Well, I noticed. I was just waiting for, you know," he said, glancing toward one of the two double beds.

Georgie sighed. "It's not just Roger and the choir," she said. "I worry about how we're going to pay the bills. The time I'm taking off from the bank for this tour is money we need. There's no financial gain in running around after Roger all the time."

Left unsaid but hanging between them stood two facts: that she made more money than he did, and that she didn't have to have come on this trip. Georgie wasn't really in the choir, even though she knew the music. She'd come because, she claimed, it was the only way to spend any time with Tyrone. That argument, however, had played out between them a week ago.

Tyrone sucked his teeth. "Georgie, you knew when you married me—you knew when we met—that gospel music is what I do. I'm gonna support my cousin. Roger needs me. And the studio and Blackstone, well, that's my dream. I *do* bring in income for us."

"Well, I need you, too," Georgie said. "And it's not about the money."

Tyrone crossed his arms. Was she finally going to say it? They'd been dancing around the issue for weeks now. He'd even started spending more time at the small recording studio he managed just to avoid the arguments. Now, though, it looked as though they were going to face the issue head-on.

2

He helps me do what honors him most.

—Psalms 23:3

For the most part, Calvin Jackson's work with the Voices of Triumphant Praise could best be described as that of gofer. He did a little of this, a little of that. He ran errands for people sometimes, and since he could sew a straight stitch, sometimes he'd repair a rip in a costume.

But mostly Calvin just reveled in the music that made him feel good. Calvin's mama had always listened to gospel music, bless her heart. Mama'd been gone now for a couple of years, and Calvin just kind of made do by working odd jobs when and where he could. He knew some people called him slow. But Mama had always said he did things the way a thinking man did: deliberately and with care.

Calvin missed Mama, but he'd been doing all right since she went on to be with Jesus. The hardest part had been moving out of the house where they'd lived for as long as Calvin could remember.

Now he lived in a rooming house. He had his radio, so he could listen to the preaching and the gospel music, and he had a little television, one that Mama had saved up for and given him for Christmas one year. The rooming house wasn't so bad. But Calvin didn't like all the cussing and the comings and goings of the other residents. So, whenever he could, he stayed near Roger McKenzie and the Voices of Triumphant Praise. They ate real good, Miss Glenna was really nice to him, and the music was always there to keep him company.

It didn't bother Calvin one bit that he shared a room with two other guys, even though he got the cot. He was happy to be on the tour with the choir. Roger took care of him and made sure he was doing okay. So did Marcus.

Right now, though, Calvin wished he'd really been asleep when his roommates opened the door with a loud "Shh" and "Calvin, you up?"

He'd been in the middle of his prayers. Mama always said not to let anything disturb your conversation with the Lord, so he didn't say anything when Scottie tiptoed over to him and said, "I think he's out."

By the time he had finished, though, and would have rolled over to greet them, the guys—Scottie, Quent, and a voice he didn't recognize—were talking about things Calvin didn't want to know. Bad things. And then they talked about some of the ladies in the choir. Nasty things that Calvin knew weren't very nice.

Calvin closed his eyes really tight, but he could still hear them talk and laugh.

And he didn't like it one bit.

In their room, the argument between Georgie and Tyrone escalated.

"You care more about him than you do me."

"Him who, Georgie? Say it; just say it."

She whirled around, a brush in her hand. "Roger. It's Roger you'd prefer to spend all of your time with. Sometimes I wonder why you even married me."

"You know why I married you, Georgie. I love you."

She stomped away. Pressing her hands flat on the dresser top, she stared, unseeing, at herself in the mirror. "You have a funny way of showing it," she said after a minute.

Tyrone came up behind her. He put his hands at her waist. When she didn't pull away, as he'd expected she would, he pressed close and caressed her slowly, sensuously. His hand inched lower. She sucked in her breath.

"I don't want to fight, Georgie," he said, nuzzling her neck. "But I do want us to talk about this."

She met his gaze in the mirror. "There's not much to say."

"I think there is. Come on."

He took her hand.

"Where are we going? I'm not dressed."

"We're not going out. Just over here," he said, leading her to the beds covered with cheerful yellow-and-blue spreads. He sat her on the edge of one and he sat on the opposite, facing her. Their hands, clasped together, were all that physically linked them now.

"Remember how it was when we first met?" Tyrone said. "We'd talk for hours, not even aware that the time had passed."

Georgie smiled. "My grandmother used to say there weren't that many words between a man and a woman."

"I don't think we used them all up yet. Do you?"

She shook her head but didn't meet his gaze.

"Look at me, Georgie."

Slowly she raised her head until their gazes locked.

"You're the most beautiful woman in the world. I think I fell in love with you when I saw you standing in that concert line."

Georgie smiled. "I was on a date with another man."

"Yeah, but you didn't marry him, did you?"

She shook her head. "No." Her eyes once again studied the floor.

"Is that what you regret, Georgie?"

She was quiet for a long time, so long that Tyrone's heart sank. He let go of her hands and leaned back on his bed.

"It's not what you think," she finally said.

"So now you're a mind reader."

Georgie winced. She folded her hands together and stared at them for a minute. Then, finally, she raised her head.

"Ty, there's something you need to know. Something I should have told you a long time ago."

He folded his arms and waited.

She reached for his hands then pulled back, hesitating as conflicting emotions warred within. Taking a shaky breath, Georgie willed herself the strength she'd need to get through the next few minutes. Maybe the next years of her lifetime. What she *needed* to tell him should have been said a long time ago, but she'd never found the right words or time. Now, though . . .

Georgie opened her mouth, ready to confess, ready to lay bare her soul before the man she loved with all the depth of her being. When they first met, she'd initially been attracted to his cover-model looks, the *GQ* clothes, and that smile. Together, she knew, they made a good-looking pair. But what she'd later discovered was that a gentle spirit and true love of God formed the core of Tyrone Thomas. He was everything she'd always wanted in a man: saved, honorable, dependable, creative, hard-working.

With a start, she realized that she shouldn't—couldn't—jeopardize the security she'd found with Tyrone, even if it meant holding on to her secret. The more she thought about it, the more she realized she couldn't, just couldn't, tell him.

"What is it, Georgie?" he asked.

She stared into his eyes, the brown depths full of love and caring for the woman he thought she was. Georgie shook her head, again rejecting the confession she wanted to make. Now was not the time for that.

But there was something else.

Clasping his hands in hers, she raised them to her mouth and pressed a kiss there. Then, with love and hope shining in her eyes, she met his gaze.

"Ty, I want a baby."

At first, Glenna didn't know what to make of Margaret's attitude. Then it dawned on her.

Usually, being around all the people in the choir made her forget about her past, the life she'd escaped. But Glenna knew there might always be somebody who'd throw the burning acid of her mistakes right back in her face.

Margaret was one of those types.

Glenna bit the inside of her mouth. Sometimes it hurt so bad to be the one everybody pointed at and whispered about. Until just now, watching Margaret wrench about, looking for a safe place to put her purse or whatever, Glenna had managed to keep the bad thoughts in the pit where they belonged.

She shook out the white blouse that was part of the choir's just-in-case wardrobe and reached for a rack. "I'm not going to steal your stuff," she said. "I may have done some stuff in my day, but I'm not a thief."

Margaret stared at Glenna. "I didn't say . . ."

Glenna tossed the garment and hanger on the bed. "You didn't have to *say* anything. I see it all over your face. Come here," she said, walking to the bathroom mirror that stretched the length of the vanity.

Cautious but curious, Margaret followed. The two women stood side by side in the bathroom, staring at their reflections. Margaret was tall, shapely in an athletic way. Almond-shaped eyes shielded by long lashes were one of her best features, but the most remarkable thing about Margaret's face was her mouth. Not too large, not too small, she had lips like the lipstick models in magazines, and her makeup, always flawless, looked as if it was professionally applied every day.

Glenna, on the other hand, was small. And she carried a street look, a hunted and haunted look that couldn't be shielded with cosmetics. But Glenna's smile made anyone who saw it smile in return. It came from the heart, where dreams and fears and hopes and eternal longings lodged. Glenna had a good heart even if she'd had a rough life. And that made all the difference between the two women.

In the mirror, one woman had the bearing and appearance of grace and leisure and opportunity, while the other looked as though tough breaks, hard times, and bad luck had come calling a few too many times.

"Look at us," Glenna said.

"What?" Margaret asked when all Glenna did was stare at their reflections.

"Two eyes, one nose, one mouth. Some eyebrows. I've got a couple of freckles. But other than that, the package is the same."

Margaret raised a perfectly arched brow. "And?"

"And I was just thinking about how alike we are," she said. "You know, two women. But look at how different, too."

Margaret barely managed to keep from rolling her eyes. "Is there a point to this?"

"Yeah. There's a point." She watched Margaret fold her arms.

"Well?"

Glenna faced the other woman. "Why do you treat me like I'm nobody? Just 'cause I ain't got money like you do and I ain't been saved all my life don't mean you should act like I'm a nobody."

"Don't be ridiculous," Margaret snapped. "We just don't know each other that well."

She reached for the bar of hand soap and ripped the paper wrapper from it. She balled up the paper, leaned back, and spotted the trash can that she then dropped it into. Next, she reached for a glass, plucked off the sanitary coaster top, and turned on the cold-water tap.

"You're doing it again," Glenna said. "Do you know what it feels like when people act like you're invisible?"

Margaret drank from the glass of water, then carefully placed the half-full glass on the vanity top. "I don't know what you're talking about. We've just never roomed together on a road trip. Maybe this is Roger's way of making sure everyone gets to know each other better."

Without again meeting Glenna's gaze, either directly or via the mirror, Margaret went back out into the room they'd been forced to share.

Glenna ran a hand over her face, then bowed her head for a moment. The prayer, a quick entreaty, was for a breakthrough.

Then she followed Margaret to the main part of their room. This time, though, she pushed her suitcase out of the way and sat on the bed while Margaret unpacked.

The women in the choir had three specially-made outfits for their engagements. For this trip, they carried all three plus a white dress and a black dress. The standard black and white—usually a black skirt and a white blouse—went along, too. The black and white was supposed to be uniform, even though they weren't all identical.

But even from where she sat watching Margaret Hall-Stuart pull and spread out her clothes, Glenna could see the difference in the quality of their garments. Glenna's clothes, always clean and neatly pressed, came from the seven-dollar store new and from the Salvation Army thrift shop used. Margaret's clothes, on the other hand, all had that department store, specialty shop, dry-clean-only look. Glenna wouldn't be at all surprised if one of Margaret's dresses cost as much or more than her rent.

Rooming with Margaret Hall-Stuart would be either a trial or a learning experience. Glenna hoped for the latter but knew the former to be the more likely scenario. She'd realized a long time ago that the advantages of learning outweighed the disadvantages of ignorance.

"I think Roger has a lot of stuff planned for this trip that is gonna be different for us," Glenna said.

"What do you mean?"

Glenna leaned back, her hands supporting her on the bed. "Well, the music, for one. Look at the type of songs we've been learning. They have a different tone and feel to them."

Pausing for a moment, Margaret's gaze connected with Glenna's. "You're right, now that you mention it. There's an urgency that wasn't there in some of his earlier work." She shrugged. "But I like it."

Glenna chuckled. "Yeah. I noticed."

Margaret, who was known as the choir member least likely to make waves or be anybody's friend, had to smile at that. "What's so funny?"

"The two sides of you," Glenna said. "I don't know if everybody else sees it, but it kind of tickles me."

"What are you talking about?"

Sitting up for a moment, Glenna switched positions and stretched out on the length of her bed and grinned at Margaret. "Actually, I think it's sweet."

"What?" Margaret said as she zipped open a cosmetics bag.

"Your crush on Roger."

That got Margaret's attention. The cosmetics bag dropped to the bed, lipsticks and compacts spilling out and rolling to the floor. Margaret stood stock-still.

"What makes you think I have a crush on Roger?"

"He doesn't know," Glenna said, ignoring Margaret's feign of innocence.

"Know what?"

"Roger doesn't know you're in love with him. But I can see it. It's written all over your spirit."

Slowly Margaret sat down on the edge of her bed, her hands clasped together one moment, then reaching for one of the fallen compacts the next. She glanced at Glenna. "I've heard that about you," she said. "That you 'see' and feel things that other people can't."

"I'm not a psychic, Margaret."

"Then why did you say you can 'see' something in my spirit?"

For a moment, Glenna didn't say anything. She just stared into Margaret's concerned brown eyes. The air and energy between the two women lifted and circled the room, changing their environment, cleansing them of the masks and the artifice they both, Margaret in particular, liked to wear.

Maybe, Glenna thought, the two of them rooming together wouldn't be so bad after all. She sensed in Margaret a shield coming down. But there was something more, something dark and potentially dangerous.

When finally Glenna spoke, her voice was barely above a whisper. "You're gonna have to be strong, Margaret. A storm is coming."

The dark shadows closed in on him, suffocating him as he slept. Roger fought, flailing his arms, kicking his legs, screaming at the top of his lungs.

But no sound came from his mouth.

His cries for help went unheeded because he'd failed, yet again, to listen and to obey.

"I'm sorry. I'm sorry!" The words echoed through his consciousness but remained locked in his soul.

From a distance, as if an ocean away, he could see the outline of a body sound asleep—or dead—on a platform. The body slowly sat up, faced him.

"Come to me, Roger." The voice sounded as clear as the day had been. "Give up. Give in."

He flinched and gathered his legs to his chest. Had he been aware of his action, the fetal position would have told him important things he needed to know. But Roger only felt his own pain, his own failing struggle. His fight was with a power that held ultimate strength, ultimate power. Knowing that, and knowing that he would ultimately be defeated, Roger continued to deny the demons.

"Yea, though I walk through the valley of the shadow of death, I will fear no evil. I will fear no evil. I will fear no evil. I will fear no evil."

He rocked as he chanted, the words a small comfort, a lifeline in the midst of a fierce storm.

"Though I walk through the valley of the shadow of death, I will fear no evil. No evil. Fear no evil."

Roger's body shook as with a fever while sweat drenched his body and the clean white sheets he lay upon. A moment later, chills ripped through him. But he continued to pray the prayer of faith, the prayer that had sustained the saints of old, the prayer that would see him through the challenge and the test of this hard night.

"Surely goodness and mercy, Lord," he hollered out. "Mercy, mercy, mercy! Mercy shall follow me all the days of my life. And I will dwell Lord, with you, with you, only with you."

"Roger! Roger!"

Hands grabbed at him, trying to pull him away, to take him under.

He had to fight. Every night he had to fight. His strength waned, though, wavering under the repeated assaults.

"Wake up, Roger."

Reverend Vince glanced about, looking for something, anything. He needed a means to help Roger shake the nightmare that gripped him. He grabbed the ice bucket from the desk and darted to the bathroom. The tap water ran tepid, but it would do the trick.

"Roger, wake up. It's a dream. Roger! Can you hear me?"

As if doing battle with unseen foes, Roger rolled around on the bed, the sheets and light blanket a tangle trapping him physically as surely as the dream spirits that assaulted him.

Vincent yelled Roger's name one more time, then dumped the bucket of water over his head.

Roger hollered and shot straight up, sputtering, gasping for breath. Arms flailing, he jumped from the bed. The lamp, telephone, and radio crashed to the floor. Hollering as if something chased him, Roger darted for the door, water dripping from his head and T-shirt. Vincent dashed after him and tackled him. The two men fell to the floor, tumbling over each other, Roger fighting and kicking the entire time.

"Roger!"

Vincent slapped his friend and saw the veil of the nightmare slowly lift from Roger's dazed gaze.

Suddenly, pounding sounded on the wall of the room next to theirs. "Shut up in there!"

Vincent grabbed Roger's face in his hands. "Wake up, Roger. It's just a dream. Talk to me, brother. Talk to me."

"Shut up!" the voice from the other side of the wall yelled. "Why don't you people go to sleep?"

"V-Vince?" Roger's voice carried vestiges of the battle still gripping him.

Tears began to fall from his eyes—first one, then another, and soon a stream even as he tried to catch his breath. "I won, Vince. I won this time."

3

"You want to talk about what happened in the room?" Vincent asked.

Roger and Vincent sat at a table in the twenty-four-hour diner adjacent to the motel. Dawn had yet to break over the horizon, but the two had been sitting there for a while, Roger sucking down black coffee. It had taken Vince nearly an hour to get him calmed down after his nightmare. A shower had worked wonders on clearing the cobwebs from his friend's head. Then a call to the front desk got them a new room after a vague explanation about water all over the mattress.

"I don't know," Roger said.

"You don't know what happened or you don't know if you want to talk about it?"

Roger smirked. "Probably a little of both." Roger sighed. "It's a recurring dream. This is the third time I've had it in as many weeks. It's scary, like I'm supposed to be getting a message and until I get the message, I'll keep having the nightmares."

Reverend Vince waved away the waitress who came with a fresh pot of coffee. "Y'all let me know if'n you need something," she said.

"Tell me about the dream," Vincent prompted.

Roger leaned back. "It always starts the same. But this time," he said, with a pointed look at Vincent, "was the first time getting drowned played a part."

Vince held up a hand. "My apologies. But you were completely out of it. I remember reading a case study about demon possessions. I'm telling you, it was straight out of *The Exorcist*. And that's how you were acting. Like something had you."

"That's just it," Roger said leaning forward. "In the dream, something always does. And this time, there were hands. No faces, but I could feel a malevolent spirit trying to engulf me."

"Do you know what the dream means?" the minister asked. His round face was open, waiting for Roger to offer some sort of explanation. "Dreams are often messages."

Roger shook his head. He had a pretty good idea what the message was supposed to be. It was always the same, no matter what form the dream demons took. He'd been having the dreams for years, but never so many in such a short period. And it wasn't something he could share with Reverend Vince.

"Well, this is a message I could do without," Roger said. "The last time, it was a mouth, actually lots of them, eating my flesh, trying to devour me. I'm always fighting, kicking. Trying to get away."

"How do you? Get away, I mean?"

Roger, quiet for a while, thought about that. He also wondered why this time he'd been able to defeat the dream demons. Well, defeat may have been too boastful a word. The truth of the matter was simple: If Reverend Vince hadn't awakened him, he would have been consumed. Again.

Roger met Reverend Vince's concerned gaze. "I don't."

The motel had a small room off the lobby that served as lounge and eating area for the complimentary continental breakfast served each morning from six o'clock until nine-thirty. About ten tables with two or three chairs around each made up the room. A sideboard held croissants, bagels, orange juice, coffee, and a bowl of fruit when the morning meal was being served. A color television mounted on a ceiling stand carried a little plaque that asked patrons to return the remote control to the front desk. Sunlight streaming in from three windows chased away the feeling of sitting in a place that seemed not much larger than a generously proportioned walk-in closet.

Roger had arranged for the Voices of Triumphant Praise to have its Bible study in the room at ten. Since the serving time was over and televisions were in every guest room, it wasn't likely that they'd be disturbed. And if anyone passed by and wanted to join in the fellowship, they were more than welcome.

In addition to being the service leader and announcer during their concerts on the road, the Reverend Vincent Hedgepeth's role was to keep the choir members focused by offering counseling and prayer when needed, and by maintaining a schedule of group study and worship. Most of the choir members were affiliated with a church at home; a couple of them, however, considered Vincent their pastor and followed him wherever he happened to be ministering.

Vincent took his role seriously, even though he and Roger didn't always see eye to eye on a couple of points. Now, for example, Vincent felt a bit conflicted. His mind still on Roger and what had transpired during the night, Vincent wanted to delay the lesson. But Calvin was there, already asking questions, this time about sin and respect for women. Hunched over her notebook, Glenna sat at the table with Calvin. Some of the others, singers and musicians Vincent planned to get to know better on this trip, sat or sprawled around. Margaret, as usual, sat slightly removed from all the others.

Was it just his imagination, or did everyone look as if the night had been full of battles mostly lost? Vincent surveyed the motley crew. To see them now, no one would ever guess that the music they made together touched the hearts of so many people.

Just as he was about to stand to make an announcement, Georgie Thomas swept into the breakfast room. Today, instead of one of her signature silk or linen suits, she wore khaki slacks and a safari-print blouse. Vincent couldn't remember whether he'd ever seen her so casually dressed. Her hair, usually done in a French roll or some other upswept look, was pulled back and clasped with a barrette. Deep circles framed her eyes, and her mouth formed a thin, tense line.

"Has anyone seen Tyrone?"

Her gaze darted about the room. She moved aside when a couple of the musicians trickled in and straddled chairs at the back.

"I saw him over at the diner when I had breakfast," Marcus said.

Georgie nodded, the motion tense. She turned to leave.

"Why don't you stay and study the Word with us, Georgie?" Vincent invited.

"I—I need to find Tyrone."

"He's never missed a Bible study," Vincent pointed out. "I'll bet he comes in here."

Georgie bit her lip and looked around. "I don't want to intrude."

Calvin hopped up and pulled a chair from an empty table. "Here's a seat for you, Miss Georgie. You can sit by me and Miss Glenna."

Georgie glanced at Reverend Vince, who nodded and smiled at her. Then, slowly she made her way to the table right in front of him and took the seat offered by Calvin.

"I don't have my Bible with me," she said.

"That's all right, Georgie," Vincent said. "Let's begin with prayer. Won't you all stand in His presence."

As the choir members rose, Reverend Vince bowed his head. "Father God, thank you for this day, Lord. . . ."

Outside the breakfast room, Tyrone stood looking in. His gaze lingered on Georgie. He wondered how she could stand there and pray when she'd turned his world upside down.

She was probably praying that he'd come around on the baby issue.

But Tyrone wasn't ready to be a father. He had too much to do before settling into that role. Down the road, once his group, Blackstone, took off, well, that would be a better time.

Besides, as much as they liked to pretend otherwise by tiptoeing around the issue, money *was* a problem. They could barely make ends meet now. Babies were expensive little buggers. Georgie was high on the Mommy and the coo-coo part, while Tyrone's mind played along hospital bills, diapers, formula, and the myriad other expenses of having an infant.

Knowing she'd want to talk about it some more, and wary of any more surprises she might have planned to trip him up, like last night's sexy nightgown, Tyrone tried to steer clear of her—at least until he got his thoughts together.

He needed a diversion, something to get Georgie's mind off the baby track.

"Morning, cuz."

He turned to face Roger and took in the man's weary and worn countenance. "You look like I feel. No sleep."

"If you're asking, the answer is no," Roger said. "If you're telling me that's how you spent the night, I can see that all over your face."

"I can't stay, Raj."

Roger grabbed his shoulder. "You mean with the tour?"

Tyrone shook his head and motioned for Roger to move away from the door so they wouldn't interrupt the prayer. A few feet away, he clarified: "I meant here, for the lesson. Just looking at her . . ."

"What happened between you two last night?"

Tyrone shook his head. "No disrespect, cousin. I just don't want to get into it. It's a husband-and-wife thing."

Nodding, Roger said, "I can understand that. Just know I'm here if you need me, Ty. I'm always available to you."

Taking a good look at Roger, Tyrone shook his head. "Looks like you're the one who needs some help."

"I didn't get a lot of sleep last night."

"Tell me about it," Tyrone mumbled.

"You sure you won't join us?"

Ty shook his head. "I got stuff on my mind. I'm gonna head to the room."

"All right. We practice at three."

Tyrone nodded as he headed to the elevator. "I'll be there."

At his makeshift lectern, Vincent finished the opening prayer and addressed those who'd come to continue their study in the Psalms.

"We're going to deviate a little bit this morning," he told them. "We had some trials just getting here yesterday. I think we need to pause a moment and think about what happened to us and what lessons we're supposed to learn about that experience."

From the place where he'd been standing at the back of the room, Roger stepped forward. While the others were dressed in casual clothes including jeans and sweats, Roger wore a light suit and a polo-style shirt underneath the jacket—a look that lent the outfit a business-casual tone.

"If I may, Reverend Vince."

Vincent ceded the floor to Roger and braced his back against the window ledge as the group turned to face their director.

"We may have gotten off on the wrong foot," Roger said. A glance in Dwayne's direction with his bandaged arm was a reminder to all. "I know the beginning of this trip has been trying, for some of you more than others," he said as he surveyed his choir, making eye contact with each member.

When he paused on Georgie, she sucked in her breath and then glanced away.

"The Lord put a calling on my life and in my heart. What I've tried to do is be true to what His will is. In the music we sing and the songs Tyrone and I write, our purpose is getting the word out about Jesus' love for us. We are just human, though. We make mistakes, but we're saved by grace."

Roger wiped his mouth with his hand, then looked up for a moment. "I know everybody's not here right now, but I'll tell you this much for now. This is something I've been thinking and praying about: a new direction for the choir. Some of you have been with me for years. Margaret. Calvin," he said with a nod to the two long-time choir members. "For some others, it's not been so long, but the fellowship we've had has made up for the years we didn't have.

"We're good. I think you know that. Our sound is top-notch. We've released a couple of CDs and have seen marginal success with them."

A few of the members exchanged glances; everyone clearly wondering where Roger was going with such a somber speech, particularly since he was saying stuff everyone already knew.

Roger folded his arms, closed his eyes, and then told them, "It's time for the Voices of Triumphant Praise to kick it to the next level."

"That's easier said than done," Marcus, the sound technician, said. With his short dreads and heavily tattooed arms, Marcus looked an unlikely sort to be hanging out with a gospel choir.

"I know," Roger said. "I also know how we can do it."

"We're going back in the studio?" Glenna asked.

"Eventually."

"So what's the plan?" someone else wanted to know.

"I'll tell you more later," Roger said. "I want everybody present, including Tyrone."

"Have you seen him?" Georgie asked.

Roger pointed toward the door. "Just a minute ago. He was headed up to the room."

"Excuse me," Georgie said as she rose, then hurried out of the breakfast room. Roger watched her retreat, then faced the choir again.

"Come on, Roger. Don't tease us like that. Give us a hint of what you've got cooking."

He smiled. "Not yet," he said. "But I do want you to start thinking about what grace means to you."

"That's easy, Roger," Calvin piped up. "My mama always told me to say grace before I eat."

Glenna patted his hand. A few people smiled.

"Not that grace, Calvin. But that's a good place to begin. I have a meeting, so I have to leave. We'll pick this up later, though. Marcus, I need to see you for a minute. Reverend Vince," he said with a finger nod, "it's all yours."

Marcus followed Roger out of the small room and into the lobby. "What's up?"

"Do you have recording equipment with you?"

Marcus shrugged. "Some. It's not the best quality. You know I tape every concert performance."

"Is it good enough to be put on tape?"

"If you mean to sell to somebody, heck no. It's just so I can get a gauge of how the sound systems are working. We had a problem when we did that show at the convocation center last month. I don't think it was us, though. The acoustics in that place aren't the best. Why you asking?"

"Just something I'm thinking about."

"Well," Marcus said. "If it's something I need to know, I'd appreciate not hearing about it two minutes before you go announcing to everybody some grand idea that's going to impact my work."

The two men stared at each other, unspoken hostility flowing from Marcus to Roger. Roger's assumption had always been that Marcus was just the surly type. But now he was beginning to wonder. Marcus had come to the group with high recommendations. He was supposedly the best sound man out there, though; that's why Roger put up with the attitude. But things were starting to get out of hand and it was time to do something about the problem.

But not this minute.

"I'll keep you posted," Roger said. "Rehearsal's at three."

"I already know that."

Roger wanted to have it out with Marcus right then and there, but he couldn't be late for his appointment. "We'll talk later."

Marcus turned to head back into Bible study. "Yeah. Whatever."

Twenty minutes later, with the Bible study in full swing, a visitor approached the morning clerk at the front desk. The clerk, riveted in his reading, barely paid the new arrival a second glance.

"I'm here to pick up a package left for me by one of the guests. It should be marked for Antonio."

The clerk walked the length of the counter and poked around for a moment underneath. "Yeah. Here it is."

Without a glance, the clerk handed the package over to the visitor and focused again on his dog-eared copy of the *National Enquirer.* The package safely delivered, the visitor glanced into the little side room off the lobby. He saw the person he was looking for and nodded. With delivery confirmed, he stuck dark wraparound sunglasses on his face and made haste out the motel's front entrance.

4

If you give up your life for my sake and for the sake of the Good News, you will find true life.

—Mark 8:35

That evening, the welcome at Jerusalem Baptist Church was more in line with what Roger had been anticipating for the tour. The Voices of Triumphant Praise were the main event. They had just two costume changes on the schedule, and for the first third of the program, they'd follow a carefully arranged playlist of the songs they would sing. The plan was simple: start slow with a praise song that put the congregation into worship mode; then, through the next three numbers, increase the tempo and the energy until the crowd was on its feet clapping, shouting, and dancing in the aisles. The ensemble would sing a few numbers, including something a cappella, while the others changed.

An artfully crafted announcement, one so skillfully woven into the concert commentary that people wouldn't recognize it as a commercial appeal, would be given about the CDs and T-shirts on sale in the vestibule. And then, finally, the entire choir would come out again and, in the words of the new gospel, "get their praise on." Pastoral announcements would follow a love offering, and then the choir would do two gospel oldies, a couple of Roger's original compositions, and then close with a sing-along medley designed for audience participation.

That was the plan.

God, however, had some other ideas.

"Marcus, what is the holdup?"

Roger and Tyrone hovered over the sound technician, their royal blue tunics and black slacks in stark contrast to the tech's jeans and T-shirt.

"I don't know," Marcus said. "We're not getting any juice." On his knees on the floor, he connected a cable, then scooted over, grabbed a microphone, and tapped the mouthpiece on a cordless mike.

Nothing.

Reverend Vince's voice at the pulpit was coming in loud and strong as he led the devotional period in the sanctuary. So it wasn't a power outage.

Annoyed, Roger looked around. "Come on, Marcus. The lights are on. The AC is on. There's power in the building. What's the problem?"

"I *said* I'm working on it," Marcus told him while leveling a telling glance at Tyrone. "I just sent Calvin out to the truck to grab our secondary amp and the headset units. I'll hook those up as a backup."

"Headset units? Half the singers don't know how to use them. We've never even practiced with them."

"That, my brother, is not my issue. I told you when we got those things that we needed to test them out. Since you kept putting it off, well, *Minister* McKenzie, this is the test."

Roger flared up. "I'm getting pretty sick and tired—"

"Come on, Raj," Tyrone interrupted, pushing Roger back.

The conflict between Roger and Marcus would come to a head soon, and the last straw would be something little and stupid like this. But with a concert about to start and technical difficulties already at hand, now was definitely not the time for them to be mixing it up.

"Come on," Tyrone said as he tugged on Roger's arm. "Walk with me. Let Marcus do his thing. If our mikes don't work, they don't work. Just like we don't need any music to sing, we also can sing without microphones."

Roger threw up his hands. "There are more than five hundred people packed into that sanctuary expecting a first-class show. Not some jerry-rigged piece of mess."

Marcus stopped working and stared up at Roger. Tyrone shook his head and held up a hand to cut off Marcus's reply.

"He didn't mean it, man," Tyrone told Marcus. "Come on, Raj. Let's go get some air."

Tyrone forcibly dragged Roger down the hallway and out a side door. Outside, the temperature had dropped a bit, but the night air remained balmy. Anyone who had to labor in the evening heat might find the air oppressive after a while, but for standing around and cooling off, it was just what Tyrone knew Roger needed right now. Besides, calming Roger down kept his mind off his own troubles.

Tyrone stood near the door while Roger paced. This preparatory time before a concert should have been spent in prayer and meditation, not anger and harsh words.

"Talk to me, cuz," Tyrone said. "You're wound up tight."

Roger stopped his frantic stride and stared at his cousin. "Did you hear anything Marcus said? We don't have any sound and his so-called backup plan is a disaster."

They didn't have a backup because Roger had kept putting off the trial run of the headset units. Now, however, wasn't the time for Tyrone to point out the obvious.

"Walk with me, Raj."

Roger glared at him. "We don't have time for your sidewalk psychology, Ty. We're supposed to be on in a few minutes."

"And the program's not gonna start without you. So come on. It's a black Baptist church, Raj. Devotions can go on for an hour; you know that. And look," he said, pointing toward the front of the church, where a long queue of cars, minivans, and SUVs waited to be directed into the church's overflow parking lots. "Folks are arriving on CP time anyway."

"Come on," Tyrone said. He started walking away from the building, secure in the knowledge that Roger would follow. Their routine, grounded in a childhood spent growing up together, was simple: walk and talk. Usually it was Roger who did the talking while Tyrone played the role of sounding board.

Tonight would be no different, even though Tyrone wanted and needed somebody to talk to regarding his own issues. Getting Roger's head straight was the priority, though. As the glue that held the Voices of Triumphant Praise together, Roger couldn't afford to come unhinged, particularly given what the two of them had in the works for the choir. The Voices seemed really close to that next move straight into the big time. Roger needed to remain focused on producing their music and honing their repertoire.

Roger fell into step beside him and Tyrone smiled. Old habits died hard.

"You know," Tyrone said: "If music hadn't called the way it did, I'd probably be a psychologist today."

"You are a headshrink," Roger said. "And I'm gonna report you for practicing without a license."

Tyrone chuckled. "All right, then, tell the good doctor what's up."

Roger stuck his hands in his pockets and stared at the ground. Quiet for a few minutes, Tyrone let him get his thoughts together.

"It's all falling apart, Ty. It's falling apart and we haven't even gotten started yet."

"You know God always has a plan, Raj. Sometimes when things aren't going right, we get frustrated, then say and do stuff we don't really mean."

Roger nodded. "I'm going to apologize to Marcus."

"That would be a good start since you jumped all into him." The cousins were nothing if not honest with each other. "The two of you also need to deal with that issue that has him blowing so much attitude your way."

"I can't help it if he thinks she—"

"That's not for now," Tyrone said, cutting him off. "And it's not just that she's the problem either. Think about it, Raj. You've been under a lot of stress. You're eating those little antacids like they're M&Ms or something. This whole trip was organized in about six weeks. It takes some groups, even some smaller than ours, months to coordinate engagements and then find sponsors to pick up the hotel and meal tabs."

"And your point?"

"Maybe this wasn't God time, cousin. Maybe it was Roger time."

Roger stopped walking and looked at Tyrone. "I have a vision for this choir, Ty. You know that. Besides, if it wasn't meant to be, things wouldn't have fallen into place the way they did. It was one open door after the other. Smooth sailing. Easy, like slicing into a piece of Sister Hedgepeth's pound cake."

Tyrone smiled at the mention of the cake they all enjoyed. But he wasn't sure about Roger's rationale, not when nagging doubt continued to assail him.

"Maybe too easy," Tyrone said. "The devil sets traps, you know. And now you're talking about launching into another major project. My work with Blackstone isn't going to leave me a lot of spare time."

"I'm taking that into consideration," Roger said. "But don't you see? We should already be up there with the Kirk Franklins and the John P. Kees of the world."

"God time, Roger. Remember, it all works out on God's time. Not my time or your time. Everything works out according to His perfect plan."

"I know that."

Tyrone nodded. "I know you do—theoretically. But what about practically?"

"I'm listening to God, Tyrone. Stop hammering on the same point. You and Vince are starting to sound like a broken record played in stereo."

"And you, cousin, are starting to look like someone we don't recognize."

Tyrone's cut hung in the air between them.

Roger was quiet for a long time. Then: "Tell me something, Ty."

"Talk to me."

"Do you, and I mean you personally, think this tour is a mistake?"

Tyrone shrugged. "I don't know, man. But we're here." He glanced at Roger before continuing. "You know me and Georgie have been having some problems."

Roger nodded.

"There was already some stuff going on and now there's more. On the road is not where I wanted us to face our future. But that's what's happening. All I can do is leave the situation in God's hands. There's a reason why we're here, Raj. All of us. There's something for us to learn here tonight at this church and on every stop of the way until we get back home. I don't know what it is. But we have to surrender to the Master to find out."

Roger took a deep breath. Then he nodded.

"That's a nice way of saying you think we shouldn't have come."

"Doesn't matter," Tyrone said. "All that matters now is that we keep our focus on our goals for this tour. The message is in the music, Roger. If there's a lesson for me, you, or anybody else to learn while we're out here, it'll happen in its own time and way."

Roger looked heavenward, but there wasn't much to see. The darkness of true night had yet to fall, and the heavy branches of large oaks shielded from view a good portion of the sky.

Maybe Satan had set a trap for them, Tyrone thought in the silence he and Roger shared. Christians were always going into, struggling in the middle of, or coming out of a trial. That was just the life cycle. But lately, Roger acted as if he was doing all three at the same time.

Tyrone glanced at Roger. "You all right, cuz?"

"Yeah. Just thinking about what you said." Roger was quiet for a while and then said, "All right, Doc. You've worked your magic. Let's go have some church."

Tyrone's spirit, however, remained heavy. The joy that usually accompanied him in his everyday walk was crushed. He'd been avoiding Georgie all day long. Tonight she'd be sitting in the congregation, her usual spot right in front, close enough to the choir to be of assistance if he needed anything.

"You go on," he told Roger. "I'll be in in a minute."

Roger studied Tyrone for a moment. "Tyrone," he said. "You've always been there for me. I hope you know I'm here for you. Anytime. Day or night."

Tyrone nodded. "I know. Thanks."

But the burden Tyrone carried was one that Roger shouldn't be saddled with right now. Besides, Roger had never been married and wouldn't really be able to offer any concrete advice. Reverend Vince, however, had been married a long time. Maybe he could be a sounding board.

Having made up his mind to confide in the minister, Tyrone went back into the church, ready to get his groove on for Jesus.

Fifteen minutes later, Reverend Vince got a nod and shrug from Marcus. The congregation, singing a spirited foot-stomping and hand-clapping rendition of "This Little Light of Mine," was primed for some good music. Vince slipped away to find Roger and located him standing at the entrance to the choir loft, just out of sight of most of the people in the sanctuary.

"What's happening? I got a cue from Marcus to stretch out the devotional period."

When Roger didn't respond, Vince touched his elbow. "Roger."

"Wha-hunh?"

"Roger, is there a concert tonight?"

"Listen to them," Roger said.

Reverend Vince looked around. "Who?"

"Them," Roger clarified, pointing toward the congregation. "They're totally into that song."

Joy lit up the faces of the congregation. Every voice lifted in celebration of letting their lights shine, shine, shine.

"Everybody knows it," Reverend Vince said. "Even little kids. But what does that have to do with anything? Is everybody ready for the opening number?"

But Roger's attention remained riveted to the faces of young and old alike, singing that they were gonna let their lights shine for Jesus.

"That's it," he said. "That's what the testimony is all about."

"What are you talking about, Roger?"

Roger looked at the preacher, seeing him clearly for the first time. "It all makes sense now, Vince. That's what we're supposed to be doing."

5

Be anxious for nothing.

—Philippians 4:6

"This all you need, Marcus?" Calvin asked. Trying to be helpful, he hovered right over Marcus's shoulder.

"Yeah, Cal, that's good," the sound technician said. "We're probably gonna start soon. You'd better hurry to get a good seat."

Calvin nodded. "Miss Georgie said she'd save a spot for me right up in front."

Marcus patted Calvin on the back. "Thanks for your help, Cal."

The younger man shuffled his feet. "It wasn't nothing," he said. "I like helping you. You don't yell at me if I get something wrong."

"No one should ever yell at you," Marcus said. "If they do, it just means they haven't learned to express themselves like human beings. You're a man, Calvin. Always remember that. Demand to be treated like one."

Calvin's chest puffed out at the encouraging compliment.

"You sure you don't need anything else?"

"I'm good. Thanks again."

With a wave, Calvin headed toward the sanctuary. Marcus watched him leave, contemplating Calvin's lot in life. He'd apparently never known his father, and from what Marcus had picked up, Calvin was pretty much set adrift after his mother died. She'd cared for him all his life, shielding him from the harsher realities of the world.

Calvin picked up on instructions pretty quickly, as long as he was told slowly and clearly and there were no more than two tasks involved at a time. Marcus understood that, unlike some others associated with the choir. With an older brother who was mentally retarded, Marcus knew more than a little about working with people who were said to be slow. Everybody had some ability, despite whatever mental or physical handicaps their bodies suffered.

What Marcus didn't appreciate was Roger McKenzie and the way he took Calvin's devotion for granted.

But before his thoughts were soiled in that musty alley, Margaret approached. A smile spread across Marcus's face.

"You're looking awfully pretty tonight, Margaret."

"Thanks, Marcus. Have you heard anything about when we're going to begin?"

He jerked his head toward the choir loft entrance. "Reverend Vince and Roger are up there. Looks like it'll be soon. Something I can help you with?"

Her smile seemed distracted and she worried at the fringe on the scarf at her neck. "No, I'm just ready to get this show on the road. I don't particularly want to see a repeat of last night."

Marcus shrugged. "Things happen for a reason."

She glanced at him sharply. "So I've been told."

The fractured tone of her voice troubled him. Margaret was something of an odd bird; maybe that was why he found her so intriguing. He'd followed in her shadow for a long time now. But a woman like her would never date a guy like him. Marcus wasn't bitter about that. Hell, if anybody looked at the women in the choir and tried to match him with somebody, they'd probably pick Glenna Anderson. But Glenna wasn't about flirting or dating or anything light. She was too intense for Marcus's tastes.

His preference ran toward delicate flowers, the type needing sunlight and nurturing to blossom. What Margaret saw in Roger, a gangly weed in the flower bed, Marcus just didn't understand. That didn't stop him from trying, though.

"I have something for you."

An eyebrow arched. "What is it?"

He reached in his jeans pocket and pulled out a tiny pin. Then he opened his palm to show her. "Do you mind?"

For a moment, she looked uncertain, unsure of his intention. He nodded toward her shoulder. "No, I don't mind," she told him.

Leaning forward, he pulled the back from the tack pin and connected it to the collar of her overblouse. "It's an angel. I saw it and thought about you. We all need a guardian angel to watch over us."

Margaret touched the angel and smiled. "That's very sweet. Thank you, Marcus."

"I'd better get this finished," he said as he looped a long extension cord around his arm.

"All right," she said as she turned to leave. A second later she faced him again. "Marcus?"

He looked up and she was right there in front of him. She leaned forward and pressed a quick kiss to his lips. "Thank you," she murmured.

A moment later she was gone. Marcus stood there, relishing the small gesture. There'd been no passion in the embrace; he knew that. But the simple and spontaneous action filled him with an incredible delight. A big grin spread across his face, transforming his normally surly features into a pleasant expression.

That was the look that made Reverend Vince pause. He backed up a step as he approached from the choir loft. His eyes widened a bit as he witnessed a flirtatious kiss between Marcus and Margaret. He'd have never put the Rasta man with the ice princess. But, he thought shaking his head, love and the Lord worked in mysterious ways.

In the men's restroom, one of the musicians was having a heated conversation on a cell phone.

"I told you, two hundred fifty bucks. Each. Take it or leave it." Scottie groaned, obviously not pleased with the answer on the other end of the line. "That is not my issue." He listened again. "Yeah, yeah, yeah. It'll all be there."

The men's-room door opened and Calvin loped in. "Hi, Scottie."

Scottie whirled around. "Gotta go," he said into the cell phone receiver. He flipped the phone shut and tucked it in his pocket.

"Hey, what's up, my main man Calvin? You ready for some singin' and shoutin'?"

Calvin nodded and reached down to pick up a piece of paper on the floor near Scottie's feet. "What's this? It has a lot of numbers on it," he said, turning the paper this way and that, trying to get a handle on the numbers.

Scottie grabbed the paper from Calvin, balled it up, and stuffed it in his pocket. "Oh, heh-heh, that's just some trash. I'll throw it away."

"Okay," Calvin said as he headed to a urinal. "The trash can's right there."

Scottie rolled his eyes and beat a retreat from the restroom.

After he was sure Margaret was gone, Reverend Vince cleared his throat and loudly called out to Marcus.

"It looks like we're ready to start," he said.

With the extra extension cord hanging from his shoulder, Marcus picked up his tool bag. "Has he decided what to do about the sound system?"

Reverend Vince smiled. "Yes. We're not going to worry about it." He put a hand on Marcus's shoulder. "Come on. We're all going to gather."

The preacher rounded up the choir members and musicians and asked everyone to get to the fellowship hall for prayer. Roger was the last to arrive. A restless energy surrounded him. Vincent hadn't seen that look in a while. He smiled, glad to again see Roger enjoying his work instead of carrying the harried and impatient countenance that had marked his features for so many weeks.

The choir members and musicians stood in a tight circle. Roger stepped into the middle of it.

"This is the day that the Lord has made. Let us rejoice and be glad in it," he said.

A couple of people nodded. Glenna, already in prayer and meditation, had her eyes closed and her head bowed.

"We've had a rocky beginning," Roger said. "But there's a fresh, new anointing for us in this place. We faced some obstacles with our sound system."

"What happened?" Krista asked.

Roger glanced at Marcus, who stoically stared him down. But Roger's expression held no animosity. "Some of our equipment isn't compatible with the electrical system here. And I want to apologize in front of everyone. I took some of my frustration out on Marcus, who has been doing, and continues to do, a terrific job on our sound."

Reverend Vince studied Marcus, whose expression hadn't changed despite the public apology from Roger. With something of a heavy heart, Vincent knew his prayer list would be growing longer and more specific tonight.

"May I join you all?"

The choir members turned to see who spoke. Calvin and Glenna stepped aside to allow the man in.

"Everybody," Roger said. "This is Pastor Joseph Armstrong, the shepherd here at Jerusalem Baptist."

"God be with you, children," the older minister said as he joined Roger in the middle of the circle. "We've been looking forward to this concert for a while now. Our own mass choir is here in full number. We like to praise God here at Jerusalem. So you all just let the Lord have his way as you minister tonight."

"Amen, brother Pastor," Tyrone said.

"We were just about to have a word of prayer," Vincent said.

"Good, good," Pastor Armstrong said. He stepped back and joined the circle as the choir members all clasped hands.

Still in the center, Roger addressed the choir again. "Tonight, we move as God says move. Follow my lead and don't worry if things seem different. Hum if you need to. But just let the spirit work within and among you."

With that, he nodded at Vincent and stepped back in the circle, taking the Reverend Armstrong's hand on one side and Georgie's on the other. She glanced at him, but put her hand in his, and bowed her head.

"Father God," Reverend Vince began. "We thank you Lord for bringing us this far on our journey. Thank you, Lord, for keeping your safeguarding angels over us. We know, Lord, that the accident we had could have been much, much worse. Lord, we pray for Brother Dwayne, whose arm was injured. Lord, tonight, as we lift our voices to sing your praises—"

A cell phone rang.

Scottie jumped. "Sorry. I'm sorry." He reached in his pocket, fumbled for the phone, and pulled it out. He quickly glanced at the number, then punched the power button off and dropped the phone back in his pocket. "My bad, Reverend Vince," he mumbled.

Vincent didn't miss a beat. ". . . let us remember that the technology you created for the advancement of our lives can also become the crutches we use to thwart your divine plan."

A couple of people snickered. Roger lifted his head and, with a look, silenced them.

"Tonight, Lord, we sing the songs of Zion, the ones that honor you. And we pray, Lord, that someone will be touched by the words, the music, and the witness we present. Thank you, Father, for all your many blessings."

Everyone said "Amen." The pastor of the church told them to "sing to the glory of God, children." Then the two preachers, talking together, went to the sanctuary.

As the choir lined up for their entrance, Roger had one more announcement. "Guys, please. The cell phones and pagers, the watches with the alarms. Turn them off."

"Roger, I'm really sorry, man," Scottie apologized again. "I thought I had it on vibrate. It won't happen again. I promise."

The concert went off without a hitch. Using the church's sound system, they sang with uncommon power. Roger didn't adhere to the program they'd planned as he played and directed. The choir followed his lead at every turn, though, from their own music to popular tunes heard on gospel radio stations.

At one point, Roger asked the mass choir of Jerusalem Baptist to join them. The combined voices sang the hand-clapping "I've Got a Testimony," followed by a tune by Kirk Franklin and the Family.

Then Roger pointed to Glenna. She stepped from the line where the Voices of Triumphant Praise stood to a microphone in front. Clasping her hands together, she bowed her head.

All eyes—those of the two choirs and the musicians—were on Roger. With one finger he pointed to the singers and the musicians, then directed two fingers to his eyes. The signal, understood by all, was for everyone to follow his lead. Roger placed his hands on his keyboard and played the opening bars of a mournful hymn. Then he switched the melody, combining the first tune with the familiar strains of "Amazing Grace."

Glenna moaned into the microphone, following his lead. When Roger's playing faded away, she began a slow, soulful solo of the cherished hymn.

As she sang the last note of the first verse, Roger cued the guitar players, the drummer, and the saxophonist as well as the combined choirs. They sang the second verse together, then, at Roger's direction, hummed it.

He cued Glenna again, then shut down the guitars and the sax. She worked through the third verse. Then, with just the saxophone as accompaniment, Glenna began the last verse of the hymn. "When we've been there, ten thousand years . . ."

The saxophone and Glenna ended on the same plaintive note. There weren't many, if any, dry eyes in the sanctuary. A woman cried out, and then another, then yet another. Soon, the main sanctuary at Jerusalem Baptist was filled with people waving their hands, crying, rocking back and forth, and shouting out "Glory to God!" and "Hallelujah!"

Tears streaming down her face, Glenna turned to return to her place in the choir line. As she took the first step, she let out a wail and fell to her knees shouting "Glory!" and "Thank you, Jesus!"

The praise continued throughout the church for fifteen minutes, Roger and Tyrone playing a soft variation of the hymn on keyboard and organ as people gave thanks. The Reverend Armstrong took his pulpit, wiped at his eyes, and adjusted the microphone.

"Saints, the Lord has put it on my heart to offer to you right now his everlasting peace. The doors of the church are open."

Twenty-seven people came forward.

6

"That was really awesome tonight," Tyrone said later that evening.

The Voices of Triumphant Praise, along with Pastor and Mrs. Armstrong and several members of the Jerusalem Baptist Church mass choir, filled the back room of a restaurant owned by one of the church members. A steady stream of chicken, ham, mashed sweet potatoes, collards, corn on the cob, and warm yeast rolls filled the stomachs of all those assembled.

Tyrone passed a basket of rolls to Georgie, who took one and set the basket down on the table.

"The Lord was really moving," the Reverend Armstrong said.

"Is 'Amazing Grace' something you all sing all the time?" someone asked Roger.

He leaned back in his chair and looked at Glenna, who sat at the next table. "Glenna, why don't you answer that?"

She looked up. "What's the question?"

"Is 'Amazing Grace' your theme song?"

She chuckled, the sound an amused rumbling. "Chile, you better believe it. That's my song and my testimony. I was a lost wretch and Jesus came and plucked me out of the mire." She waved her hand, accenting her words.

"Amen, sister."

"Where are you headed next, Brother Roger?" Pastor Armstrong asked.

"We have one more night here; then after breakfast and Bible study the next day, we're going up the road a bit to the University of Maryland for a workshop and an afternoon concert. Then we'll be right outside Baltimore for a couple of nights. We have several engagements up there."

"Well, let me tell you this. If you all minister there the way you did at Jerusalem tonight, souls will be saved. Your ministry is a blessing."

Roger nodded his thanks.

Georgie leaned into Tyrone. "Honey, it's after midnight," she whispered. "How much longer are we going to be here?"

"Shh," he said.

Georgie breathed deeply and sat back in her chair, folding her arms across her chest.

Scottie reached for their server's hand. "Hey, Miss Pretty. Can you direct me to the facilities?"

The young woman smiled at him, then pointed toward a rear exit. When Scottie rose, so did Marcus. The two headed toward the restroom. Krista and Dwayne both stretched and yawned.

"It's been a long day," Krista said. "How's your arm?"

"Doing all right," Dwayne said. "My sister picked me up last night at the hotel and she took a look at it. She sprayed something on it and told me to keep it dry."

"Are you staying at the hotel tonight or are you going back to your sister's?"

He glanced at her, then leaned forward with a small smile curving his mouth. "You suggesting something more interesting?" he said, just loud enough for her ears only.

Krista met his gaze and slowly licked her lips. "Maybe."

Dwayne nodded, his gaze on her appreciative in a purely male sort of way. "I've been, you know, noticing you."

"Have you?"

He stroked his chin. "Yeah, girl."

She smiled at him. Then, with a fingernail on the back of his hand, lightly formed her room number on his skin. Dwayne smiled.

The tryst was set.

Three tables over, Margaret sat with some of the musicians. She'd tried to finagle a seat next to Roger, but the church pastor and first lady claimed his right side and Reverend Vince was on his left. When she'd turned to unhook her purse strap from a chair it had gotten tangled up in, the last seats at that table were taken by Georgie, Tyrone, and the Jerusalem Baptist mass choir director.

Margaret glanced up and saw Reverend Vince looking at her. He'd been giving her strange little looks all night, and as far as Margaret was concerned, it was time to end. She'd have a talk with him first thing in the morning. Right now, though, all she wanted to do was get back to the room so she could do her nightly reading and go to bed.

"Is there a late-night drug store or something around here?" Glenna asked. She hadn't eaten much and was looking more worn out than usual.

"Yeah," one of the Jerusalem folks said. "And Wal-Mart's always open."

"Perfect. I need to pick up some pantyhose."

"I can run you over there and drop you back off at the hotel, Sister Glenna," one of the ladies from the Jerusalem Baptist mass choir said.

"Ooh, would you? Bless your heart." Glenna grabbed her handbag and Bible and stood up. "Anybody else need anything?"

That was the wrong question to ask.

Toothpaste. Deodorant. The latest *Ebony* magazine. Some Tylenol. NyQuil. Nacho-cheese Doritos.

"Hey, if it's a Wal-Mart with the grocery store, get me some Oreo cookies and a pint of chocolate milk."

The list got so long that Glenna held up her hands. "Wait a minute, now. You all acting like I'm Mrs. Wal-Mart or something. They ain't giving the stuff away in there. Somebody need to pass some cash this way. And while I'm thinking about it, I'm gonna charge a service-and-delivery fee."

A couple of people laughed. In the end, two carloads headed to Wal-Mart for everything from cough drops to styling gel. Roger and Vincent rode back to the motel with the Armstrongs, and the remaining members of the choir, after saying farewell to their hosts from Jerusalem, boarded the bus.

"Whoo-ee. It's a good thing you all don't have an early morning appointment," Jerry, the bus driver, said. "You all act like ya'll don't need any sleep."

"Tell me about it," Georgie mumbled as she boarded.

"Come on stragglers," Jerry called to Scottie and Marcus, who were taking their time about getting to the bus. "There don't appear to be any cabs running in this part of town this late. All aboard."

But Marcus stopped Scottie before he reached the front door of the bus. "I want to talk to you," he told Scottie.

Scottie bobbed his head and slapped Marcus on the back. "Cool, man. We can chill in the room. I'm in with Quent and Calvin. Room two-oh-five. I think."

He hopped onto the first step. "Yo, Calvin. What's our room number?"

"Two. Oh. Five," Calvin answered. "On the second floor. Up the middle stairs. Make a right after the elevator door opens."

Scottie grinned and leaned down toward Marcus. "Yeah. That's it."

Marcus jerked a finger at Scottie, who jumped down. "Whassup, man? Jerry's ready to bounce."

"What I want to talk to you about is something I don't think you want everybody else hearing. You dig?"

Scottie sized Marcus up. He was all muscle and not prone to having a little fun. Scottie rolled his shoulders. "Yeah. All right. I hear you."

He backed onto the bus. When his leg hit the bottom stair he turned around. With a final, uncertain look at Marcus, who was headed toward the panel truck, Scottie boarded the bus.

Had Marcus overheard something?

With the room free while Glenna did her Wal-Mart run, Margaret pulled out her cell phone and pressed the speed-dial function. Sister Amelia's number was one she could have dialed in her sleep. It was late, but not too late to call. Particularly given the circumstances.

The machine picked up. Margaret frowned.

"You have reached Reverend Sister Amelia, Prophetess of the True Light. I am on the other line right now, ministering to a soul in need. Please leave your name and a number and I shall return your important telephone call with all due speed. Grace and peace of the heavens and Our Father to you, my child."

Margaret didn't leave a message. She'd call back in a few minutes.

She snapped the phone shut, tossed it on her bed, then went to her small carry-on bag. After carefully turning the combination that would open the lock, she pulled out a leather case. It, too, had a lock on it.

Settling on her bed with her back propped against the headboard, she opened the leather case, taking comfort in its familiar feel and worn-leather smell. Setting aside the deck of cards, she pulled out a thick book. Part journal, part astrological forecast, Margaret consulted its pages every day.

She opened the volume to today's page, already bookmarked with a thin blue ribbon. With Glenna in the room, she hadn't had a chance to do the reading first thing, so now, at day's end, she'd see what the stars had to say about the day she'd had.

Margaret frowned as she read the detailed horoscope message, wondering what the passage about "a mistaken alliance" might mean. Nothing out of the ordinary had happened during the day—except for the spectacular concert at Jerusalem Baptist.

For a moment, she felt a twinge of guilt at relying on an astrological reading when she should have been relying on God. But Margaret had long ago reconciled her two belief systems, even though she didn't flaunt to others her reliance on the alternative faith method.

God granted all kinds of gifts. To some he gave a talent for singing or preaching or teaching or art. And some got the word of knowledge, which, to Margaret's thinking, included psychics like the Prophetess of the True Light, who had a true talent for divining the meaning of the stars and of the life journey.

Not in the mood to write a lot, she jotted down a couple of lines about the day on the journal side of the page. Then she reached for her phone, flipped it open, and pressed the redial button. The Reverend Sister Amelia's number remained busy. Daunted but not discouraged, Margaret put the phone aside and picked up the deck of cards.

Sitting cross-legged on her hotel room bed, she lay down the tarot, hoping to get a message about how to proceed with Roger.

Marcus stood outside, hands draped over the balcony rail. The balmy night was just right for a little come-to-Jesus talk with Scottie. The brother had no clue how close he'd come to getting busted. Marcus had a good mind to turn him in himself.

Scottie thought his little game was safe, that no one knew what he did on the side. But Marcus knew, and he didn't at all like it that Scottie put all of their lives—and futures—in jeopardy by running numbers and maybe even drugs from the confines of the choir.

He'd been out here waiting for Scottie and Quent to show up.

They'd taken off the moment the bus hit the motel parking lot. Neither one had been seen since.

What Scottie didn't know, though, was that Marcus had the patience of Job. And like Solomon, he didn't take any mess. Like Paul, he'd call you out. And just like Moses, he'd lay down the law.

Georgie and Tyrone Thomas were preparing for bed. "Why don't you want to talk about this?" Georgie said. "You'd think I'd asked for a mink coat and a mansion."

Tyrone spit out the toothpaste, then rinsed his mouth. He dried his hands on a white hand towel and met her gaze in the bathroom mirror. She'd paused in rolling up her hair to hear his response.

"Georgie, think about it. You're actually asking for more. A child is a big responsibility. Raising a child takes a lot of time and money. And we're short on both. You're at the bank a lot, sometimes even on Saturdays. And you know what I'm trying to do with Blackstone. Not to mention the work I have at the studio and with Roger."

Georgie stamped her foot and threw the yellow curler on the vanity. "Roger. It always comes back to Roger."

For a long moment, Tyrone didn't say anything. Then he turned around, crossed his arms over his bare chest, and leaned against the sink top. She'd never pretended to like Roger. Until recently, though, her sometimes coolness could be attributed to getting to know all of Tyrone and Roger's large and close-knit family. Their mothers were sisters. Roger and Tyrone had grown up as close as brothers.

Georgie, for a reason he'd been unable to fathom, had taken an immediate dislike to Roger but shielded her feelings most of the time. Now, though, in the past few weeks, she'd been openly hostile. Tyrone wanted to get to the bottom of it before one of them, probably Georgie, did or said something that they'd later regret.

"We started talking about this last night," he told her. "Then I shifted direction. I won't make that mistake again, Georgie," he said, taking in her lushly full-figured body. The pale-pink see-through nightie was designed to be a distraction. "Roger is my family, my blood. And you don't like him. I need to know why."

Georgie turned her back to him, unwilling or unable to meet his intense gaze. Tyrone wasn't about to let her off this time, though. He reached for her and turned her around, quickly releasing his hands from her smooth skin. He loved touching her, making love with her.

She could so easily distract him. And he needed to focus, completely, on what she had to say.

"I'm waiting, Georgie."

"It's late," she said, her voice taking on almost a purr. "We can talk about this some other time." In a swirl of negligee and duster, she swept past him and went to the bed closest to the wall. Tyrone followed her. She turned the spread down, slipped out of the robe, and got into bed.

"You look awful sexy wearing nothing but those pajama bottoms," she said.

He leaned against the desk chair watching her.

Patting the space beside her, she smiled at him. "Come to bed, Ty."

"Georgie, we're gonna talk about this if it takes all night. You can have it your way or my way."

Her eyes narrowed. "What's your way?"

He went to the other bed, yanked the covers down, and got in.

"Ty! What are you doing?"

"I'm going to bed. You don't want to talk; I'm going to sleep."

"You know I don't sleep well without you beside me."

"Sleep isn't what you're over there plotting."

Georgie pouted. "I am tired, Ty. It's been a long day."

"Fine," he said, reaching for the light switch on the lamp between their beds. He turned it out and the room was bathed in darkness.

A split second later, he heard a click and light danced across the room. "Thought you were tired," he said dryly.

"Just shut up."

He raised an eyebrow at that.

"I'm sorry," she quickly apologized. "This isn't easy for me, Ty."

He sat up, swinging his legs over the side of the bed. "Start at the beginning."

She glanced at her hands for a moment, then met his gaze. "That's just it," she said. "I'm not sure where the beginning is."

7

The wisdom that comes from heaven is first of all pure; then peace-loving, considerate, submissive, full of mercy and good fruit, impartial and sincere.

—James 3:17

"Well, just start somewhere," Ty said.

Georgie looked at him, sure that this wasn't a particularly good idea, but not sure how to redirect his thinking. Her prior relationship with Roger was complicated—complicated in ways that shed no good light on her own character.

Tyrone, she knew, would jump to conclusions, and many of them would be right on target. Others though would be off, way off the mark. In many ways, her two-year marriage had been similar to the children's guessing game in which the person designated as "it" lets the participants know whether they are warm or cold in their guessing. Georgie had deliberately and with forethought led Ty down a cold path.

On some level she knew that she was the cause of his increased curiosity. But it was getting close to the date and her anxiety grew. This year was, for some reason, much worse than last year's had been. A year ago, she'd spent the day crying. Now, instead of crying, she was lashing out. And her pain, manifest in digs directed toward Roger, was making things apparent to Tyrone.

"Well," he said. "Are you going to get to it?"

"I'm trying to figure out where to start."

"Start with 'I don't like Roger because . . .' "

"Because he takes up too much of your time," she blurted out, relieved to have an ancillary issue to dwell on—at least for now.

"A few weeks ago, I had tickets for us to see that new gospel play in Portsmouth. I'd been looking forward to us having an evening together. It was a Thursday. Perfect, I thought. There were no church meetings, no choir rehearsals, nothing on the calendar."

Tyrone's brow creased. "What play? What are you talking about?"

"It was a surprise," she said as she stomped away. "Or at least it was supposed to be. But I was the one who got the surprise, and a bad one at that. You came home and took a shower and before I could open my mouth about the dinner reservations and tickets, *Roger called,*" she said, emphasizing the last two words.

"Baby, I'm sorry. I didn't know. You should have said something."

"When, Ty? When am I supposed to be able to get a word in when all it takes is a phone call from Roger and boof!" she said, snapping a finger. "You're out the door running to him like he's a fix you need to survive. How do you think it makes me feel to know I'm your wife and I obviously have to make an appointment to spend some one-on-one time with you?"

"I'm trying to make a living for us, Georgie."

"Well, from this side of the fence, it looks more like he comes first in your life. My understanding of marriage and the vows we took before God was that man and wife were to cleave first to each other. The way I see it, the lineup should be God first, me and our marriage second, a career or job third, then friends, family, hobbies, and whatever else."

Ty rubbed his temples.

"But you know what, I don't even come after your job," Georgie said, her mouth trembling. "I take like fifth place with you. And that's not right, Ty. That's not right."

"It's also not true, Georgie."

Determined not to cry, she took a deep breath, folded her arms under her ample bosom, and glared at him, putting all the bravado she could muster in the look. "Then what is it?" she said. "We obviously are looking through different lenses."

Tyrone pushed the covers aside and stood up. He padded to the desk chair, where he reached for his shirt. After buttoning it, he walked back to his bed and sat on the edge, facing Georgie who stood staring down at him.

She waited, knowing he needed the time to get his thoughts together. She was right on this point, and she knew that deep down,
Tyrone had to know it, too. That other issue, well, it wasn't really all
that important—as long as Roger kept his trap shut.

Ty folded his hands. "I love you, Georgie. I've always loved you.
From the moment we met in line to see that Gospel Explosion concert. I took one look at you and it was like Bam! All the stuff Luther
and Teddy and Smokey have been singing about all these years, it just
hit me. I knew you were the one and only woman for me."

Georgie's mouth trembled; this time, though, she held back tears
of joy. She reached for his hand. "Ty."

But he got up, putting distance between them. "It cuts me,
Georgie." He pounded his chest with his fist. "It cuts me like a knife
to hear you saying you think I don't love you. You put the melody in
my music. You're why I work so hard every day. You," he said, pointing at her. "You're the one I thank God for every night before I go
to sleep."

Tyrone closed his eyes and shook his head. When he looked at her
again, his eyes glistened with a dampness Georgie hadn't seen since
the day they stood before God and their families. Tyrone had cried at
their wedding as he said his vows. It was the sweetest gift he could ever
have given her.

He pulled the chair out, straddled it and looked everywhere in the
motel room but at her. Then, taking a deep breath, he ran his hands
over his eyes and faced her.

"So, what you're telling me, Georgie, is that you want a baby or
else?"

She nodded.

He looked at her. "What's the 'or else?' "

"You all go on," Glenna told the two ladies from Jerusalem Baptist.
"I need to get something over here."

They'd been in Wal-Mart about thirty minutes already. Glenna's
basket was filled with the requests of the choir members who'd gone
on back to the motel. She watched the two women from Jerusalem
head down the main aisle toward the check-out lines. When she was
sure they weren't turning back, Glenna headed to the pharmacy department—the real reason she'd needed to come to the store.

She turned a corner and . . . it was closed!

Her heart sank. "What now?" she said, looking around. The pharmacy hours were clearly posted, eight A.M. until nine P.M. It was way past midnight.

Then she remembered that someone said an all-night drug store was around. Glenna quickly made her way to the check-out and paid for her hose and all the other stuff for the choir members. Back in the car with the ladies from Jerusalem Baptist, she vaguely explained about needing to see a pharmacist. About ten minutes later, they arrived at a drug store with a twenty-four-hour pharmacy. Promising not to be long, Glenna went inside.

She had to wait behind a man picking up a prescription, but soon found herself facing the clerk. "Is a pharmacist still on duty?"

"One minute. Hey, Max. A customer wants to see you."

A moment later, a black man in his mid-forties appeared before Glenna, his wire-rimmed glasses perched on his nose. With both hands flat on the slightly raised counter, he smiled at Glenna.

"How can I help you, ma'am?"

She unzipped her purse and pulled out a small orange-brown medicine bottle. "I'm up here on tour with my choir for a week. I thought I had a refill with me, but I can't find it. I got about enough in there for the next three days. Is it possible to get this refilled here?"

The pharmacist peered at the bottle and then at Glenna.

"How much pain are you in?"

"It's okay right now," she said. "I'm just worried about when that runs out. I figured if I had to, I could maybe take half of the daily dose every day and stretch it out."

He looked at the bottle again, then opened it and shook the few remaining pills. "That's not advised." He rubbed his cheek, then looked at Glenna again.

She sighed. "I understand," she said. "It's my own fault for not double-checking before I left home." Her shoulders slumped and she glanced around the pharmacy area blinking back sudden tears.

Then, getting a hold of herself: "Can you recommend something over the counter that I can take that'll maybe keep me stabilized enough? I'm with a group and I can't leave and go back."

"Do you have your insurance card with you?"

Hope flared in Glenna's eyes. "It's here. Yes. My medical card. Wait a minute." She dug in her purse, pulling out all manner of miscellaneous items until she found what she was looking for. "Whew, praise the Lord," she said. "For a minute I thought I'd left it at home."

She handed over the card, her ID card, and driver's license.

The pharmacist assessed her again with a long look; then he took a deep breath. "Just a moment."

He disappeared with her prescription bottle and cards.

It took him longer than a minute. Glenna could see him on the phone. He spied her watching him and she stepped away from the counter to hunt for the pain relievers. She looked at the many packages, searching for something that was super-duper extra-strength.

"Miss?"

Glancing up, Glenna looked toward the pharmacist's counter. He motioned for her to approach.

"Yes? I'm right here." She hurried back to him.

He handed her her original prescription bottle. Accepting it, Glenna was about to drop it back in her purse when she paused. She shook the bottle. If she'd been hoping for a miracle, she'd been let down. It wasn't the first time in her life, and probably wouldn't be the last.

She turned to leave.

"Miss?"

"Huh?"

"Your prescription." The pharmacist held out a small medicine bottle.

Glenna stared at it and then her gaze shot up to the pharmacist's. "You were able to call in the refill?"

"Yes," he said. "There are just enough to get you home. That's all that was authorized."

Glenna wanted to kiss his feet. "Thank you, mister. Thank you. You don't know how much . . ." She glanced at the bottle, then at him. "Well, I guess you do, huh?"

He nodded.

She reached for her wallet. "How much?"

"I was told it's already been taken care of. You just need to sign here."

She turned wide eyes to him. Glenna's mouth trembled. She reached for his hand. "Bless you, mister. Bless you."

In the room he shared with Roger, Reverend Vince finished up his personal Bible study, then put together the notes he'd need for the choir's morning devotional period. He stepped around the power cords that ran along the floor leading from an electrical outlet on the wall to the keyboard Roger had set up.

Roger stood at the keyboard, working on a song. He jotted notes in a black notebook, then fiddled with a different melody. The sound, slightly muted, wasn't loud enough to disturb anyone in the adjoining rooms.

"How's it coming?" Vince said.

"All right. Tonight just really got me thinking about the future. God was moving in that church tonight. Everybody felt it."

"What are you working on?"

Roger stuck his pencil in his mouth. "I'm not sure. It's just kind of coming in spurts. So I'm rolling with it."

Vincent nodded. In his months working with the Voices of Triumphant Praise, he'd learned a few things about creative types. The first being that the muse didn't always strike between nine and five, and sometimes it didn't come when it was most needed.

He'd met Roger several years ago at the Ministers' Conference at Hampton University. They'd struck up a friendship. Then, later, when Roger called asking if Vincent would be spiritual adviser to the choir, he readily accepted. He liked the idea of being able to work with the small group.

He was also a pretty good judge of character. This was his first extended road trip with the choir, and with the exception of tonight, things just didn't seem to be going well. The Bible study sessions went off without a hitch. They spent the first fifteen minutes of each rehearsal doing a quick lesson. On the road, though, things were different. There was an underlying tension among the choir members. And that bothered Vincent.

"Tell me about the relationships in the choir," he said.

"What do you mean?" Roger answered without looking up from the keyboard.

"Well, I know you and Tyrone Thomas are cousins. He's married to Georgie. Margaret and Marcus seem to be a pair."

A discordant chord squawked from the keyboard. Roger's hands splayed across the keys. "What was that?"

Vincent eyed him, gauging his reaction. "Margaret. And Marcus?"

"Marcus with the dreads and the tattoos? The sound guy?" Roger clarified, as if they had more than one person who fit that description.

Vincent nodded.

"I don't think so. He's not her type."

Vincent didn't say anything about the thread of animosity he heard in Roger's voice. And he kept quiet on the kiss he'd witnessed between Marcus and Margaret. But he did give voice to something he'd suspected for a while. "You like her?"

"Yeah, she's all right," Roger said, turning back to his work. "We go way back. To college. We were in the gospel choir. Ty, too."

"But you didn't answer my question," Vince said.

Roger looked up. "We have some history," he said. "Not *that* kind of history. Margaret's a friend. I am, however, planning to hook up with someone who is, shall we say, *more* than a friend."

Vince smiled. "I see. And who might this mystery lady be?"

Roger smiled and wagged a finger but didn't say anything. Vincent let the subject drop and got back to the one on his mind.

"I'm thinking about setting up some one-on-one counseling with the choir members."

"Sounds like a good idea," Roger said. "Some of 'em could use it."

"That's why I was wondering about some of the relationships."

"With a couple of exceptions, everybody pretty much gets along."

"What are the exceptions?"

"Marcus has an attitude problem. But I'm gonna deal with that pretty soon."

"Tell me about Glenna."

Roger's face split into a smile. "She's my angel."

Vincent plopped onto his bed and scooted up until his back braced against the headboard. "Where did you guys meet?"

Roger looked at Vince, then stared beyond him, a ghost of a smile at his mouth. "An alley. We met in a dark, rat-infested alley."

8

The name of the Lord is a strong tower; the righteous run to it and are safe.

—Proverbs 18:10

"It was not quite two years ago," Roger said. "I remember because one of our cousins had just gotten married. The alley was about three blocks away from the reception hall. I was out getting some air, talking a walk, when I heard this noise."

Roger shook his head, remembering the scene as if it were just yesterday. "At first I thought it was a cat mewling in the alley and kept walking. Something, though, and you know, I'm not sure what, but something made me pause. I listened closer and realized it wasn't a cat. It sounded like a person, like somebody whimpering."

"What was it?" Vincent asked.

"Glenna. Although I didn't know her or her name at the time. Vince, that was the nastiest place I've ever seen in my life. It was like hogs lived there, or at least in the apartments above. It looked like nobody bothered with the trash bins, even though a big rusted Dumpster stood nearby. It was actually blocking the entrance to the alley, so it's a wonder I heard anything at all. I went around it and the smell hit me.

"Garbage everywhere, rotting food. I heard something skitter and saw a rat. God almighty, it was as big as a cat. I stomped my foot and yelled at it. Then kicked a can on the ground."

Roger shivered. "What'd I do that for? All of a sudden there was a lot of rustling. God, you should have seen me jumping out of the way when those rodents scattered. Jesus."

He shook his head. "I couldn't believe it. Still can't," he added. "And then I heard the sound again."

"Glenna?"

Roger nodded. "I didn't see her at first. There was so much trash all over the place. It was like the people just opened their apartment windows and tossed stuff out, some of it in bags, but a lot of it not. Food, dirty diapers, sanitary pads, cat litter."

Turning off the keyboard, Roger rounded the instrument and sat in a chair, his hands dangling between his knees. He stared first at his hands and then at the floor covered in a dark green carpeting.

"She was half-propped against a broken-down chair. Jesus, Vince, you should have seen her. You wouldn't have recognized her as the woman you know today. Her face was swollen, and black and blue in some places. Her clothes were torn and ripped up like someone had been yanking them from her. She was caked in dirt and garbage. To this day I think someone tossed some trash out of a window and Glenna didn't have the energy to get out of the way before it landed on her."

"How long had she been out there?"

Roger shook his head. "I don't know. Neither does she. She thinks it could have been a couple of days, a week. She had rat bites on her arms and legs."

"Sweet mercy."

"You know the most remarkable thing?"

"What?"

"She had a tract. It was in her hand, clutched like it was her last will and testament."

"A tract? Where'd she get it?"

"She later said it was on top of a metal trash can lid she'd picked up to beat off the rats."

Vincent just stared at Roger.

"You know the sound I'd heard, the one that drew me into the alley in the first place? It was Glenna praying. 'Save me, Jesus. Save me. Save me.'"

"She has a powerful testimony."

Roger nodded. "That's why people weep when she sings 'Amazing

Grace.' She knows what she's singing about. That testimony is coming from a place that a lot of people can't even imagine."

Marcus finally gave up waiting for Scottie to return. The little hustler thought he was so smooth. But Marcus knew his game. And he knew hard brothers much smarter than Scottie thought he was.

The night had turned cool—not enough to need a jacket, but the temperature had dropped just enough to notice it.

Making his way to his room, Marcus thought about the kiss he'd shared with Margaret Hall-Stuart earlier in the day. It came as something of a surprise to him to realize that all these hours later, his mind was still on the woman and the sweetness of her touch. The memory of that touch aroused him.

Margaret was a woman who had secrets. That was something Marcus recognized as a given. He, too, had secrets.

"Kindred spirits," he said as he shut and locked the door.

Marcus didn't share a room with anyone. That was part of the deal he'd made with Roger. His lip curled at just the thought of McKenzie. The man was talented; he'd give him that. But that was all Marcus would concede.

He wouldn't go so far as to call Roger an enemy. But if Roger ever needed to be bailed out of something, Marcus definitely didn't have his back.

Then there was the issue of Margaret. Sweet, beautiful Margaret. Marcus knew that he'd long ago lost his detachment where she was concerned.

He slapped his room key onto the bureau and went to the window. His motel room overlooked the side parking lot of the diner next door. Its red-and-yellow neon sign proclaimed "ALL-YOU-CAN-EAT PANCAKES FOR $3.99" and "OPEN 24 HOURS."

It was close to two in the morning, but Marcus wasn't sleepy. He'd learned a long time ago to get by on very little sleep. Far from needing any rest, he was keyed up. Needing to burn some energy, he reached into his bag and pulled out a set of free weights and dropped them on the bed.

Marcus tugged off his shirt, straddled the desk chair, then lifted the weights, ready to do three hundred curls. Exercise always got his mind off things he couldn't have . . . like Margaret Hall-Stuart.

* * *

Krista turned the deadbolt lock, then put the chain on the door.
"What about your roommate?" Dwayne asked.

"What about her?"

"Won't she be coming back?"

Krista followed him into the room. "Not for a while."

Dwayne's wide mouth split into a grin. "What kind of view do you
all have?"

"We're looking out at the parking lot. Real exciting. At least we can
see the bus and the truck and know nobody's ripped off our transpo
and equipment."

She came up behind him and touched his uninjured arm. "How's
your arm feeling?"

He faced her. "Just fine." A small smile played at his mouth. "Why'd
you invite me in?"

She shrugged, but her fingers stroked his arm. "I've been watching
you, Dwayne. I think I'd like to get to know you better."

"Whatcha want to know?"

She stepped away for a moment. "Would you like something to
drink? We have some soda—Sprite and either Coke or Pepsi."

"Sprite sounds good."

She picked up the ice bucket on the dresser. "Why don't you get
comfortable. I'll go get us some ice."

His gaze met hers. "When you say comfortable, just how *comfortable*
do you mean?"

Her answering smile held promise, and more than a touch of sass.
"You be the judge."

Margaret didn't at all like what the cards predicted. But tomorrow
was another day. Maybe they'd turn better after sunrise. She quickly
put everything away and dressed for bed. The moment she slipped
under the covers, she heard Glenna at the door.

For a moment, Margaret thought to play as if she were asleep. But
there was something she needed to say to the other woman.

Glenna tiptoed into the room, careful not to wake her roommate.

"Hello," Margaret said.

"Oh," Glenna said, whirling around. "I was trying not to wake you
up."

"You didn't. I was waiting for you."

Glenna's eyebrow arched. "Why?"

Margaret sat up in bed, bringing the sheet and light blanket with her. "I just wanted to say . . . I mean you were really terrific at the concert tonight. I was moved by your singing."

Glenna deposited her purse on her bed, and a blue plastic Wal-Mart bag on the desk chair.

"Thank you," she said. "God gets the glory, though."

Margaret folded her arms. "I don't understand you."

"What do you mean?"

"You sing like you're anointed, yet . . ."

"Yet I come from the street and that bothers you."

Margaret didn't say anything.

At the closet, Glenna shrugged out of her clothes and reached for her robe. She came back and sat on her bed, facing Margaret. "You said you were moved by my singing. What did it feel like?"

"What do you mean?"

"What did you feel? Here," she said, tapping her heart. "And here," she said, pointing to her head.

Margaret shrugged, the motion an unnatural one for her. "I don't rely on feelings to run my life; I look at facts."

"And what facts did you get tonight at that church?"

Their gazes locked for a moment. Margaret was the first to look away. "I don't know," she said. "I'm sorry I brought it up."

She whipped the covers over her shoulder and turned her back to Glenna. "Good night."

Glenna sat staring at Margaret's back for a while. Her spirit ached at the turmoil she sensed in the other woman. Her prayers tonight would be for Margaret—and for the pharmacist who'd blessed her with the medication she needed to ease the pain that tormented her body.

———

9

There is wonderful joy ahead, even though it is necessary for you to endure many trials for a while.

—1 Peter 1:6

The note arrived late in the morning after the group's Bible study. The front desk clerk rang Roger and Vincent's room saying a letter had been delivered for Roger McKenzie.

"Tell them I'll pick it up when I come down," Roger said, as he stroked his razor along his jaw. He was dressed in just his pants and a white T-shirt.

Vincent relayed the message, then replaced the receiver. He looked at a copy of the group's itinerary for the day. "It's going to be a long day."

"Tell me about it," Roger said. "And with just three people at Bible study, I somehow get the feeling that we weren't the only ones who had a late night. After the concert at Jerusalem and then that terrific dinner, everybody was bouncing off the walls."

Vincent chuckled. "And Lord only knows how long that Wal-Mart contingent stayed out. When my wife goes in there, I don't count on seeing her for a long, long time."

"We're gonna need to hit the road just as soon as Bible study is done tomorrow. It won't take long to get to Baltimore, but I definitely don't want us to be late."

Roger rinsed traces of shaving cream from his face, then wiped his face and hands on a towel. Vincent's image appeared in the mirror when Roger looked up.

"One day at a time, Roger. Take one day at a time."

Roger grinned. "Too late, Rev. I'm already into the middle of next week."

Vincent held the group's itinerary. "Today," he said, emphasizing the word, "everyone has the morning and lunch free. Then at three we go to Riverview Convalescent Center for ministry and music. And we're due at Howard University at seven tonight. What's the deal at Howard?"

"Gospel Jamboree. It's really awesome," Roger said. "An annual thing at the student center. The university's gospel choir and one of the fraternities host it every year. It's a fund-raiser for the Alphas. Some of the frat brothers form a little group to sing, too."

"How many choirs participate?"

Roger reached for his shirt. "Varies. Sometimes as few as three. This year, though, according to the schedule I was sent, there are eight. We're fifth in line."

As he buttoned his shirt, he walked to the dresser and pulled out a pair of black socks.

Vincent took in the suit jacket draped over the chair. "Date?"

Roger glanced at him and grinned. "Actually, yeah."

"Oh." The single word held question, comment, and amazement. "Roger McKenzie is making time for a personal relationship. God apparently is still working miracles."

"You don't have to act so shocked," Roger said. "Camille is someone that I've known for a while. We try to get together whenever I'm up here or she's down the way."

"And how often does this 'trying' happen?"

Roger grinned. "About three or four times a year."

"Late breakfast or early lunch?"

"Lot of questions today, Reverend Vince."

Vincent nodded at the censure. "Just curious."

Roger slapped his back as he passed by and snatched up his tie. After tying a perfect Windsor knot, he brushed his hair again, then lifted the suit jacket from the chair and shrugged into it.

"Lot of detail going into this casual date," Vincent observed, a touch of amusement evident in his voice.

Roger turned to his friend. "That's because things could be heading in another direction for us."

Roger hoped that was the case. He'd been doing a lot of thinking about Camille lately. They'd met on-line in a Christian singles chat room about three years ago and had eventually met. Their friendship had boundaries that they'd set in the first e-mails they'd exchanged. Now, though, Roger was thinking about changing the nature of their relationship.

Tucked in his pocket was a small gift for Camille. Nothing so dramatic as a ring, but the kind of jewelry that would let her know his intentions were serious.

He took the stairs to the motel's first floor and stopped at the desk to get the letter the clerk had called about. Through the front doors he could see the cab he'd ordered waiting for him.

"Roger McKenzie," he announced to the clerk. "You said I had a delivery."

The clerk looked up from his magazine, took a glance at Roger, and reached for the plain white envelope.

His mind on Camille and their lunch date, Roger glanced at the envelope, and tucked it in his inside jacket pocket. His contact at Howard University had said he'd send over parking passes for the choir's vehicles.

"Thanks," he told the clerk. "I was waiting for this."

Not too much later, he stood with Camille in a DuPont Circle restaurant near the office where Camille worked as an aide to a lobbyist.

"You look great," he told her. She was dressed in a blue silk dress and medium-heeled pumps. A multicolored scarf intricately tied around her neck added a touch of color and flair to her conservative look.

"Thank you," she said, leaning forward. As was his custom, Roger kissed her on the cheek as they hugged.

"Are you sure this isn't too early for you?" he asked.

Camille shook her head. "I have a reception tonight on the Hill. I don't know if I'll be able to slip away to get to your concert."

"That's okay," he said. "Just seeing you now is great."

She reached for his hand. "Having lunch with you is the best part of my day, the best part of my week," she added with a smile.

"Your table's ready. Right this way."

Still holding hands, Roger and Camille followed the restaurant hostess.

"Where's Roger?" Margaret asked.

A few people from the choir were standing in the lobby. They'd decided to make a trip to the Mall area to sightsee for a few hours.

"I haven't seen him since breakfast," Krista said.

Margaret knew that today would be a good one. She'd willed it, despite the message she'd gotten from her cards last night. She'd been unable to do a reading this morning because Glenna was up and moving around.

A sightseeing van pulled up and the choir members surged forward.

"You want to come with us?" Krista asked. "There's room."

Margaret glanced about. Normally, she didn't socialize with the choir members. She didn't always feel at ease with some of them. But, she thought, maybe going along on this little side trip would show Roger that she was capable of being a team player. That, above all, seemed to be what held him back from really accepting her as a potential life partner.

"Sure," Margaret said. "I'd like that."

A couple of people exchanged glances, but no one said anything.

Moments later, they were all aboard the van headed to the Mall.

In her room, Glenna leaned against the bathroom vanity and wiped her mouth. The acrid taste of vomit still lingered, even though she'd swished several mouthfuls of water around her mouth.

Getting up this morning had been hard, very hard. But she refused to give in to the weakness. She had too much to do.

Life had dealt a cruel and unfair hand, but Glenna had decided long ago that she would go out fighting. She'd give as much as she could in the time she had left. She knew she couldn't make up the wasted years, but she could spend her remaining days being a soldier in the Lord's army.

"Just let me get to that chair, Lord," she prayed.

Clutching her stomach, she lurched around, aiming for the chair that seemed three miles away. She sucked in her breath and took one halting step forward.

She toppled over, hitting the floor hard.

Glenna cried out in pain.

Then, she just cried.

Marcus paused in his stride. Had someone called out for help? He looked behind him but didn't see anything on the walkway outside the rooms. A housekeeper's cart was at the far end, too far away to have made the heavy thud that sounded like someone or something falling. Marcus's mind was on the things he needed to accomplish today, before the choir's engagement up at Howard.

He'd left his room and was headed to the equipment truck to take a look at those headset units. If Roger pulled another stunt like the one he'd done earlier, Marcus planned to be ready for him. They didn't need any sound equipment in the afternoon, so he didn't have to work the engagement at the seniors' center. That was just as well. He had plenty to do.

Everything had worked out all right last night. No thanks to Roger, though. The only reason he'd even signed on to this gig was to . . .

A door opened and shut in front of him.

"Oh, hello. You scared me," an older white woman said as she came out of her room.

"Morning, ma'am," Marcus replied. "Did you just drop something? I thought I heard a noise."

The woman looked askance at him, drew her purse closer to her body, and skittered by without another word.

Marcus rolled his eyes. People saw what they wanted to see. Few, if any, ever looked below the surface. The dreads that he'd grown for just that purpose obviously worked. That scared white woman saw a big black man with dreadlocks and tattoos and probably thought *threat*. He grinned. Her assessment wouldn't have been too far off the mark on that particular fact.

Again surveying the closed room doors, he dismissed the sound he'd heard and took the stairs two at a time. Now was not the time to get distracted from his mission.

Tyrone's question still ate at Georgie. Last night, she'd evaded answering. But she wondered what she might say if he eventually demanded to know what her "or else" threat would be.

She'd been a good wife. They were well suited. Everybody said so. And Georgie truly did love him—even if she hadn't when they'd first gotten together.

Georgie's love for Tyrone Thomas was something that had evolved over time. They'd been married for two years now. And Georgie didn't regret a single day of it. Ty was a loving and devoted husband. If anything, she knew, it was she who wasn't deserving of him and his love.

If he knew everything, such as her secret, he probably wouldn't love her anymore. More than likely, he'd demand a divorce. He'd be justified if he did; that fact Georgie well knew.

No one in her entire family had ever been divorced—even when some of them should have been. But then, no one, to her knowledge, had done what she'd done.

"What God has put together, let no man put asunder," she whispered.

Yet, she had to admit, was it God who had put her with Ty? Or was it her own doing that had led to their dating and eventual wedding? Had she just wanted it so badly that she'd willed it, or was Tyrone the man she was supposed to grow old with?

Georgie didn't have any answers to the questions that plagued her. And she didn't know where she and Ty stood. She did love him, though. With all her heart and mind and body she loved him.

Would he still love her if he knew?

Probably not. And that fact ate at her.

Last night was the first time they'd ever slept apart. When she wouldn't answer his question, Tyrone got dressed and left their room. When he'd returned about an hour later, Georgie had pretended to be asleep. She'd expected him to get into the bed and draw her body to his as he did every night. Instead, though, she'd felt him standing over her for a long time. Then, he yanked the covers up on the other bed and climbed into it, leaving Georgie alone and afraid of what had become of their marriage.

Now, she let the hot water in the shower beat her back. The running water masked the sound of her anguish and washed away the hot tears of regret that fell from her eyes.

The Reverend Vincent Hedgepeth opened his hotel room door, surprised to see Tyrone Thomas standing there. He'd expected

Calvin, who always had a follow-up question to whatever the Bible study lesson had been about.

"Tyrone. This is a surprise. What can I do for you?" he said, shaking the man's hand and guiding him into the room.

"Hey, Reverend Vince," Ty said as he came in.

Vincent closed the door and waited near it.

"You know how you're always saying you have an open ear if anyone in the choir ever wants to talk about anything?"

The minister nodded.

"Well, I'm here. I want to talk."

Nodding, Vincent motioned for Tyrone to take a seat. He waited to see where the man would settle. First Vincent went to the keyboard Roger still had set up. He looked at the music Roger had been working on. Then, shaking his head, he finally took a seat at one of the two chairs at the room's small round table. Vincent sat in the other one.

"How long have you been married, Reverend Vince?"

"This year will be twenty-three years."

Tyrone shook his head and whistled. "That's a long time."

"Yes. It is."

Tyrone steepled his fingers. Quiet for a long moment, his gaze eventually met Vincent's. "I don't think I'm gonna make the three-year mark, let alone twenty-three."

For a moment Vincent didn't say anything. The quiet between the two men remained companionable, though. Vincent waited for Tyrone to get his thoughts together. After a few minutes he quietly asked, "Want to talk about it?"

Tyrone shook his head. "I don't know. I don't know what to say. I don't even know what's wrong."

"Why don't you start at the beginning?"

Tyrone's answering laugh was brittle. "Which beginning? The one where we met, or the beginning of what's looking like the end?"

Vincent regarded the younger man. "Why don't you just start wherever you want to."

Tyrone nodded. "I fell in love with her the moment I saw her."

Vince smiled.

"She was beautiful. She was with another brother, though. We were in line to see a gospel show." Tyrone stopped talking for a moment; then his direct gaze connected with the minister's. "Reverend Vince, do you think Roger and I spend an excessive amount of time together and focused on music?"

He shrugged. "Depends on what your definition of 'excessive' is. Roger is in full-time ministry. You work another job, you have the Blackstone group, and you have a fairly new marriage you're still working at. Is time what's bothering you and Georgie?"

"Yeah. That's one of the things."

"Have you tried talking to each other? Communication—"

"Yeah, our talking led me straight here." Vincent sighed. "It's like all we do these days is argue. And it's over stupid stuff." He shook his head. "It's like we're dancing around something and I can never get a handle on what it is. Almost like whatever it *really* is, neither one of us wants to come out and just say it."

"Say what?"

Tyrone looked at the minister. All of the tiredness, emptiness, and even the loneliness he'd been feeling lately reflected in his eyes. Ty had never failed at anything. Not one single thing. When he put his mind and his heart to a matter, it always, *always* came out right for him. Whether playing on the basketball court in school, writing a piece of music, or dealing with the mood swings and personalities of singers, Ty knew how to turn a bad situation around.

Now, though, now that it mattered, the one thing that meant the most to him seemed to be slipping from his grasp right before his eyes. The chasm between him and Georgie grew wider every day. Ty didn't know what had caused the earthquake and he didn't know how to shore up the fault line. His gut told him that their problems were about more than having a baby.

He did, however, harbor a suspicion. It was ugly. Unkind. And he hoped to God it was untrue.

He looked at Vincent, anguish burning at his heart like a brand. "I think she's either having or had an affair."

Stunned, Vincent blinked. "That's a serious charge," he said slowly. "Georgie doesn't seem like the type who . . ."

Vincent's gaze leveled on the minister's. Then he hopped up and paced the area between the door and the chairs. "It's the only thing that makes any sense."

If Georgie wanted a baby, fine. What did that have to do with Roger? Unless . . .

"Reverend Vince, Georgie barely tolerates Roger. You've seen the tension between them."

"Well, yes, but . . . Where are you going with this?"

Tyrone suddenly stopped pacing. He shook his head, not wanting to put voice to his speculation. It made sense, though. It would explain so much, like why Roger had seemed so distant at their wedding. When the preacher said the speak-now-or-forever-hold-your-peace bit, Roger had started coughing, and Georgie gripped Tyrone's hand so hard he thought she'd broken one of his fingers.

What were they hiding?

There was some kind of history between Roger and Georgie. That was the only thing that would or could account for the defensive way she always acted around him. The rest of the time, she acted as if she could barely stand to be in the same room with him.

He didn't think she'd stepped out on him since they were made husband and wife. But that didn't mean Georgie hadn't been eaten up by the black specter of guilt over whatever had happened between her and Roger.

"Tyrone?"

Ty, who'd been standing stock-still as if he'd turned into a pillar of salt, turned and stared at Reverend Vince.

"Reverend Vince, I don't mean to get in your business or anything, but when you and Sister Hedgepeth have a really big fight—something that shakes the very foundation of your relationship—what's the first thing you do after it's over?"

"Talk to God first. Then I talk to my wife."

"That's what I thought. Reverend Vince, I've got some God-talking to do. Excuse me."

Taking another look around the hotel room, as if seeing it for the first time, his gaze paused on his cousin's keyboard. Tyrone snorted, mumbled something Vincent couldn't make out, then left the room without another word.

10

Serve each other in humility, for God sets Himself against the proud, but He shows favor to the humble.

—1 Peter 5:5

Margaret's face flushed with excitement when she burst through the door. What a wonderful day! Touring Washington had been fun. Of course, she'd been to the nation's capital many, many times, usually for a performance at the Kennedy Center or to visit friends in Georgetown. But she'd never taken a tour like a tourist. And then to see the president and the first black secretary of state at the White House. It was just too much.

She dropped her purse on the table and was about to swing her White House souvenir bag onto her bed when she saw Glenna.

"Oh, my God."

Margaret rushed to Glenna's side. She lay sprawled on the floor, her back propped against the bed.

The telephone was on the floor and off the hook. The edge of the bedspread clutched in Glenna's hand showed the effort she'd given to try to rise.

"Glenna! Glenna!" Margaret shook the other woman.

"Margaret. Stop. Please."

A huge sigh of relief rushed through Margaret. She put her arm under Glenna's and tried to raise her.

"Wait," Glenna said. "Rest."

"Is there some medicine? Should I call nine-one-one?"

Glenna shook her head. "Just need to rest. For a minute."

Margaret picked up the pillows on the floor and replaced the telephone receiver. Then she went to the sink at the vanity and ran a glass of water for Glenna.

"Pills in my bag."

Spying the large tote that Glenna carried, she brought it with the water to Glenna. Margaret settled on the floor next to Glenna.

"Prescription bottle," Glenna said.

Margaret rummaged for the bottle and came up with three. "Which one?"

Glenna closed her eyes. "Small pills."

Her hands fumbled as she opened the bottle. Glenna looked exhausted. Her face was mottled and deep circles ringed her eyes. Margaret shook out a pill.

"How many?"

"Just one. For now," Glenna added.

She helped Glenna with the water. The other woman swallowed the pill, then leaned her head back on the bed. Eyes closed, breathing deeply, Glenna sat there.

As she recapped the bottle, Margaret took a look at the label. The long name of the drug meant nothing to her. But she glanced at Glenna after reading the directions: "Take as needed for pain."

"Should I get Roger or Reverend Hedgepeth?"

Glenna shook her head. "No. I'll be all right. This episode just . . ." She shook her head. "It came without warning. Took me by surprise, that's all."

"How long have you been on the floor?"

"Don't know. I just prayed that somebody would come."

"Do you think you can get up now?"

Glenna nodded.

Together they managed. Margaret got Glenna onto the bed, then pulled the sheet over her and got the pillows situated.

Glenna tried to ward her off. "I'm fine now. Really. You don't have to do all of this."

Margaret paid her no attention. When she was satisfied that Glenna was resting comfortably, she sat on the edge of her bed. "What's wrong with you?"

When Glenna smiled, Margaret realized how presumptuous the question had been.

"It's nothing contagious, if that's what you're worried about."

Margaret's eyes widened. Until Glenna mentioned it, she hadn't even thought about that. She glanced at her hands and suddenly felt compelled to wash them.

That she'd spent a few minutes selflessly helping another person didn't cross her mind. All she wanted right now was to disinfect her entire body, then find another room to stay in.

"I have pain episodes. Sometimes it feels like my bones are on fire, but mostly my stomach hurts." She managed a small smile. "Dealing with this, I know what Jeremiah was talking about."

"Jeremiah?"

"The prophet. You know, he said he was so filled with the Holy Spirit that it felt like he had fire caught up in his bones."

Margaret looked at Glenna.

Glenna sighed. "I'll be fine. I don't think I'm going to make that afternoon program, though." She took a deep breath and closed her eyes.

Margaret watched her for a moment, then asked, "What do you have? Lupus? Sickle-cell?"

When she didn't answer, Margaret leaned forward.

Glenna had fallen asleep.

An ensemble went to the convalescent home. With his keyboard as their only accompaniment, Roger and four others entertained the mostly black and elderly residents with songs from the Baptist tradition. Foot tapping and hand clapping filled the day room where the residents gathered to hear the singers. When it was over, Roger accepted the good wishes of the attendees and pocketed the check from the home's activities director.

The full choir didn't have to gather until five-thirty. Roger and the ensemble arrived back at the hotel with just about twenty minutes to spare.

Glenna, who'd exacted a promise from Margaret not to mention her illness, dressed for the evening engagement. She didn't want to chance it that Roger might recommend she skip this performance. In the time she had left, Glenna wanted to get in all the singing for the Lord that she could.

When everyone was loaded onto the bus for the trek to Howard, and with a scan in the direction of Roger and Tyrone, the Reverend Hedgepeth prayed.

"Father God, we thank you for the mercy you've given to us this day. Lord, some of us have heavy hearts tonight. If we haven't walked uprightly in your spirit, we pray that you will lead us and guide us to the truth of your everlasting power."

At those words, several things happened at once:

Tyrone, thinking about Georgie, pressed his eyes shut tighter.

Georgie, thinking about Tyrone, suppressed a shiver and tears that welled.

Scottie smirked.

Glenna's loud "Yes, Lord" echoed through the bus.

And with guilty looks across the aisle, Krista and Dwayne glanced at each other.

Jerry wheeled the big bus through the streets of Washington, D.C. When he turned onto Georgia Avenue he called for Roger.

"Where am I going on campus?"

"Just a sec," Roger said, pulling up his briefcase. "The concert is at the student center. I have some parking info right here."

He'd tucked the parking passes in his appointment book where he kept all of the tour contact materials. He slipped a finger under the flap and slit open the edge of the envelope that had been dropped off at their motel.

"All righty, let's see," he said, flipping open the piece of white paper.

His face paled when he read the single line of type. "Jesus!"

"What's wrong, Roger?" Krista asked.

He quickly folded the paper, jammed it in his briefcase, and slammed it shut. "Nothing," he said. "Nothing."

But his hands were trembling and his heart beat as if he'd just run a marathon.

"Roger?" the bus driver called. "Where to?"

Roger shoved his briefcase onto the floor at his feet, then leaned forward and gave Jerry some directions.

A few minutes later, they arrived at their destination. With the usual jostling and commentary, the choir members and musicians filed off the bus and gathered outside. Roger still sat in his front-row seat, staring out the big expanse of bus window.

Dwayne's head popped up from the stairs. "Roger, man. You coming? There's some people out here asking for you."

"I . . . Tell them I'll be right there."

Dwayne disappeared and Roger reached for his briefcase. He didn't want to look at that envelope again. Its message was burned onto his brain. Carefully locking the case, he then joined his choir members.

"Do you think he was talking about us?" Krista whispered to Dwayne.

They were in the room designated as the dressing area for the Voices of Triumphant Praise. The choir would have a warm-up and prayer before they went to the stage.

"Who?"

"Reverend Vince. You heard that prayer on the bus. You think he was specifically talking about us?"

Dwayne shrugged. "I don't know, baby. He could have been talkin' 'bout any old body." With a nod in Scottie's direction, he added. "You know all the stuff that's always going on in this choir. Shoot," he said, stepping close to her for a quick feel. "For all we know, we ain't the only ones—"

"Shh!" Krista elbowed him as her frantic gaze darted around.

"Oww!"

Immediately she looked contrite. "Sorry," she said. "But keep your voice down. If everybody doesn't already know, they will with you broadcasting our business all over the place."

Dwayne rubbed his arm where she'd poked him, the same arm that had been injured on the bus. "I'm going to get something to drink."

He walked away, leaving Krista standing there with hands on hips and a scowl on her face.

"I wouldn't worry too much about that, Sister Krista," Glenna said.

Krista jumped and whirled around. She bit her lip, guilt making her wonder just how much of the conversation Glenna had overheard. She plastered a bright smile on her face. "Worry about what?"

Glenna nodded toward Dwayne's back as he studied the selections in a soda machine across the way.

Deciding to play ignorant, Krista said, "What do you mean?"

Used to playing the game, but not willing to tip her hand or to embarrass the girl, Glenna just nodded. "The Lord has a word for you, Sister Krista. Don't miss the message."

Glenna slowly made her way to a table, where she leaned heavily on the surface for support before sitting down. Krista watched her, her expression troubled and unsure. She'd heard some things about Glenna. Maybe the stories were true after all.

"Hey, Krista, you have a safety pin?"

Krista turned to Danita, one of the newest members of the choir. "Yeah. I'll get it for you."

With another look, first at Dwayne and then toward Glenna, Krista joined the other woman who'd set up a makeup kit on one of the tables.

Across the room, Marcus had cornered Scottie.

"I know what you're doing, man. And you need to take that shit away from here."

Scottie eyed Marcus. "I know you ain't standing there trying to get in *my* business."

"If you know what's good for you, my brother, you will straighten up and fly right before your little entrepreneurial venture brings more trouble than you can handle."

Scottie folded his arms, challenging the stronger man. "This is the perfect set-up," he said, jerking his head back toward the choir. "You and what posse are gonna page the po-lease?"

Marcus stared at him for a moment. Scottie glared back.

"Watch your back," Marcus warned. "You aren't as slick as you think you are."

From the center of the room, Roger called the choir members together. They did a warm-up exercise, running through scales and harmony; then he gave them the line-up for the evening.

"Basically, I just want you to follow either my lead or Tyrone's tonight. We're here to spread the word about the gospel. So let's just focus on that." That particular message, Roger knew, was directed more toward himself than the choir members.

It was important that he focus on their ministry that night, not the threat in his briefcase.

Georgie's attempts to talk to Tyrone weren't at all successful. When she first approached him, he said he needed to consult with the musicians about something. When she tried again, Glenna came up at the same time.

"I'm not feeling too good tonight, Brother Tyrone," the small woman said. "I don't think I better do a solo, okay?"

Tyrone nodded. "I'll let Roger know." He looked at Glenna, concern in his eyes. "Is there something I can get for you?"

It hurt Georgie that Ty hadn't shown that much care for her feelings or well-being.

Glenna shook her head. She reached for and squeezed Georgie's hand. "You're looking sharp as usual, Sister Georgie."

"Thank you," Georgie said. Ty hadn't mentioned a word about the lavender-and-cream suit that accented her full curves. She reached for his arm. "Ty, do you have a minute?"

"Not now," he said, the words curt enough that even Glenna noticed.

"I'll, uh, leave y'all," she said. The couple watched her slower-than-normal progress to a chair.

Georgie again faced her husband. "Tyrone . . ."

"I said not now, Georgie." He walked away, leaving her standing there alone.

Reverend Vince, who had witnessed the exchange, hesitated a moment before approaching Georgie. He liked Georgie and Tyrone Thomas, and didn't at all like seeing them like this. Maybe he could help in some way.

"Sister Georgie," he called. "There you are. I don't have to make the choir's intro tonight. I've staked out a couple of seats in the reserved section. Would you like to join me?"

Right before the choir went on, Camille showed up. She waved at Roger from where she stood near the front of the musicians' entrance. Roger's face lit up. He gave her the thumbs-up sign as he accepted a microphone.

"Good evening, Howard!"

Margaret Hall-Stuart frowned. Her gaze moved from Roger to the woman she didn't recognize, a woman Roger looked all too happy to be seeing. Once she started singing, though, Margaret forgot about the woman. The music she loved singing swept her up.

The Voices of Triumphant Praise's five-song set went off without a problem. The choir members enjoyed themselves. The audience gave them a rousing applause when they finished. The choir members made their way offstage and to the seats reserved for them while the next group did their setup.

The woman Margaret had seen stepped forward. Roger embraced her in a big hug.

Witnessing the greeting, Margaret relaxed. That was a brotherly hug. The woman was probably one of Roger and Tyrone's relatives.

Content that she had nothing to worry about on that front, Margaret settled into her seat to enjoy the rest of the Gospel Jamboree.

11

In the day of my trouble I will call to you, for you will answer me.
—Psalm 86:7

Roger's thoughts were still on Camille by the time he and Vincent returned to the motel. He'd been pleased to see her wearing the necklace he'd given her that afternoon.

Their conversation at lunch ran through his mind, mostly her surprise about the gift, a pearl surrounded by tiny sapphires on a gold chain. Pearls were her favorite and she was born in September, the sapphire month, so he figured he was safe. Diamonds and rings meant promises, and Roger very much wanted to make that life-long promise with Camille. But it was too soon, their in-person relationship still too new to make that leap just yet.

So he'd wait. And in the meantime, he'd get up to Washington, D.C., a little more often.

"That was a good concert," Reverend Vince said as he flicked on the lights in their motel room.

Roger nodded.

When he didn't hear anything from the man behind him, Vincent turned around. "You all right?"

"I was just thinking about Camille."

Vincent grinned. "So, how'd it go with your lady love this afternoon?"

Roger shrugged, not really ready to talk about things between them, but at the same time desperately in need of some reassurance.

"She said she needed time to think. Said I took her by surprise."

"What'd you do?"

It was Roger's turn to grin. "I gave her some jewelry."

"A ring?"

"No," Roger said drawing out the word. "But more than a little something, particularly since it's not her birthday or anything. She was there tonight."

"Your lady love? Up at the college?"

Roger nodded.

"Well, I'll be," Vincent said. "You didn't say a word. Must be serious."

Vincent took off his jacket. When Roger didn't say anything, he went to the closet area to pull out his suitcase. Hefting the large rolling bag, Vincent moved back to the bed, opened it, and began packing his clothes.

"Did she say anything about this piece of jewelry when you saw her tonight?"

Roger ducked his head and smiled. "She was wearing it."

"Hmm," Vincent said.

"What's 'hmm' mean?"

"Means she's doing what women tend to do."

"Which is?"

"Trying to figure out where you're coming from, wondering what else you're asking and wanting by giving her the jewelry. Trying to decide if she wants to go to the next step in the relationship."

Roger frowned. "All that?"

The older man nodded. "All that."

After coming out of his own suit jacket, Roger loosened his tie and pulled it off. He reached for and unzipped a black leather duffel bag. "You and Tyrone need to enroll in the same head-shrinkers class."

A quick smile curved Vincent's mouth. He said, "I sat with Georgie up at Howard tonight."

When Roger didn't say anything, Vincent tried another approach. "You and Georgie get along?"

Roger glanced up from unbuttoning and rolling up his shirt-sleeves. "Sure. But I'm kind of worried about them. Ty didn't say much of anything all night."

Normally, Tyrone kept everyone's spirits up; his jokes or words or encouragement were always just what someone needed. Tonight, though, now that Roger thought about it, Ty looked as though *he* could have used a good word from somebody.

Roger went to the drawer where he'd stashed his underwear, socks, and shirts, and scooped up all of the contents. "Keep them in your prayers, Reverend Vince. Ty and Georgie are . . . well, they're going through a rough patch right now."

"How long have you known Georgie?"

Roger thought about it for a moment. "It's been a little while, since before they got married. You might know her father. He's chairman of the deacon board over at First Goodwill Baptist on Taylor Road."

"That's that little church on the corner. Dwight Johnson's place, right?"

Roger nodded.

"I know of it. Heard Johnson speak at a ministers' council prayer breakfast, but I've never been over there."

"Real conservative group. Worse than GOGIC ever was back in their early days. They adhere to a lot of 'thou shalt nots.' The folks over at Goodwill are what my grandmother used to call Old Testament saints."

"Nothing wrong with that," Vincent said.

Roger shrugged. "Some of it is . . . well, let's just put it this way. The Voices of Triumphant Praise will be gray and in their graves before we ever get an invite to sing over there."

Vincent finished up his packing. He left slacks, a polo shirt, and a sport jacket out for the morning. "I'm going to call Sister Hedgepeth, let her know where we'll be tomorrow."

"Tell her I said hi and thanks for the treats."

Moving to the closet to give Vincent a bit of privacy, Roger picked up the tie he'd worn earlier. In his haste to get back from his lunch date with Camille and to the afternoon engagement at the convalescent home, Roger had shed his clothes and thrown them in a heap across the luggage stand. He shook out the slacks and then folded them up to go in his bag.

When he picked up the jacket he'd had on that afternoon, his good mood evaporated in an instant as he remembered what he'd tucked into that jacket—the envelope he'd mistakenly believed held campus parking passes.

He quickly made his way across the room to snatch up his briefcase.

"Hi, honey. We're back from Howard University."

With a glance at Reverend Vince, Roger went to the bathroom vanity. He unlocked the case and plucked the offensive envelope from his appointment book.

Roger stared at the note, his skin growing clammy all over again.

He quickly glanced over at Vincent, who was kicked up on his bed talking to his wife in low tones.

Roger read the letter again, then looked at the envelope. It, like the note, had no return address, no writing, nothing to identify the sender.

With another furtive glance at Reverend Vince, Roger went to the bathroom, where he shut the door, sat on the toilet, and stared at the letter.

He'd always been afraid that something like this would happen. That someone would find out what he'd done and make him pay for his sin; as if his nightmares weren't enough reminder.

The ramifications of that night so long ago still haunted him all these years later. He balled his fists. The paper scrunched and crinkled in his hands. But the message burned on his brain: *Do you really think nobody knows?*

Someone knew his secret.

And it was someone who'd waited ever so patiently until Roger was just on the cusp of making it big. He had nowhere to hide, and no defense that would acquit him in a court of law. Despair washed through him. Pain and regret followed. But he couldn't change the outcome of that night so long ago.

He couldn't bring back the life he'd taken on a dark road.

Roger rocked on the toilet seat, trying to get his thoughts together, trying to figure out what to do. In an attempt to make the images disappear, he squeezed his eyes shut. The picture, however, remained as clear as it had always been: a car, a dark road, the sticky warmth of blood, and the stench of liquor strong on his breath . . .

He sat there. Stunned. Cold. Tired. Confused.

An annoying and persistent wail echoed in his ears. The sound grated through his central nervous system. Slowly he sat up, wondering why his head felt as if a thousand bricks had been lowered onto the back of his neck, one at a time until the weight became an unbearable burden. His mouth, thick and cottony, didn't feel at all like his own.

He blinked his eyes, the grit of sandpaper scratching his irises. Then, suddenly, he realized the wail no longer echoed through the night. The only sound he heard was the rush of his own breathing, staccato, panicked. And then he realized.

"Oh, my God."

He cried out again. His plea was for divine intervention, for a miracle of time and place. Maybe, he hoped, wished, prayed, just maybe it was all a horrible dream, a nightmare in which he'd become the central victim, trapped in a gruesome tale and spirited away by the demons of hell.

Slowly, he became aware of a scent. Unfamiliar at first, it became stronger, more definite. And he knew. He glanced to the left, at the passenger seat of the small car. His new car. The blue Escort he'd saved money to buy. It had taken six months of overtime and extra church gigs to save the cash.

Gin.

We thin gin.

The line from the Gwendolyn Brooks poem floated through his consciousness. He'd walked into the liquor store and asked for gin. It was the only liquor he knew by name. He knew it from the poem.

We die soon.

Would he die this night? A part of him wondered if he'd already died. Was hell a place where eternal nightmares came to the damned? Was hell a place at all?

He thought he knew. Now, though, he wasn't so sure.

He moved his mouth, trying to work his jaw. His hand fell forward and the wailing siren sounded again, this time in a short, angry blare.

He belatedly recognized the car horn as the source of the long, angry noise he'd first heard. He ran his hand over his face. His fingers came back warm, sticky. Slowly he brought his hand down. He had to blink several times to focus on what he was actually seeing.

Blood. Thick, red, warm blood covered his hand.

His?

He reached for the rearview mirror. The small rectangle of glass sat askew on its mount in the windshield. He turned it to face him. A crack ran along the side of the mirror.

He stared at the image staring back at him.

He didn't recognize the man.

He closed his eyes before looking again. Thick eyebrows matted with blood, a broad nose, scared eyes. The eyes in the reflection frightened him most. The eyes knew, and he didn't want to know what they knew. But the knowledge was there.

Stark. Deadly. Cold.

Taking a deep breath, he coughed. His breathing suddenly labored as the last few minutes—or had it been hours?—came back to him.

The ABC store where he'd bought the bottle of gin. Twisting the cap as he drove along the dark streets, turning here and there at will. Music on the radio: loud, glaring rock that grated on his nerves as much or more than anything. He'd never listened to hard rock before. For that matter, he'd never touched alcohol either. Neither fact mattered tonight.

Nothing had been going right: not his music, his classes, or his life. He was broke and another late month's rent away from being evicted. Then, to lose not one, but two talent shows! He'd banked on the winnings from those shows to tide him over. But when the judge's scores were tallied, Roger McKenzie had come in second in one show and third in the other. Losing out both times to that no-talent, posturing . . .

The screech of a guitar emboldened him. He screamed the repeated lyrics along with singer: "Walk this way," and he'd followed, speeding, giddy, released from the strictures of his role, his time, his place, and his pain.

And out of nowhere she appeared, darting across the road.

He tried to stop—or did he press the accelerator?

The bottle fell from his hand as he reached for the radio knob. *Turn it down. Turn the wheel.*

First a thump. Then a screech of tires . . . and then nothing.

Nothing.

Until now. Blood and glass and gin on his body.

He had to make sure she was all right. He'd hit her, he was certain. He reached for the door handle, but pain arced through his arm.

Wincing, he prayed for help to come. Then, realizing the full ramifications of his actions, he prayed that no one would ever come. Not until he'd made sure she was okay, not until the pungent odor of spilled gin faded. Not until . . .

Roger shook his head, willing that night away from his memory, away from his past. But it was there.

And someone knew.

He balled the paper up, rose, and threw it in the toilet. Then he plunged his hand into the cold water of the commode, retrieving the letter. Its one line of type burned onto his memory like a brand on his brain.

He ripped the paper into tiny pieces, as small as he could tear the wet paper. Then he flushed it all down the toilet.

Forgiveness had been granted. He knew, he trusted, he believed that God had forgiven him his sin.

But someone else hadn't.

Tyrone didn't know what to do about his suspicions. He watched Georgie putter about the hotel room. There was nothing for her to clean, fix, or fool with, so she spent the time touching things. She had something she wanted to say; he could sense that. But she didn't know how to say it. He wasn't making it easy, either. And then the solution, at least a temporary one, came to him.

"Georgie."

She whipped around, her face caught in an expression somewhere between joy and sorrow. She really was beautiful. Her rounded face reminded him again of why he'd fallen for her that first night. She looked like a cherub.

"Yes, Ty."

"I think you should go home."

Her face fell. "What do you mean?"

"We're headed to Baltimore tomorrow and then the rest of the tour. This is work for me. For you, it's a vacation."

"You think that arguing every night—"

He held up a finger. "My point exactly, Georgie. We have some problems. Issues we're either gonna have to work out or not. But this is not the time or the place for those discussions. You have a beautiful voice and you know all the music because you come to rehearsals. Yet you refuse to sing with the choir."

"You know I don't care for all that—"

He continued as if she hadn't interrupted. "You say you want a baby, but you don't want to consider the cost and strain it'll put on our finances. When I point out the reality of the situation, you get that look and that attitude."

"Who are you to talk about attitude? You're the one who always closes down and clams up. I want to talk about us. I want to plan for the future. We should be in a house, Ty. Instead, we're cramped up in a four-room duplex with the next-door neighbor's big-screen television set blaring through the walls."

That hurt, as she knew it would.

"I'm doing the best I can for us, Georgie."

She shook her head. "No, you're not." The words were soft and therefore all the more devastating.

He cocked his head to the side. "I know you didn't just say that." He shook his head as if to clear it. "I *know* I didn't hear that."

Georgie folded her arms. "I did say it. And you know it's the truth. You spend all of your time—time that should be ours—with Roger."

He threw his hands in the air. "Here we go again. Back to Roger. Tell me, Georgie. How did he make such an impact on you that every time you see me, you're comparing what you could have had with him to what you have with me?"

"What?"

"You heard me. And you know exactly what I'm talking about."

"Tyrone Blackstone Thomas, I swear to God sometimes you make me so mad I could scream."

"Go ahead. Scream. Swear. Yell all you want," he said, flopping into the room's easy chair. "I'm sure Roger will come running to your rescue."

She stared at him, hands on her broad hips, her mouth open in either surprise or fury. Tyrone didn't know which, and at this point he didn't much care.

"I hate you for this, Tyrone."

"Ah, the truth finally comes out of your lying mouth."

She jerked as if he'd slapped her. Her mouth trembled and Tyrone steeled himself. Her tears always made him putty, a fact she obviously knew because she used the ploy often.

He watched her swallow hard and stare at him. Then, without a word and without a single tear falling, she turned around and ran to the bathroom.

The door slammed. He smirked.

He got off the bed and walked over to the bathroom door. He could hear her crying. This time, Tyrone wasn't moved by her tears.

He'd let her sulk for a while and then maybe they'd be able to have an adult conversation.

Still dressed in the tunic and slacks he'd worn up at Howard, Tyrone grabbed the hotel key from the dresser and let himself out of the room.

He'd give her time to cool down; then he'd come back. With no place to go and no one he wanted to talk to, he went over to the diner and sucked down coffee while he waited for Georgie to see the right way—his way.

But when he returned to their room about an hour later, it was empty.

"Georgie?"

He dashed to the closet area, knowing what he'd see yet hoping he was wrong.

Empty hangers dangled on the rod next to his clothes. Her makeup and toiletries were gone from the bathroom countertop. The two drawers she'd put her things in were bare.

Tyrone looked around, trying to spot a note or something. But nothing remained. It was as if she'd never even been there. The barest trace of her perfume lingered in the air, but maybe that was a figment of his imagination.

He sat on the edge of a bed and rubbed his eyes. His sigh echoed through the empty room. When he'd suggested that she go home, he'd meant it as a way for them to put a little distance on their running argument. He hadn't meant or even thought that they might part in anger. Well, he amended to himself, at least not this kind of anger.

Things weren't looking good. Not at all. His suspicions were eating him up. But she hadn't *denied* having a relationship with Roger. The only thing she had done was cut him down.

Angry, he flopped onto the bed where he'd slept and stared at her bed. She'd get home all right. He had no doubt about it. She'd probably go to the airport and get a first-class ticket just to spite him. Georgie had a credit card—as a matter of fact, she had too many. That was one of the reasons they were always broke. He had no doubt that she'd get home safely. She was a resourceful woman.

What he hadn't counted on was missing her already.

*   *   *

Roger dreamed that night. The demons came at him. They promised he'd never get away. They laughed at his feeble attempts, first to protect himself and then to hide.

And then he was drowning. In a lake in a car in the fog. Water filled the small car, covering his entire body and then his neck and then his head and then he was floating, floating on a river of thick, red blood.

He woke up sweating and coughing.

He called out to Vincent, but no answer came.

Stumbling from his bed, Roger lurched toward the bathroom. He fell to his knees and vomited into the commode.

It was late and the motel lobby was quiet. In the breakfast room, Reverend Vince sat with Tyrone. The two men prayed together, the minister's leather-bound Bible on the table between them.

With nowhere else to turn, Tyrone had gone to Reverend Vince for help. They'd come down here so as not to disturb Roger's sleep.

After the prayer, Tyrone sat back in his chair. "I think it's time for a change in my life."

"What do you mean?"

"I'm leaving the choir."

Vincent's eyebrows rose. "Where'd that come from?"

Tyrone shrugged. "I didn't like how she said it, but Georgie was right about one thing: I act like Roger is my keeper. I'm not subservient to him. We're blood and all, but there's a limit to a man's loyalty."

The minister nodded. "So you've decided to be judge and jury without hearing the other side's case."

A hard glint shot through Tyrone's eyes. "That's right."

"Then I think you need to talk to the Lord some more."

Before Tyrone could respond, a woman interrupted.

"Uh, 'scuse me."

The two men looked toward the door where a black woman with burgundy hair, large hoop earrings, and a stud in her nose stood.

"Yes?" Vincent said.

"Is one of y'all a Reverend Hodgepodge-something or other?"

Vincent rose. "I'm Reverend Vincent Hedgepeth."

"There's a lady on the line for you, says it's an emergency."

Grabbing his Bible, Vincent quickly followed the front desk

overnight clerk. She went back to her reception desk and pointed to a house phone on the wall near a rack of tourism brochures.

"Just press that blinking light," she said.

He snatched the receiver off the hook and punched the flashing button. "This is Reverend Hedgepeth."

"Oh, my God," Margaret cried. "Come quick. Call an ambulance. Reverend Vince, it's Glenna. I don't think she's breathing."

12

In just a little while the world will not see me again, but you will. For I will live again, and you will, too.

—John 14:19

Margaret Hall-Stuart, Roger McKenzie, the Reverend Vincent Hedgepeth, and Tyrone Thomas paced the floor of the hospital waiting room. Glenna had been in the emergency room for more than forty minutes and they'd gotten no word on her condition.

In Glenna's big purse they'd found her prescription bottles. Not readily recognizing the drugs, they'd handed them all over to the paramedics who arrived at the motel.

"What do you think is wrong with her?" Tyrone said to no one in particular.

"She's sick," Margaret snapped. "I found her on the floor when we got back from the tour this afternoon. After resting for a while, she insisted she was okay to go to the engagement tonight."

Roger rounded on Margaret. "You found her on the floor? Why didn't you say something?"

"I . . . I . . . What does it matter now?"

Reverend Vince glanced at Roger but kept quiet, at least for the moment. Now wasn't the time to point out that he'd found Roger slumped on the bathroom floor, his back pressed against the tub.

From sick bodies to sick spirits, there were a lot of things that bothered Reverend Vince about the members of the Voices of Triumphant Praise—the main thing being that its members weren't on an even spiritual keel. The drama in their lives, from the little he'd seen so far, was the sort that kept people out of the will of God if they let the problems overcome the faith in their lives. In his years as a counselor before coming to the ministry, Vincent had seen this sort of thing play out time and time again.

What the Voices of Triumphant Praise needed right now was to re-group.

He glanced at Roger, who was having a hushed but heated conversation with Margaret. His gaze then moved to Tyrone, whose animosity seemed to be growing exponentially to the point where it was almost as palpable as the tension between Roger and Marcus, the group's sound technician.

Roger.

Vincent's eyes widened. The key to it all was Roger.

He'd never really thought about it before, but everything seemed to revolve around Roger McKenzie's relationships with the people in the choir. From what he'd gleaned to date, every person in the choir had some story and connection with Roger that went beyond the confines of the singing and the music.

"Excuse me," a voice said, breaking into his thoughts.

All eyes went to the ER attendant in scrubs.

"Which one of you is Roger McKenzie?"

Roger strode forward, confident but worried. His brows arched together, forming something of an accent to the question obviously on his mind and everyone else's. "Is she okay? Is Glenna going to be all right?"

The doctor nodded but didn't say anything about Glenna's condition. "She's asking for you."

Roger glanced around at the others, then quickly followed the man.

Glenna lay on a table, surrounded by machines and medical apparatus. An IV slowly dripped into her arm. Her skin was pale, her hair askew.

Roger smiled. "You gave me a scare."

She smiled back, but the effort cost her. She swallowed. "Told them you're my cousin," she said, her voice weak, her breathing labored. "Said only family."

Roger took her free hand and squeezed it. "We are family, Glenna. You know that." Except for the night they'd met, he'd never known her to be weak or to show any fear. Glenna was strong. She was a fighter. Glenna had always been strong, even during the lowest point of her life.

In many ways, her life reflected the hope and the glory of being forgiven, saved by grace, baptized in the spirit. She'd come so far, had endured so much. Seeing her this way frightened Roger. But he refused to give in to the fear.

"Is there something I can do for you?" he said. "Something I can get?"

She paused for a long time before answering. Roger wasn't sure if it was because she was thinking of what to say, or if she needed the time to gather her strength. Then, finally, came her one-word request.

"Pray."

Roger leaned forward, closer. He placed his other hand atop hers so her hand was completely encased in his. He closed his eyes and began. "Father God, Sister Glenna needs you now."

He prayed for her strength, for the doctors and nurses as they worked. Roger prayed for grace from God and for mercy. He prayed for healing. And he prayed for endurance. When he finished, tears rolled from the corners of Glenna's eyes.

He squeezed her hand, then kissed her cheek.

Her eyes drifted closed and Roger's heart stopped. "Nurse?"

The attending nurse reassured him. "She's just resting. Why don't you talk to the doctor." The nurse pointed toward a man who stood reading a chart.

With a final look at Glenna and another quick prayer sent up for her, Roger sought the doctor.

"Is she going to be all right?"

The physician glanced back at Glenna, then motioned for Roger to step away a bit.

"Well, given her condition, yes."

"Condition. What condition?"

The doctor's sympathetic gaze fell on Roger. "From what we can tell based on the medication and the dosages she's taken, it's just a matter of time."

"Before what?" Roger said. But he knew. Deep down he'd always known, just as Glenna had, that she was living on borrowed time.

"I'm sorry," the doctor said. "The best we can do is get her comfortable and stabilized. I'd like to hold her overnight. We can give you the names of some hospice care centers in your area."

"Hospice care centers."

The information was coming too fast. It was too much to absorb, more than he wanted to know or accept.

Glenna was dying. Of what, it didn't really matter. Not the way the doctor looked at him.

She'd known she didn't have much time left, yet she'd come on this tour knowing the demands the travel would put on her body. And she'd never said one word. Not a single complaint.

Roger's shoulders sagged.

The doctor put a comforting hand out. "We'll do what we can."

"Thank you," Roger said.

He slowly made his way back to the waiting room, where the others awaited word on Glenna's condition. Roger realized he didn't know what to tell them.

He wished there were someone he could call, some of her family. But there was no one. The choir was Glenna's family.

Roger didn't know whether that made him feel blessed or stressed.

Later that morning Roger told the rest of the choir members that Glenna had been rushed to the hospital during the night. Several of them wanted to go straightaway to see her. So they roused Jerry and piled onto the choir bus. Roger, Tyrone, and Reverend Vince, who with Margaret had spent much of the night at the hospital, remained at the motel.

Margaret was in her room asleep.

After the choir pulled away, the three men sat in the breakfast room.

"You were right, Ty," Roger said. "You, too, Reverend Vince."

Tyrone, looking the worse for wear, leaned back in his chair. "Right about what?"

"This being a trip we never should have taken."

"Well, it's kind of late for that revelation," Tyrone said.

Roger glanced at his cousin. "Something up with you?"

Tyrone glared at him for a moment, then apparently decided to have it out here and now.

"Yeah," he said. "As a matter of fact, there is."

Roger's shoulders rose at the aggression.

"Georgie's gone," Tyrone said.

"What do you mean 'gone'?" both Roger and Vincent said at the same time.

"Gone. I mean she packed her bags and she's gone."

"Where?" Roger asked.

"You tell me."

"Guys, I don't think . . ."

Roger ran his hands over his face and rubbed his eyes. "What's *that* supposed to mean?" he said to Tyrone across Vincent's words.

"It means that everything wrong with my marriage comes back to you."

"Me?" Roger was clearly bewildered. "What do I have to do with it? Georgie acts like she doesn't like me. I respect her because she's your wife, but there's no love lost between us."

"Yeah, and why is that, huh? Why is that?"

Roger looked at the belligerent Tyrone but remained silent.

"Brothers . . ." Reverend Vince said. "We've had a long night. Why don't you—"

Tyrone hopped up from his chair. "What is it, Roger? You look like you've got something to say."

"It's not my story to tell," Roger said, fronting his cousin.

"What is *that* supposed to mean?"

Roger ignored the question. "Did she go home?"

"I don't know where she went. All we've been doing on this trip is fighting. And it's funny how your name is always up in the mix."

Reverend Vince put a hand between the two men, then stepped into the breach. "Roger. Tyrone. That's enough."

The two men turned toward Reverend Vince.

"I think there's a bigger issue at work here," the minister said.

Tyrone turned away. "You got that right."

Roger waited for Vincent to finish his thought.

"I know you have contracts and commitments, Roger, but given everything that's happened so far on this trip, I think you need to seriously consider if this tour and everything that's happened so far is in your best interest, in the choir's best interest."

"That's what I was doing before Ty here—"

Reverend Vince held a hand up again to ward off the angry words.

"Assess the damage that's already been done," Vincent continued. "We started off with a blown tire and an injury that could have been much worse. Then there was that disastrous concert at the community college. Microphones not working. Problems between Tyrone and Georgie, now Georgie's gone. And Glenna's sick. Maybe these are signs you need to heed."

Roger closed his eyes and tried to focus. They didn't understand. No one seemed to understand. He had a vision for the choir. This was the trip that would propel them into the limelight. Roger knew it just as he knew his name. He could feel it. This was just a storm they were passing through. The blessing and the rainbow were both on the other side.

He couldn't quit now. Not after they'd come this far.

"No," he said quietly. Then, with the conviction he felt in his heart, he emphatically made the declaration. "No. We go forward. We have to go forward."

Tyrone glared at him. "You can go wherever you want."

"Tyrone," Reverend Vince said, hoping to thwart words that would surely be regretted later.

Tyrone looked at the preacher, then glared at his cousin. "I'm going to bed."

In her room, Margaret wasn't sleeping. She'd come in and packed up Glenna's belongings as Roger had asked. Then she'd taken a long, hot shower before pulling out her journal and tarot cards.

What a day it had been. She wrote for a while and then shuffled and sorted her cards to lay down the tarot.

She needed some assurance that things were going to be okay, but she wasn't at all liking what she was seeing.

The Fool card and the Chariot were there. The way Margaret divined the cards, neither portended well. The fool could have meant the beginning of a great adventure, but its reverse meaning meant bad decisions had been made.

In the Marseilles deck she used, the one favored by the Reverend Sister Amelia, Prophetess of the True Light, the Chariot coupled with the Fool predicted defeat and failure.

Margaret took a deep breath before she put down the next card. She very much wanted to see the Lover or the Sun, cards of light and happiness.

She turned the next card on the top of the deck.

"Damn!"

Despite a TV game show of the same name, the Wheel of Fortune card wasn't one she wanted to see with the other grim cards.

Did the Wheel of Fortune mean her destiny would be one of perpetual misfortune?

Frustrated, Margaret decided to focus on someone other than herself. She snatched up all the cards, shuffled them, cut them, then read first for Glenna and then for Roger.

She stared at the cards, not at all believing what she was seeing. She got up, went to her purse for her phone, and called her psychic.

After a twenty-minute conversation, Margaret sighed. The Prophetess of the True Light had had similar readings. She recommended that Margaret do a cleansing ceremony to help shield herself from the bad spirits.

From her bag Margaret pulled out a purification candle. She lit the candle, placed it in the center of the chair in the center of the room. Then, she sat on the floor crosslegged and began the chanting prayer the prophetess recommended.

She finally had part of what she'd wanted at the beginning of this trip: a hotel room to herself. But Glenna's absence and hospitalization made Margaret sad, even sadder than the prophecy she'd read in the tarot.

Later that day, Roger walked the perimeter of the small church in Baltimore, Maryland. The Voices of Triumphant Praise were supposed to be singing soon. Roger felt everything but triumphant. Anxious, worried, tired, and on the verge of collapse were how he most felt.

He hadn't had a decent night's sleep since they'd started out. His stomach was giving him fits, and the antacids no longer seemed to do much good.

The ride to Baltimore from Washington, D.C., had been quiet. Most of the choir members had Glenna on their minds. She'd been transported back home and would be admitted into a care facility until she got her strength back.

This was his quiet time, the time when he and Tyrone usually walked a bit, talked together, prayed before a ministry in song. Tonight was different, though. There was no quiet banter between the cousins, and Roger's thoughts were in turmoil.

Tyrone wasn't talking to him and had elected to ride in the truck with Marcus rather than be on the bus with Roger.

Then there was Reverend Vince, who was on a mission to get him to throw in the towel on the tour. Even Margaret, who usually agreed with anything he said, had pulled Roger aside and quietly suggested that maybe they needed to cut their losses and go home.

But Roger had seen the Promised Land. The spies with the bad reports weren't going to dissuade him. He had the promise, or what he thought was a promise, from God.

He ran his hand over his head and sighed. "Now I'm questioning you, Lord. And that's not right."

The promise was that his ministry would go places. Touch people. Make a difference in the world. Roger clung to that promise, had embraced it, nurtured it, and let it feed his ego and his head until his only purpose in life was seeing the promise to fruition.

He would be a force to be reckoned with in gospel music. That he knew to be true. He'd win the big awards, land the mega contracts. The obstacles and pitfalls along the way, though, were also forces to be reckoned with. But they, he believed, would just be a part of the testimony when he emerged victorious.

Glancing at his watch, Roger turned back to go inside the church. It was time to minister, even though he felt that he himself needed to be ministered to.

"Hey, Roger," Krista said when he appeared in the doorway. "One of the ushers said this came a little while ago."

She held out a white envelope.

Roger stared at it as if it were a poisonous snake. "Who brought this?"

Krista shrugged. "I don't know. Some guy. He said it was dropped off right before we got here."

She wiggled the envelope in her hand. "Come on, Raj. I need to check my makeup and do my nails."

He took the envelope but held it between two pinched fingers as if the contents might explode in his face. Krista hurried back to the women's dressing room.

Roger watched her leave, then stared at the envelope. An icy fear arced through him. Someone knew. And they wanted to make sure he knew they knew.

Another realization hit him at that moment: It had to be someone close to him, someone *in* or connected to the choir.

The first envelope was delivered to the motel's front desk in Washington. Now, here at this little country church, another one had been delivered. That meant the person who was sending the notes knew his schedule.

Roger didn't quite know how to handle this situation, but taking a deep breath, steeling himself against whatever fiery dart Satan was about to throw his way, he carefully opened the envelope.

Inside was another envelope, a small tan one like the ones usher boards and choirs used to give love offerings to the preacher on pastor's anniversary. A small note was neatly folded inside the second envelope.

With shaking hands, Roger pulled it out and slowly opened it.

It's offering time. I'll be leading off the $500 line. A "timely cash tithe" should be behind the mirror in the men's room. Selah.

Blackmail. Was that what this was all about?

Roger glanced around but saw no one watching him. He pocketed both envelopes even as he calculated how fast he might be able to replace five hundred dollars of the choir's money if he used it to make this payoff.

13

When you go through deep waters and great trouble, I will be with you.
—Isaiah 43:2

"It's been a trying few days for us," Roger said when he finally took the microphone that night. He glanced back at the singers and musicians of the Voices of Triumphant Praise. "I think everybody can testify to that."

"Yes, Lord," a couple of people said at the same time.

"That's the truth," Danita called out with a wave of her hand.

Roger took a deep breath, facing the congregation again. "As we minister to you tonight, please pray our strength in the Lord."

He put the microphone down and went to his keyboard. He played the introduction to a song, then with a start realized it was one that Glenna usually led. He pointed to Ti'Nisha, who sang the backup. She'd never sung solo before, though, and cast wide, unsure eyes at Roger. She didn't move from her spot in the line and tried to shake her head.

"Take your time, children. Let the Lord have his way," one of the mothers of the church said in a deep voice.

Tyrone, on the church's organ, looked at Roger, shook his head, and deftly changed the melody to an original composition that everyone knew and that required no solo voices. Realizing what Tyrone was doing, Roger nodded and then gave a finger signal for the choir to follow Tyrone's lead and direction.

The concert was at a small church. The Voices of Triumphant

Praise were the only choir on the program. The church's sanctuary, which seated about two hundred, wasn't quite full, but there was a good showing.

Reverend Vince sat with the church's pastor and associate minister.

Even as he played and directed, Roger watched and listened to the choir singing music that should have been songs of praise and worship even as they lifted Glenna up. The edge they should have had singing as one body didn't seem to gel. Instead, their fractured voices rang out in disharmony.

It was not that they suddenly lost the ability to sing. The words were there. The right harmonies blended together. It was just that the spirit was lost or gone or absent. Their witness was not effective. And there wasn't a choir member who didn't realize it, not with Roger's occasional wince when someone missed a cue, or the awkward glances thrown about among the choir as they sang.

They could claim it was just an off night, particularly since everyone remembered how well the program at Jerusalem Baptist had turned out. But the ones who were honest with themselves knew it was much more than being off. They had issues, personal issues and issues as a choir that were adversely affecting the music and the ministry.

The audience's polite smattering of applause followed what was usually a soul-stirring, foot-stomping praise song.

Roger bowed his head and sighed. Then, with about everybody looking on, he walked to the center aisle of the church. Calvin hopped up and handed him a cordless microphone. "It's okay, Brother Roger," Calvin stage-whispered.

For a long minute Roger stood there. A woman coughed. A baby whined. Someone cleared his throat.

"That's all right, brother," a sister hollered out. "Take your time."

A few people said "Amen" as the choir members looked among themselves and at Roger. All eyes were on Roger McKenzie. And not even he knew what he was going to say.

Roger turned back to the choir, smiled a small smile, and shook his head. Then he again faced the congregation.

"It's been a rough road for us this week. This is our third day out on a seven-day tour. I tell you, it feels like day thirty."

That got loud "Amens" from the choir members.

Off to the side, where he sat with the pastor of the church and the ministerial staff, Reverend Vince cupped his chin in his hand.

Roger shook his head. "We need prayer, church. If there's anybody in here who can get a prayer through, we need you right here. Right now."

A couple of the choir members stepped forward, then slowly all of the others followed. They formed a close circle around Roger as Tyrone, on the organ, played softly. The church's organist slipped onto the bench and did a seamless exchange, allowing Tyrone to make his way to the circle for prayer.

Reverend Vince rose, as did the pastor and associate minister of the church. Before long, most of the people in the sanctuary had pressed forward, surrounding the Voices of Triumphant Praise in a cocoon of spiritual power during the impromptu altar prayer.

When the preacher asked everyone to bow their heads to approach the throne of grace, Scottie took that moment to slip away.

A message was supposed to have come for him. But it was almost time to go and he hadn't gotten it. In the hallway, he checked his voice mail. He had two messages, both of which could wait.

Remembering how and where he'd made contact before, Scottie slipped his cell phone back in his pocket and went to the men's restroom. His boy always included a little joke for him in the notes they exchanged, but tonight it just looked like he was being all business.

Scottie looked all over the restroom. There was no place to hide anything at the urinals, so he checked the stalls and then the paper towel dispenser.

"Where the hell?"

He stood in the middle of the floor and slowly surveyed the room. "Door. Urinals. Stalls. Wash the nasty hands there. Profile there." He stopped as he faced the mirror. A grin filled his face.

"My man."

If he hadn't been looking, he'd have missed the tiny bit of white edge peeking out. He stepped forward and pulled the envelope out from behind the mirror frame. A small brown envelope fell, too.

Scottie frowned. He opened the large envelope, counted the money he was expecting; then ripped open the small envelope. An extra five hundred was there.

Scottie laughed. "A tip for good service." His boy thought it was funny that he'd gotten a nice cozy set-up with the choir and always hooked him up with a little church-folk humor. But none tonight apparently. He had some free money though and a brother could always do with some extra Benjamins.

He pocketed all the cash, balled up and tossed the envelopes in the trash, and then made his way back to the sanctuary in time to hear the preacher say, "In the precious name of your son Jesus, Amen. And Amen."

"Amen," Scottie said.

Later that night, Roger sat in his hotel room staring at his hands. He didn't want to accept that he'd made a mistake; the acknowledgment was a bitter pill to swallow.

He pulled out his appointment book and stared at the six remaining engagements they had scheduled: two more concerts, three programs, and an assembly at a private school.

Roger hated admitting it, but Reverend Vince was right. This trip wasn't meant to be. Everything that had gone wrong so far was just confirmation of that fact—not, as he once believed, merely a test of his faith.

On top of everything else, what kind of threatening or blackmail notes awaited him when they reached Philadelphia?

Roger was tired and his heart was heavy. He hated going back on his word. But tonight had proven that there were some obstacles that couldn't be overcome. Being an ineffective witness was worse than being no witness at all.

He felt defeated, deflated. But in his heart of hearts he knew what he had to do. He'd make the necessary calls. At their Bible study in the morning, he'd tell the choir members what he'd decided.

PART TWO

SOLO

GEORGIE AND TYRONE

14

Barefoot, Georgie padded from the bedroom to the living room. She paused at the sight of Tyrone stuffing a sheet and blanket into the side of the pull-out sofa. He was bare-chested but wore the blue pajama pants of the set she'd given him last Christmas. Georgie wondered if their marriage would hold on until this Christmas. At the rate they were going, that didn't seem at all likely.

"Ty, we need to . . ." She cleared her throat and started over. "We should talk."

He glanced at the small alarm clock he'd placed on the end table as he put the sofa pillows back in place. "It's seven-thirty. You're gonna be late for work."

"I called in sick," she said.

Reaching for a throw pillow, Tyrone paused. He turned and looked at her. "You don't look sick."

She studied him for a moment, remembering all the love they had shared at the beginning of their relationship. In the six weeks since Roger had abruptly canceled the rest of the choir's tour, she'd watched Tyrone retreat further and further away from her, and from his cousin, Roger.

If their marriage truly was over, she owed him an explanation of what really had gone wrong, of why her animosity toward Roger was like a cancer spreading throughout her body. And if there was an outside chance they could salvage what they had and create a new beginning, then now was the time for total honesty and all its accompanying pain.

She stepped forward, closer to him. She wanted to touch him, wanted to feel his warmth, but she didn't know how, or whether he'd rebuff her. These past few weeks they'd been living like painfully polite roommates, neither willing to upset the delicate balance of a platonic relationship teetering on the brink of full collapse.

"I'm sick of us being like this," she said. "I'm sick of not having you as a husband. It pains me that I'm no longer your wife."

Tyrone took a deep breath. He didn't look at her, though. He stared at the sofa pillow.

He was quiet for so long that Georgie sighed. She pulled the edges of her chenille robe closer, as if garnering the warmth from it that she couldn't get from Tyrone. Finally, she turned, moving toward the kitchen, ready to make breakfast to give her idle hands something to do.

"I don't like it either," he said.

Georgie looked up, a sudden light shining in her eyes.

Their gazes met, hers hopeful, his sad.

"I'm moving out today," he said. "I was gonna leave you a note."

The joy that had been building in Georgie withered and died. She shivered as if from cold. Then, too weary to go on, she pulled a chair out from the dining room table and sat down.

She couldn't let it end this way. Not without a fight.

"I love you, Tyrone. I've loved you as long as I've known you."

He dropped the pillow he'd been holding and looked at his wife. "I love you, too, Georgie."

She wanted to scream. She wanted to holler. But in the end, she could only quietly ask, "Then why are we doing this?"

Tyrone walked the few steps to the table and pulled out the chair opposite hers. He sat down with as much weariness as she had. His face was drawn; dark circles under his eyes told of how well he'd been sleeping on the sofa the past few weeks. When he turned his full gaze on her, Georgie saw pain and hurt in his eyes. But she also saw resignation. He'd made up his mind about leaving, and there was nothing, she knew, that she could say or do to dissuade him.

"Because you might love me," he said, finally answering her. "But you're still in love with Roger."

For a long, confused moment, Georgie just stared at him. "What did you say?"

Tyrone hopped up, his chair toppling behind him. "How do you think it makes me feel, Georgie, knowing that my own wife chose me because she couldn't have the man she wanted?"

Georgie stood. "What are you talking about? Have you lost your mind?"

"Yeah." He whirled around and got in her face. "I have lost my mind. It's been hell knowing you've been kissing me, making love to me, and all the time thinking about Roger."

She grabbed his arm. "Tyrone . . ."

He yanked free, ran his hands over his head, then started pacing the area between the living room and the dining table. "On that trip up to D.C. it all became clear to me. Your little act. Well, you're not as good an actress as you think you are, Miss Georgie."

Her world was collapsing all around her and she didn't have a clue as to what he was talking about. Her thoughts ran in a thousand different directions trying to make sense of what he was saying, trying to shape out of his accusations a kernel of coherence.

"You had me fooled, Georgie," he snorted. "Hell, you played me for a fool."

She covered her hands with her ears. "Stop swearing. You don't swear. And I don't know what you're talking about."

The hurt in his eyes seared her, but it was the barely controlled anger in his voice that frightened her. Tyrone had never so much as raised his voice at her in all the time she'd known him.

He stopped his frantic movement and faced her. "I'm talking about the affair you had with Roger," he said, advancing on her.

Georgie flinched as if he'd hit her.

"I know it had to have been before we got married," he said. "I'd like to think you wouldn't go so far as to dishonor our vows."

"Affair? I never had an affair with Roger. I can't stand him. The only reason I've been able to tolerate him is because he's your cousin."

Tyrone smirked. "Yeah, right."

Something in Georgie snapped.

She'd been tried and convicted on trumped-up charges. She was guilty, all right, but not even remotely guilty of what Ty accused her of. He was so far off base that it was ludicrous. As bizarre as this accusation was, she wished her problem was that cut and dried. She wasn't about to stand by and have the only man she'd ever truly loved walk out the door thinking that she'd been after his cousin.

Georgie grabbed his arm. "What kind of idiot are you? There's nothing between me and Roger. There never has been."

He yanked free. "Please, Georgie. Just stop, all right. Roger already told me that the story wasn't his to tell. So, since I'm not getting it from you, that just leaves one conclusion."

Georgie grabbed her head. "Oh, my God. I don't believe this." The stress of their estrangement, the guilt, the lies. It was all just too much to bear.

"I hate him!" she shrieked. "I hate him. Does that make you happy?"

"Why? There aren't but so many things that would cause you, little miss pure-and-righteous church girl, to hate anybody."

Georgie's eyes filled with the tears she'd been holding back. "Because he knows," she said. "He's been lording it over me all these years and I was afraid he was going to tell you."

"Tell me what?"

"He knows about my baby."

The room became deathly still.

Georgie hugged herself, tears falling from her eyes. She couldn't meet his gaze. She couldn't do anything but regret that he'd found out this way. She hugged her robe to herself and waited for the explosion.

It took about ten seconds coming.

"What baby?" Tyrone asked. He was too stunned to say much else. He glanced at her stomach, wondering if she carried his child. A hope flared within him. Then her words registered. She'd said "all these years."

He and Georgie dated for about six months before marrying two years ago. They'd talked about children and the family they'd have one day. But the finances hadn't been right. They'd spent most of their marriage barely making ends meet. The last thing they could afford was a baby and she knew it.

Tyrone looked at Georgie, confusion warring away at his insides. "What baby, Georgie? You were a virgin when we married. Did you get pregnant and abort my child?"

The pain in his voice was palpable.

Georgie shook her head but didn't meet his gaze. "No," she said. "No, what?"

"No, I wasn't a virgin," she said, her voice quiet, flat. Dead like all her emotions.

Tyrone shook his head. "I was there. I remember the blood on the sheet. You cried when we first . . ."

Georgie pressed her eyes closed and bit her lips. She reached for the chair and slowly lowered herself onto it again.

"What are you saying?" he asked.

She opened her eyes to see him. He stood a few yards away, next to the sofa. He looked strong, invincible. She loved this man with all her heart. And she'd hoped and prayed she would never have to tell him this. She'd guarded the secret and her shame so carefully that she'd fooled herself into believing it wasn't really that big a deal.

Her marriage was over now. If Tyrone hadn't been ready to leave before, he'd surely leave now. But this time, he'd have the truth. He'd know she wasn't the chaste Christian woman he thought he'd married.

She twisted in the chair so that she faced him. For a moment, neither said anything. Then, taking a deep breath, Georgie opened her mouth.

No words came.

She swallowed, then blurted it out. "Tyrone, I was pregnant that night when we met."

He staggered back as if she'd slammed him with a wrecking ball. His eyes darted back and forth. She watched as he tried to process the information.

"Don't be ridiculous," he said. "You didn't look . . ."

"Ty. I was pregnant."

He stared at her as if she were a stranger, a woman he didn't know. The implication and ramifications of her words rocked the foundation of their marriage, a union that supposedly had been built on love and trust, a union ordained by God and maintained by faith and grace.

Ty. I was pregnant.

He didn't want to believe it, but the finality in her voice as she said those four damning words convinced him. He backed away, taking small steps until he backed into the edge of the wood-grained coffee table. Tyrone sat on the edge of the sofa, his head bowed, his hands dangling between his legs. His back was to her.

"I'm not understanding this, Georgie."

"It was an accident. The first and only time I'd ever—"

"Who is he?"

Georgie closed her eyes. "Was, Tyrone. That relationship was over before we started going out."

He pursed his lips but didn't say anything.

"I . . ." In the face of his animosity, she faltered. "The reason you saw blood on our wedding night . . ."

He raised his head, waiting for the explanation.

"After you fell asleep, I pricked my fingers and smeared it on the sheet."

Tyrone let out a long, unsteady breath. He closed his eyes and leaned his head back on the sofa. "I see," he said after a long time. "What other lies were there?"

Before she could open her mouth to answer, he confronted her. "The baby. What'd you do with the baby?"

"I lost it," she said, her voice barely above a whisper.

Tyrone recoiled. "You had an abortion?"

Georgie jumped up. "No. No, Ty. I'd never do anything like that. I lost the baby. I had a miscarriage. We . . . we'd been fighting about what to do, though. I wanted to get married. He didn't. When I miscarried, it made things easier."

"Easier." He shook his head. "That's a hell of a choice of words, Georgie."

"When did you start swearing so much?"

"When did you start lying to me?"

Georgie looked away. "I never meant to hurt you, Ty. You weren't ever supposed to find out."

"Obviously."

"I didn't want to lose you," Georgie said, trying to explain her actions, a course that had seemed so true then. "Would you have married me if you'd known?"

Tyrone didn't say anything.

"That's what I thought," she said. "You were so adamant about wanting a 'pure' wife and us waiting. I wanted to tell you. I even tried a couple of times. And then you proposed, and well, I . . . it seemed better to just try to forget as best I could."

He ran a hand over his face. "Why are you telling me this now?"

Georgie sat in the chair again, her hands clasped together tightly. "You accused me of having an affair with Roger."

He snorted. "It's six of one, half a dozen of the other with your true confessions, Georgie."

"I wanted us to be happy together," she said. "I'd hoped we, you and me, that we'd have our own babies together."

"That's not freaking likely now."

Georgie started crying. "I love you, Ty."

"Don't," he said. "Don't even walk that path right now."

He stomped to their bedroom. A few minutes later, he returned, completely dressed and with a hastily packed gym bag.

Georgie jumped up and took three steps toward him. "Ty, where are you going?"

He stared at her for a long time, looking at her as if he were seeing for the very first time the real woman he'd pledged his life and his heart to. The filter on the lens was cracked and out of focus. *What God has put together, let no man put asunder.*

"Ty?"

Georgie stood there, not sure what to do, what to say. Was there anything she *could* say to redeem herself in his eyes?

Without a word, Tyrone snatched his wallet and his keys from the end table.

A moment later, the front door slammed behind him.

Georgie crumpled to the floor, her anguished wail filling the empty room.

15

Tyrone walked around the block taking long angry steps, hoping the air would clear his head. That tears fell from his face the entire time was a fact he didn't notice or care about. His world had completely fallen apart.

All this time he'd been despising his cousin, letting his suspicions and his anger fester.

Roger wasn't even the guilty one.

Belatedly he realized he still didn't know how Roger fit into the picture. Right now, though, he wasn't sure he wanted to know. He felt like kicking something, hitting something. He wanted to destroy something tangible, just like he'd been destroyed.

When he looked up, he stood in front of the duplex where he and Georgie lived. Her car, a late-model fully loaded Toyota Camry, still sat in its designated spot. His beat-up Chevy Impala was parked next to it. The AC in his car had conked out some time last summer. His car needed a new muffler and two new tires.

He glanced between the two vehicles—one shiny, new, and pristine; the other a tune-up away from being a clunker. The cars seemed to represent everything that was wrong with their marriage and his life.

Ty pulled his keys from his jeans pocket. Hoisting his gym bag on his shoulder, he positioned a key in his hand and stepped toward her car. He positioned the key just so, right in the middle of the driver's side door. With a good keying, he could destroy something *she* cared about.

A moment later, he had a better idea. He searched through the key ring until he found the keys to her car.

Then, without another thought about it, he got in Georgie's car and drove away.

Ten minutes later, he pulled up at Roger's house. There was some more to Georgie's story, and he wanted to know the rest of it. Right now.

"Hey, man. Come on in," Roger said in answering Tyrone's knock. "I was downstairs working on a song. I could use some help."

"I'm not here to help you. I want some answers."

Roger turned around, the anger in Tyrone's voice making him cock an eyebrow. "What's up, cuz?"

Tyrone folded his arms and stared at Roger. "Tell me about this baby Georgie supposedly miscarried."

"Hmm." Roger put down the pencil in his hand and pushed his reading glasses to the top of his head. "She finally told you."

"Were you the father?"

Roger's eyes widened. "Good heavens, no. What would make you think something like that?"

The tension in Tyrone seemed to dissipate. His shoulders sagged, and much of the fight and the anger left him. All that remained was a bitter, disillusioned disappointment. The worst of his fears had just been put to rest. That didn't mean he wasn't still angry.

Roger peered at him. "You look like something the cat dragged in. Come on out to the kitchen. I'll make some coffee."

A few minutes later, the two men settled at the round table in Roger's kitchen. Mugs of steaming coffee sat before them.

"What happened between you and Georgie?" Roger asked.

Tyrone explained that they'd been sleeping separately since the Washington trip, that the only reason Ty hadn't moved out already was because he had nowhere else to go. If he went home to his parents' house, he'd have to answer questions he wasn't ready to deal with.

"*Mi casa, su casa,*" Roger said. "You know that, right? There's a bunch of music in boxes in the spare room, but it's yours as long as you need it. I don't know how well that pullout bed sleeps, though."

Tyrone nodded his thanks. He took a sip of coffee; then he looked Roger straight in the eye. "How'd you know about this pregnancy of hers, and who was the man?"

He'd tried, but was unable to keep the note of hostility out of his voice. Whether it was directed at Roger, at Georgie, or at himself for being played, he didn't know. Part of him wanted to confront the man who'd defiled his precious Georgie while the other part viciously reminded him that Georgie was far from innocent in this drama. She'd said she wanted to marry the bastard.

Rebound man.

Is that what he'd been to Georgie?

Bile rose in his throat. The thought sickened him. Had he been so in love that he'd been blinded to signs that may have been there?

"Ty?"

Tyrone blinked several times before focusing in on Roger. He shook his head. "I've got so many things on my mind right now."

Roger sat forward. "Ty, there's a lot we need to talk about. But right now, I think you probably need some time to just sit."

Tyrone visibly tensed. "You know something bad, don't you?"

"Bad?" Roger shook his head. "It just is."

"Spit it out, then. I want it all," he said, tapping the table with his forefinger. "Right here. Right now."

Roger sighed and sat back.

"Talk, Raj."

"I knew Georgie from her music. She played the piano at her church. Competent, nothing fancy. She read music and played straight from the hymn book." Roger shook his head. "Remember that little gospel doo-wop quartet I had a while back?"

Tyrone's brows scrunched together.

"Oh, yeah. You may have been in Memphis then. Anyway, we ministered over at Georgie's church one night. I thought those people were going to spit prunes, they were so puckered up."

Ty smiled. "They're still like that."

Roger nodded. "Well, after the program, we made tracks, but Georgie caught me at the door and gave me what for. How dare I bring club music into the church. She said I owed her, the pastor, and her father, who was and still is chairman of the deacons' board, an apology, etcetera, etcetera. She went on for about five minutes."

"Then what happened?"

"I told her I'd keep her in prayer and walked out the door."

Tyrone laughed in spite of himself. "That must've set her off."

"I didn't stick around to see. But I ran into her a month or so later at a prayer breakfast and she gave me the seriously cold shoulder. With that as an introduction, it's pretty needless to say that when you started dating her I had my doubts."

Tyrone folded his arms.

Apparently noticing the frost, Roger added, "But people change. God moves in their lives." He shrugged.

"Get to the pregnant part."

"Well, fast-forward a few years," Roger said. "By this time, artists like the Winans were on the scene. Then, Kirk Franklin exploded out of nowhere and changed gospel music."

"He wasn't the first."

Roger nodded. "No, Edwin Hawkins set the industry on fire back in the day with 'Oh, Happy Day.' But a lot of time had passed since then. Anyway, I mention Kirk because churches like Georgie's still don't accept the new gospel."

"Georgie's not too hip to it, but she knew what I did from the jump."

"Well, anyway, a few years ago," Roger paused and scratched his head. "Maybe it was three years ago. Yeah, because I was visiting Aunt Selia at Riverside right before she died. I came out of the hospital and there was Georgie, just standing there looking lost. I went up to her and asked her if everything was all right, and she burst into tears."

Tyrone frowned but remained quiet.

"I kept asking her 'What's wrong? What's wrong?' She was doing that hyperventilating kind of crying. So I led her over to a bench and sat her down. I couldn't leave her like that. I just sat there with her while she cried and then she started talking. She said she'd lost her baby. God was punishing her for her sin. She just kept saying the same thing over and over."

Roger took a sip of his coffee, then got up to top off his cup. He hovered the coffee pot over Tyrone's mug, but when Tyrone shook his head he placed it back in the coffeemaker.

"I was able to figure out that she'd just been released from the hospital—probably outpatient, because she didn't have one of those hospital bracelets on." Roger shrugged. "That's it."

Tyrone looked up. "What do you mean, 'That's it'?"

"I don't know anything else. She eventually stopped crying. She looked really embarrassed to have been telling me that stuff. She begged me not to ever say anything, and then she ran off."

Tyrone scowled.

"Ty, I'd tell you more if there was more to tell."

"And when was all this?"

"Well, Aunt Selia died in April, so some time that month. I just know it was warm outside. Hot almost, because we sat outside. A while after that you were showing up in church with Georgie on your arm."

"And soon after that, we were married," Tyrone said, not even trying to keep the disgust out of his voice. "Why didn't you say something?"

"What was I supposed to say? I thought you knew. To tell you the truth, I thought you and she . . ." He didn't finish. "Georgie was a church girl and has been all her life, for all I know. Pregnancies, miscarriages, that's the sort of thing couples keep between themselves. Besides, what would you have done if I'd said something anyway?"

Tyrone's gaze connected with Roger's. "Probably knocked your lights out."

"Exactly."

Georgie crawled to the sofa. She didn't know how long she'd been on the floor crying. Her bathrobe gaped open and she stared down at the angel on the T-shirt she'd worn to bed. Since Ty had left their bedroom, Georgie didn't bother with any of her sexy nighties. She'd put one of them on one night two weeks ago, hoping to entice Ty back to their bed. He'd flicked his eyes over her sprawled out on the bed, then stomped into the bathroom, slamming the door in his wake.

The rejection still stung.

Maybe he no longer found her sexy. She'd lost ten pounds in the past few weeks, but that had been a result of stress and not eating rather than any conscious effort to lose weight.

In her misery, Georgie had searched for any excuse, any reason for Ty to be so distant.

Didn't all couples have communication problems? That's what all the talk shows said. That's what her gossipy coworkers at the bank talked about when they didn't think she was around to hear. Georgie had made it pretty clear when she started working at First National

Bank and Trust that she didn't believe in gossiping and refused to participate in the little cliques that formed in the office.

As a consequence, she had very few, if any, close associates at work. She did her job and she did it well. She worked overtime when it was available, to help with the finances. And she tried to make a home that was warm, inviting, and sheltering for her husband.

Georgie wanted a baby and had let Ty know. He refused, though, always saying they couldn't afford it.

Now, though, it looked as though she'd be starting her life all over again. Again.

She stared at the curtains in front of the picture window in the living room and wondered if she'd be in a better place if she hadn't fallen for the sweet talk of Deacon Arthur Logan. He was from a sister church and almost old enough to be her father. The maturity and the suaveness coupled with the whispered promises: that, ultimately, was why she'd succumbed so easily.

Her virtue should have been given to the man she married. All those years of waiting. And then, in one heated moment, it was over. And she'd gotten pregnant to boot.

Georgie closed her eyes tight, willing the mistakes she'd made to vanish. But her sin and her lies finally caught up with her. And more than two years later, she was still paying the price. God took her baby and now he was taking her husband.

But it wasn't God's fault. She knew that.

"You're the one to blame, Georgie. Just you."

She toppled over on the sofa and curled into a fetal position. She didn't think she had any more tears to cry, but they fell nonetheless.

"So, all this time," Tyrone said. "All this time, the tension between you and Georgie dates back to a confrontation about music that you had six or seven years ago."

Roger shrugged. He drained his coffee cup, got up and rinsed it out, and put it in the dishwasher. "Far as I know. But cousin," he said, folding his arms and leaning against the counter. "What's up with you thinking I had gotten with Georgie?"

Rubbing his eyes, Tyrone sighed. "I don't know, man. I mean, when we were on the road, it was like she couldn't stand being within two feet of you. And you were just as hostile toward her. I saw something, came to some conclusions, and *bam!* I put a bunch of pieces together."

"Is that why Georgie disappeared from the tour? You guys had a fight and she went home?"

Expelling a breath, Tyrone nodded. "This is just a big mess."

"Don't you think if I had *that* kind of history with a woman that I'd say *something* before you up and married her?"

"I'm sorry, man. And yeah, you would have. But I wasn't thinking straight. Haven't been for weeks."

"What are you going to do now?"

Tyrone sighed. "I don't know. Crash here at the crib till you kick me to the curb."

Roger threw a dish towel at Tyrone's head. "Earn your keep, then, boy. I'm headed back downstairs to get some work done."

After Roger returned to the garage he'd converted into a studio and office for his music, Tyrone sat at the kitchen table, thinking about the future and contemplating the past.

For the past two and a half years Georgie had been his life, his all. He loved her more than life itself. But if she'd lied—even by omission—about something as fundamental to their relationship as all this, what else had she lied about?

His thoughts turned to the day they'd met. Had the half-truth and fabrications begun even then?

He'd been waiting in line to get into the Gospel Explosion concert at the Coliseum when he spotted her. She was smiling up at a brother he'd seen around; Clyde was the dude's name. Her hair was all done up as if she'd just been to the beauty parlor that day. And the dress she had on highlighted all the lush curves on her body.

Even though he knew he shouldn't be thinking that way, Tyrone's eyes and his mind kept wandering back to the pretty woman. He liked 'em big. He'd always liked a woman he could wrap his arms around.

Just more to love, he thought with a grin.

An usher told people to break the line in two, directing some of the waiting crowd to another entrance so they could get in faster. Ty stayed in his own line, quickly closing the gap between himself and the woman he'd been admiring.

Tickets were reserved seating, so there was no need to bum-rush the door.

Tyrone watched the man lean down and whisper something in the woman's ear. She laughed, then tapped his arm with her ticket. "Clyde, you ought to be ashamed."

The ticket slipped from her grasp and fluttered to the ground, landing at Tyrone's feet.

"Oh!"

Ty had quickly retrieved the ticket.

"Here you go, miss. They won't let you in without it." He handed her the ticket but held it a second too long. Her gaze connected with his. He smiled. She smiled right back.

"Thank you," she murmured.

Out of the corner of his eye, Tyrone saw the man scowl at him.

"Georgie, let's go." The man wrapped a possessive arm around Georgie's waist, letting Tyrone know that the property already had a claim on it.

She snaked an arm around the man's waist and together they stepped up to hand the usher their show tickets. But before disappearing into the dark hall, she turned back and flashed Tyrone a brilliantly dazzling smile.

He was gone. Right then and right there, Tyrone knew he'd have to find her.

When he saw her in the audience at an afternoon church program less than a week later, Tyrone knew he'd been given an opportunity. Never one to let blessings or opportunities slip away, he decided he'd make a move. He didn't care one bit that she sat right next to Clyde.

Then Ty had paused, checking himself. For all he knew, that was a union God had ordained. Just because he was liking what he was seeing didn't at all mean that he was supposed to be with her. That other brother had obviously been putting in work. They looked close.

But Ty found that he couldn't seem to get her off his mind.

When she showed up—alone—at the church where he was playing the next Sunday, Ty knew that what he'd been feeling had been shared. She came up, said hello, and after service they went out for coffee. Clyde, she said, was just a friend.

In his cousin's kitchen, Tyrone shook his head. He'd been a sucker, through and through.

"Clyde was the one," he said through gritted teeth, coming to the most likely conclusion.

He couldn't stand that Clyde had been there, between Georgie's legs, before he had. The mental image ate at his soul. The hurt of it wounded his pride.

In this day and age, Tyrone hadn't truly expected to marry a virgin. So it had been an extra-special delight to find on their wedding night that she'd never been with another man. The blood on the sheet proved it. She'd cried, too. But now he realized those tears had nothing to do with a woman losing her virginity.

He slammed his palm on the table. "Lies. Nothing but damn lies."

MARGARET

16

Margaret Hall-Stuart knew that some people would think what she was doing was wrong. She'd spent enough years in church, enough Sunday mornings in Sunday school, and enough Wednesday nights in prayer meetings to know that nowhere in traditional Baptist doctrine was there anything about tarot cards and psychics.

As a matter of fact, she'd heard plenty of sermons specifically saying that that sort of thing was an abomination unto God.

But somewhere along the way, Margaret had managed to merge her faith in an unseen Almighty God with her belief in and reliance on the predictions and premonitions of her psychic, the Reverend Sister Amelia, Prophetess of the True Light. Rare was the morning when Margaret didn't reach for her customized horoscope book, a volume that combined her numerology chart with her astrological readings. And usually, she did that reading before she prayed to the God she'd grown up with.

Her transformation had come slowly; her dependence on the cards and psychic energy and sometimes even tea leaves had developed over time. She'd been married once, a disaster that was eventually annulled. Looking for a lifeline in the middle of that heartache, she'd called a 1-900 psychic line, one of the many featured on late-night TV. After racking up several hundred dollars in phone charges and with no real answers or solutions to any of her problems, she decided the psychic lines were fake.

Then she saw an article in the newspaper about a psychic fair in Virginia Beach. The psychics would be there, in person, doing readings. So she went and wandered around trying to figure out how to choose from the twenty-five or so seers who were set up at tables and booths in a large ballroom.

Unable to decide which one to approach, Margaret picked up a copy of the profiles and went to find a quiet spot to read them in the hotel lobby. She overheard a couple of women exclaiming about the Prophetess of the True Light. Margaret leaned in closer, then got up and asked them about this so-called prophetess. Their testimonials convinced her.

Margaret had scheduled a fifteen-minute session.

The Reverend Sister Amelia's table was set apart from the others. Candles burned all around her.

Having never seen a psychic in the flesh, Margaret wasn't sure what to do or expect. So she put her money on the table and just sat there.

"Surely, the Omnipotent One wants to see you happy, not a miserable shell of a woman. This relationship of yours, it is not happy."

Margaret's mouth dropped open. She hadn't said a single word, yet this woman, this prophetess, knew. Stunned, Margaret nodded.

And that was the beginning of her long-term association with the Reverend Sister Amelia, Prophetess of the True Light.

Now, Margaret turned the handle on the door leading to her altar room. Sometimes she called it her holy place. Usually, though, she just called it her prayer closet. That's what it was in reality. A spare walk-in closet at her house, one large enough for her to fit a comfortable chair, a small table, and a stand where she kept her holy books.

Stepping into the closet, Margaret closed her eyes, letting the sweet scent of the potpourri she'd placed about the room sink into her consciousness. After a few minutes, she took a deep breath and slowly opened her eyes. From a polished brass container she pulled out matches and lit the candles that lent light to the room. She'd long ago removed the shelving and the white light fixture that hung overhead. It had been replaced by a soft-pink bulb, but she rarely used that light.

Candles of all lengths and shapes filled the room: tall ones on thin stands, short fat ones on flat holders, votive candles in tiny cups, triangular wicks, and long, elegant tapers. The largest candle, though, sat in the middle of the table, its three wicks representing to Margaret so many things: the holy Trinity; the past, present, and future; and her three belief systems.

When she had company at the house, Margaret kept her prayer room locked. It was a private place, her special retreat, and she didn't want anyone stumbling in and defiling her holy place.

Right now, she had a lot on her mind. She needed to meditate. Settling into the chair, she placed her hands on the arms and took a deep calming breath, gentling her troubled spirit, and opening herself to messages and new energy from the Universe.

She'd spent a lot of time thinking lately. A lot of time meditating and wondering, hoping, praying. Margaret's attention had been divided the past few weeks. She hadn't spent a lot of time focusing on Roger, and so she felt a disconnect. One she hoped . . . no, one she *knew* would be reunited again if only she put her mind and her energy on the right situation.

She blocked from her mind the turmoil at work. She erased from her consciousness the housework that needed to be done. She even focused her thinking away from Marcus, the choir's sound man who'd been so nice to her.

A smile curved her mouth when he came to mind.

But then she remembered.

"Peace . . . peace . . . peace," she chanted.

For twenty minutes Margaret sat in her prayer room. She chanted, she meditated, and she prayed. When she was finished, she slowly opened her eyes and took several deep breaths to refresh and purify her spirit; then she methodically tamped out all of the candles.

When she emerged she felt centered, energized, ready to tackle the issues of the day. She read her horoscope in the newspaper, carefully checking it against the one in her customized astrological forecast. The Reverend Sister Amelia had told her time and again that she shouldn't put stock in those generic readings, but Margaret always checked anyway. She wanted to be armed with all the right information when she stepped out into a new day.

Her day would be a full one. It started with a meeting at work at eight-thirty. She would run a few errands at lunch. After work she'd

have time for a fast dinner, for personal Bible study, and then she'd
head to choir rehearsal.

She was reading the Bible straight though—a year-long effort—
and checked to make sure she was still on target. She opened her
Bible study booklet on the gospel of Mark and made sure her special
pen and notebook were handy. She always did her personal Bible
study in the evening. Tonight, because of rehearsal and the outfit she
planned to change into, by the time she got home she'd have barely
enough time to get through the complete reading before dashing out
the door again.

After eating a quick breakfast of grapefruit, toast, and coffee, she
showered and dressed in a conservative gray-and-pink dress and was
out the door by 7:45.

The day she'd carefully mapped out and anticipated was not the
one she would get.

In her Cadillac, she cued the CD player to the eighth track of
Spread the Word. She loved listening to Roger play the piano and
organ. The eighth song on the latest Voices of Triumphant Praise CD
was one of Roger's original tunes that featured him playing the
organ.

She'd been in love with him as long as she could remember.

He'd been one of the first people she met when she arrived at the
University. Her parents' connections and hefty contributions ensured
Margaret a private room in a hall typically reserved for upperclass-
men. That fact didn't earn her any points with the other women in
the dormitory. Her freshman classmates were standoffish, so Margaret had fully expected to spend her time in college ensconced in loneliness.

Then she had met Roger McKenzie.

She'd been sitting in the chapel, the only truly quiet place on campus, feeling sorry for herself. She'd been missing home with her
queen-size canopy bed and sitting room that overlooked the pool.
Her dorm room was just barely the size of her walk-in closet at home,
and sharing a bathroom with twenty other women was the most dis-
gusting thing she'd ever encountered in her life.

She missed her best friend, who'd gone off to Spelman, the college
Margaret wanted to attend. But her parents, both alumni of this uni-

versity, wouldn't even consider sending their beloved only child off to Atlanta.

In addition to her minuscule dorm room, Margaret's list of woes included the cafeteria food, the laundry service—she was actually expected to wash clothes!—and the fact that her parents were planning to go to Europe without her just because the trip happened to coincide with mid-term exams.

She didn't realize she was crying until a white handkerchief appeared before her face.

"Whatever the problem is, sister, give it up to God."

She sniffed, accepting the hankie and dabbing at her eyes. "I don't think my problems are quite what God specializes in."

The man sat down on the pew but kept a respectable space between them. "The Lord specializes in everything, sister."

She glanced at him. "Even pity parties?"

He smiled. "Even pity parties."

She neatly folded the handkerchief and offered it back to him. "Thank you."

"Why don't you hold on to that? Just in case," he added with a wink. "Listen, I came in here to get some practice on the organ. I don't want to disturb you, though."

"Go on," she said. "I'm fine."

He nodded and, with a small wave, left her and headed to the choir loft. He settled at the organ, turned it on, and began to play. Margaret listened for a while, then lifted her voice up to sing the lyrics of "Lift Ev'ry Voice and Sing," her strong but sweet soprano echoing through the chapel.

He glanced back at her, smiled, and motioned for her to come up and join him.

She sang all three verses. When he finished playing, they sat together for a moment before he played "Amazing Grace," then a couple of contemporary gospel tunes.

"You have an incredible voice," he said.

"Thank you. You're not so bad yourself," she said, indicating the organ.

"Roger McKenzie," he said, introducing himself.

"Hello. I'm Margaret. Margaret Hall-Stuart."

His eyes widened. "As in the Hall-Stuart Cadillac dealerships?"

She nodded.

"Wow."

Margaret shrugged. "It's no big deal," she said. "It's what my parents do."

"Are you in the concert choir?"

She shook her head. "No."

"Good," he said, a grin spreading over his features.

She laughed. "Why is that good?"

"It means you're free to join the gospel choir."

And that was the beginning of their friendship, a relationship that for Margaret was much, much more.

Lately, though, Margaret wondered. She'd invited Roger to dinner several times, but he'd begged off. Remembering her resolve to have as stress-free a day as possible, she banished Roger from her mind.

The drive to work, mercilessly tangled with fender benders, took thirty-five minutes instead of the usual fifteen. That left Margaret precious little time to get her thoughts together before the morning meeting.

Muttering about cell phones, distracted drivers, and endless VDOT road construction projects, she stomped to her desk. Before she had time to drop her bag or her briefcase, Sheila Cross swooped in. Sheila occupied the cubicle next to Margaret's.

"Hawthorne wants to see you ASAP," Sheila said.

Margaret winced. *What's wrong now?* she wondered.

"And he's in a foul mood," Sheila added, a sympathetic grimace marring her too-wide mouth.

Taking a deep breath and shaking her head, Margaret grabbed two folders from her desk. One had the latest projections on a grant she was writing. The other was a project Hawthorne had dumped on her late yesterday. She'd barely had a chance to go through it, but what she had gleaned from the quick overview was that it was already two weeks behind schedule.

"Thanks," she told her coworker.

"I put some coffee on," Sheila said. "I'll have a cup waiting for you. Good luck."

With that bit of well-wishing to propel her, Margaret squared her shoulders and headed to the project director's office. Nate Hawthorne, named for the writer, would have made his employees a lot happier if he quit his job and pursued his dreams of becoming the next great American novelist. Unfortunately for Margaret, Sheila, and the other two grant writers in the division, Hawthorne was apparently an abysmal writer. His employees suffered with every rejection he got.

It was a known fact that Margaret did the work in the office, Hawthorne's included. He was too busy in his corner office writing novels—on the foundation's time. How he got the job in the first place was a constant source of speculation among his staff.

Margaret made her way though the maze of tables that held reference materials and approached Hawthorne's closed door. She knocked, two sharp raps, and waited for his bellow.

When it didn't come, she knocked again.

Silence.

Margaret let out an exasperated huff. She rapped again and called out, "Mr. Hawthorne."

When he still didn't answer, Margaret turned and glanced at Sheila, who stood across the big room. Sheila shrugged.

Muttering under her breath, Margaret went back to her desk and booted up her computer. She called Hawthorne's extension, left a message on voice mail, and then grabbed the material she needed for the morning meeting.

Sheila showed up at her cubicle with a cup of coffee. Carefully balancing their cups, the two women went to the conference room, one they shared with the foundation's research and development department.

Eight people were already seated around the table. Margaret and Sheila took the two empty seats.

"Good morning," she said to the man at her left, a stranger. He was clean shaven, both his face and his head. He was also tieless; that alone branded him as someone just passing through. But it was the gold hoop in his ear that definitely marked him as a visitor and not a new employee at the very conservative Brinker Foundation.

He nodded.

"Margaret," Ed Johnson, the foundation's assistant manager, called from the head of the table.

She looked up. "Yes?"

"Where's Hawthorne?"

As if she were supposed to know where her boss was.

"I left a message for him."

Johnson frowned. "Well, you'll have to give his summary of the youth pathways project."

"Youth pathways project? What is—?"

But Johnson cut her off and called the meeting to order.

Margaret glanced at Sheila, who shrugged. Then she looked at Tim Wright, the other grant writer from their division who attended these monthly status meetings. Tim looked as baffled as Sheila.

Sighing, Margaret sat back in her chair. She could either bluff her way through this—which wouldn't be a good idea since she had no idea what the youth pathways project was—or she could just lay the blame for the lack of information right where it belonged, at Nate Hawthorne's feet.

The first rule of business, however, made her pause: Never make your boss look bad. Since this wasn't the first time Nate Hawthorne had pulled one of his disappearing acts, Margaret was less than inclined to offer him any good employee points.

Unfortunately, her time to present would be at hand very soon.

Sheila slipped a note a few inches toward Margaret. "What are you going to do?" it read.

Margaret answered by drawing a question mark.

"Our team is at something of a loss, Mr. Johnson," she began when she was called on. "Mr. Hawthorne didn't brief any of us on this project. We'll be happy to—"

Johnson scowled. "You know, Ms. Hall-Stuart, all I ever seem to get out of your department is 'I don't know' and 'we're not yet prepared with that data.'"

Margaret's hackles rose. First of all, it wasn't *her* department, even though it should have been. Second, there was only so much that could be done about a totally incompetent and clueless supervisor.

"Mr. Johnson, I assure you—"

He cut her off by flinging a large file folder of documents her way. The man she didn't recognize caught it before it went careening off the smooth surface of the table. He pushed it to Margaret.

"That mess is what you all have produced so far on this project," Johnson said. "Clean it up. Write it in English this time, please. And make sure that it's in my office by Friday."

Margaret was pissed off. She was taking a public berating for something she knew nothing about and had no control over. "This project is not one we were briefed on, sir," she said. The "sir" came out through clenched teeth and barely controlled anger.

The look Johnson sent her way would have melted the polar ice cap. "That'll be all, Ms. Hall-Stuart."

Seething, Margaret sat back in her chair. Being blindsided by something that Hawthorne had neglected to mention made her see red.

She loved what she did, but it was time—way past time—to get another job. The meeting went on around her, Johnson getting glowing progress reports from the various teams. Everyone's work was on track, moving forward, making headway. Every team except the one she was on.

Margaret thought about ways she could get back at Hawthorne for being such a pain in the rear end. He was a brick wall in the middle of a thriving forest. As long as she, Sheila, and Tim could figure out what information he was withholding, they could do end runs that mitigated whatever damage Hawthorne may have created. Not today, though.

Her head was pounding with a headache that only this sort of situation could bring on. The headaches came far too frequently these days, and always while at work.

With her complaints about Hawthorne, she could go straight to the foundation's director. She could ask for a transfer to another division; that would quickly show Johnson just who was doing the work in the grants department. She could even confront Hawthorne when he crawled back out from under whatever rock he'd slithered under this morning.

The image of a snake emerging from a black pit came to mind. A smile curved Margaret's mouth when she thought about crushing the slimy creature's head. Then, realizing that that particular train of thought was serving no good purpose—at least not right now—she tuned in again to the proceedings.

"We have a special guest with us today," Johnson said from his chair at the head of the table.

Margaret watched the stranger lean forward.

Positively beaming now, the assistant manager sent a large smile Margaret's way. Belatedly she realized it was meant for the man sitting next to her.

"I'd like to introduce to you David Underwood. David will be with us for the next three weeks. He's going to be evaluating work flow, efficiency, and the way we do things here."

Margaret's heart stopped beating for a moment. Her mouth grew dry. She'd been in this business long enough to know that down the road somewhere an efficiency expert meant one thing: consolidation. And consolidation usually led to layoffs.

Just one person had been crucified during the hour-long meeting. One person had been left looking like an incompetent finger-pointer. With a sick stomach, Margaret realized she'd been set up.

17

Margaret opened the folder Johnson had tossed her way. She read the top sheet and cried out.

All eyes turned her way.

David Underwood, who was about to address the group, closed his mouth and turned toward her.

Sheila leaned forward, whispering, "What's wrong?"

"Is there a problem, Ms. Hall-Stuart?" Johnson intoned from the head of the table.

Margaret slammed the folder shut. "No, sir."

Johnson snorted. Then he turned his attention back to the guest, smiled solicitously, and gestured for him to begin.

With a glance at Margaret, David Underwood stood to address the group. He had handouts and a Powerpoint presentation. But Margaret didn't hear a word of it. Her anger roiled and churned.

That low-down, good-for-nothing, backstabbing son of a bitch had totally set her up. The only thing that kept Margaret in her chair was the fact that enough negative attention had already been sent her way today. What she wanted to do, though, even more than she wanted to draw her next breath, was to hunt down Nate Hawthorne and give him a piece of her mind.

Not normally driven to violence or even violent thoughts, Margaret's anger bubbled and churned and ate at her gut like a poison.

She had backup. Both Sheila and Tim knew just how inefficient and incompetent Hawthorne was. They could testify to the man's slack record-keeping, his indifference toward deadlines, his total disregard for the foundation's established policies and procedures. He'd left them all in the lurch more times than Margaret could count.

But this . . . this treachery beat it all.

She stared at the folder on the conference table. Nate Hawthorne had written that she, Margaret Hall-Stuart, was the senior grant writer for this youth pathways project. He'd signed her name on the cover sheet and then initialed his own on a line as if he'd signed off on her work before sending it up to the director's office.

Margaret's eyes narrowed as her gaze keyed in on Ed Johnson. He'd never been friendly toward her. She'd always assumed it had something to do with the auto dealerships. He'd probably been turned down for a loan when he tried to buy a car, and was unjustifiably taking that anger out on Margaret. But now, another far more plausible explanation came to mind. Nate Hawthorne had probably been sending her work up under his name, and his shoddy work he pawned off as hers.

That was the only explanation that made sense. It would explain Johnson's open hostility toward her. It would explain why and how Nate Hawthorne not only hadn't been fired long before now, but why he'd actually been promoted to the head of the team, a job that everyone in the office thought was Margaret's.

She glanced at Underwood, the efficiency expert. He, she knew, was here to cull the ranks. Margaret had some culling of her own in mind, though.

She picked up her pen and made a short list, just three to-do items.

Twenty minutes later, Johnson adjourned the meeting. Without a glance at either Johnson or Underwood and not a word to her coworkers, Margaret walked out of the conference room, her head held high, her back straight, her determination set . . . and her hit list in her hand.

Hawthorne never did put in an appearance at the office that morning. It was probably just as well, Margaret realized. By lunchtime she'd calmed down enough to shred her hit list and to come up with a more practical—not to mention legal—way to vent.

She drafted a six-page letter to Mrs. Brinker, with copies to the Brinker Foundation's director and managing partner, and a blind copy of the letter addressed to the local newspaper.

For the better part of the morning, Sheila tried to get out of Margaret details about what was in that folder and what she'd been up to while digging in the files where they stored old project information. But Margaret put the other woman off, explaining that it was an issue between her and Hawthorne.

"I'd come in a little late tomorrow if I were you," Margaret did say.

Sheila grabbed her arm. "Margaret, please don't do anything rash."

"I'm not. As a matter of fact," Margaret said as she gathered her purse, her briefcase, and several files from her desk, "I've never been more clear-headed in my life." She smiled brightly. "It's time we got credit for the work we do around here."

"We do get credit," Sheila said. "Our names are on the grants that go up to the fourth floor."

Margaret, who'd spent the morning doing a bit of research in the grant division's files, knew better. But she wasn't going to drag Sheila into this fight. It was hers, and she relished the battle—particularly since right was on her side.

Watching Margaret stuff several file folders into her briefcase, Sheila asked, "Where are you going with all that stuff?"

"Home," Margaret answered simply. "I'm taking the afternoon off." She placed her fingers over her mouth and delicately issued forth two fake coughs. "Not feeling well," she said. "I'll take a sick day. Or two."

Sheila eyed her. "You're up to something."

Margaret raised an eyebrow but said nothing. She snapped her briefcase closed, secured the small lock, and picked up her shoulder bag. "Ta-ta," she said with a small wave.

A moment later, Margaret sailed out of the office, a bemused Sheila staring after her.

Margaret stopped off at Starbucks, ordered a double-shot espresso, and contemplated her options while she sipped her coffee. She essentially had two. She could send the letter she'd written, thereby exposing Hawthorne for what he was. Or she could simply cut her losses and leave, recognizing that even if she exposed Hawthorne, little would be done unless they could prove malfeasance on his part.

She'd been working at the foundation for four years, enough time to prove to her parents—and, more important, to herself—that she could live an independent life, could take care of herself. After a disastrous marriage that had lasted all of thirteen months, she'd run home to Mommy and Daddy and the security of their wealth. They nurtured her and took care of her, and everything was again all right in Margaret's world.

While at home, she'd fallen into the habit of doing community public relations work for the dealership, organizing events that put the Hall-Stuart Cadillac name in front of potential customers. That meant arranging everything from scholarship dinners and black-tie galas to sponsoring drill teams that proudly sported the Hall-Stuart auto empire logos on their jackets and T-shirts. She schmoozed in all the right circles and went to the right church, where her parents were big financial supporters.

Over time the rut became the routine.

There had to be more, though. And so, with her extremely nervous and overprotective parents looking on, she'd bought a house and got a job and cut the apron strings. The first job lasted a year; the second one lasted two years. And then she'd seen the ad for the grant writers' position at the Brinker Foundation.

"Excuse me," a man said.

Margaret glanced up, then moved her briefcase on the table so the man could get by.

"Margaret? Margaret Hall-Stuart, is that you?"

She blinked and looked up. The man held a large Starbucks cup, a bag with a pastry in it, and a *Wall Street Journal* tucked under his arm.

For a moment, she didn't recognize him. Then he smiled, a sexy dimple appearing in his right cheek.

"Rondell. Rondell Isaacs. Oh, my goodness." She rose, her smile as broad as his. He placed his coffee and pastry on her table and they embraced.

"Margaret, it's been what?" he said. "Five or six years?"

"Seven, Rondell. Seven years." She shook her head. "I was just sitting here thinking about that first job. I learned a lot about nonprofits, thanks to you."

His appreciative smile took in all of her. "And I learned that I let the best thing that ever happened to me walk right out of my life."

She laughed, even as the awareness rippled through her. If ever there was a man who'd turned her head even more than Roger

McKenzie, it was Rondell Isaacs. The years had been good to him. He was still sexy. Still tall, dark, and confident. And he looked like a million bucks.

"Join me," she said, indicating the chair at the table. "So, are you still with the Community Action Fund?"

He shook his head. "I left about five years ago."

"And you were running it when you left, right?"

He chuckled. "You always did know me better than anyone."

"So what are you up to these days?"

"Working in development."

She waited.

He shook his head. "Director of Development."

"At?" she prompted.

His answering smile was just as playful as her tone. "At a certain very large research university not too far from here."

She guessed.

He nodded.

"You are the man," she said.

"And you're as beautiful as you were seven years ago. More so."

Margaret's smile was coy. "Thank you," she murmured.

Coffees forgotten, they stared at each other. The chemistry between them had always been right. At the time, though, seven years ago when she still carried the emotional wounds from her failed marriage, Margaret hadn't been open to Rondell's subtle advances.

Now, though . . .

He was still a very good-looking man. His hair was cropped short, his eyes a dark brown, filled with intelligence, depth, and honesty. His suits, then Saville Row, now Armani, always fit his frame in a way that made Margaret realize just how well clothes could make the man. Rondell, though, could make a suit talk. He still did.

"I'm in town for a conference," he said. "But I finished early today. When I drove by and saw this Starbucks I kept driving. Then, something told me to turn around. So I listened."

She reached for his hands. He took her hand and raised it to his mouth, placing a small kiss there.

Margaret's breath caught. They stared into each other's eyes.

"We have some unfinished business," he said.

"Yes, we do."

They were quiet for a few moments.

"So what happens next, Margaret?"

She lifted her hand and caressed his cheek. "I think we should explore the potential conclusions to our mutually unexplored territory."

He smiled. "You always did have a way with words."

A minute later, they gathered their belongings and left the coffee shop. Rondell's golden Lexus followed Margaret's white DeVille back to her house.

They talked for a while, catching up, filling in the gaps the years had left. Margaret even told him about her problems at the Brinker Foundation.

"So come work for me," he said.

They were sitting close on one of the sofas in Margaret's large, sunny day room. He'd shed his jacket and loosened his tie. Her feet were tucked under her, her shoes neatly to the side.

"Don't joke like that," she said, tapping his shoulder with a finger.

"I'm not joking," he said, turning so they faced each other. He took her hands in his. "You said you're not appreciated there. So walk away. Come to Charlottesville."

"And do what?"

"Head up my institutional giving department." He filled in the details, including the fact that she'd hire a staff of six. "That's why we met up today," he said.

Her brow creased.

He quickly explained. "This conference I'm attending: one of the things I'd hoped to get out of it was a candidate, or at least a lead on a candidate, for this job. It's newly created. I thought I'd run into someone who might be the right fit. I've been here two days and haven't come close. Then, out of the blue, I walk into a Starbucks and there you are. Someone I know who is savvy, creative, and exactly what I'm looking for."

A chill ran down Margaret's spine, but the feeling wasn't an unpleasant one. It felt like the answer to a question she'd been asking for some time. It felt as if the stars smiled down on her. It felt right. But so did his hand on her thigh.

"Rondell, what about this?" she said, dipping her gaze to the place where his hand rested easily on her.

"What about it?" he said, leaning into her, running one finger along the smooth expanse of her thigh while the other teased the sensitive hairline on her face.

Her breath caught as sensations washed through her. "We couldn't work together and . . ."

"And what? Continue our friendship? Have it develop into something more? I think we can."

Margaret's mind was racing. His touch felt so right. And the Reverend Sister Amelia, Prophetess of the True Light, had said that a change was looming on her horizon. Was this the answer to both the singleness she loathed and the job situation she'd grown to despise?

She thought about Roger. Where was *that* relationship going?

The mental image of the choir director brought her to her senses. She slid away from Rondell.

"What?"

Margaret paced the area in front of the facing sofas, her arms folded under her breasts. "I have friends here, a church family. I sing in a choir."

"You'll make friends in Charlottesville. We have churches and choirs there, too."

She smiled. "This is so sudden."

He rose and stood in front of her, halting her pacing. "Is it? Or is it, as I'd like to think, just what was meant to be?"

She glanced at him, they were practically the same height. "I don't know, Rondell. The house, I'd have to sell it."

"I'll buy it."

She blinked. "Excuse me?"

"As part of your relocation package."

"You can do that?"

He grinned. "I'm the man."

"Oh, really? Well, Mister Man, how much are you paying for this newly created position of yours?"

He named a figure. A *very* generous figure. It was more than double what she made right now, and that wasn't shabby.

Without hesitating, Margaret named another figure, ten thousand dollars higher than his original.

"Done," he said.

She cocked her head. "And the house?"

"Already done."

"Why are you doing this?" she asked him.

He pulled her to him and wrapped a hand around her waist. "Because I let you walk out of my life once before. I don't want to make the same mistake a second time."

And then his lips covered hers. Margaret closed her eyes, kissing him back. But the image in her mind was not of Rondell Isaacs, the man who held her. It was of Roger McKenzie, a man who'd become her obsession.

Rondell shifted, drew her closer. The evidence of just how much he wanted her couldn't be more evident. He ran his hand along her back and then lower. Margaret moaned as he deepened the kiss. A moment later, the only man on Margaret's mind was the one in her arms, the one making her feel cherished.

18

By the time she had to leave for choir rehearsal, Margaret's mind was still a jumble of the day's events. That horrible meeting at work, then preparing the case against her boss, then running into Rondell after all these years, and then having him offer her both a dream job and happiness with him.

But more than all of that, her mouth still tingled at the memory of his kiss.

Margaret wondered, though, as she stood in her dressing room, if she could really make it work with Rondell. She'd claimed to have friends. But the truth of it was, she had no friends at work, even though she and Sheila were relatively close. Her strongest tie to the area was her church and choir life. Her parents, now thinking about retiring, divided their time between the dealership and a home they'd built in South Carolina.

As she opened a scarf drawer, looking for something to accent the slacks and silk blouse she'd donned, Margaret had to pause.

"You have no life," she said.

The realization made her rather sad. She went to work. She went to church. She went to choir rehearsal. Her entire social life revolved around singing and traveling with Roger McKenzie and the Voices of Triumphant Praise. Yet still, she felt friendless.

She thought about Glenna and the overture of friendship the other woman had made while they were on the road several weeks ago. Other than the updates she'd gotten at choir rehearsal, Margaret had not thought much about Glenna. The woman was ill; that much was known. But Margaret had not once called, sent a card, or stopped by to see if there was anything Glenna needed.

It had never crossed her mind to do so.

Why her thoughts seemed so focused on Glenna was a mystery. But for some reason, Margaret felt compelled to see the woman.

Snatching up a brown-and-orange scarf, she went to her study, where she'd tucked the choir roster in a small filing cabinet. She found Glenna's address, jotted it down on a piece of paper, then grabbed her purse and keys.

Reverend Sister Amelia had encouraged her to go with the moments of insight and clarity that the spirits sent as gifts. Except for the few hours at work, much of today seemed like a gift.

If memory served correctly, Glenna, too, had some sort of power. Margaret sensed—and feared—the psychic energy that seemed to flow in and around the street woman. If nothing else, Margaret wanted to set to rights the mysterious warning Glenna had given her when they briefly shared a hotel room.

You're gonna have to be strong, Margaret. A storm is coming, Glenna had said.

What storm? she wondered. The situation with Hawthorne? Or did Glenna mean something else?

Curiosity getting the best of her, Margaret drove straight to Glenna's house, a run-down duplex in the city's southeast section. Glancing around, she pressed the key lock on her car and set the alarm. Then, delicately picking her way across a sidewalk littered with beer bottles and empty potato-chip bags, she made her way to a rusted-out gate. She'd double-checked the address, so she knew she had the right house.

Not in a million years could Margaret imagine living in this sort of squalor. She was so far removed from poverty that she couldn't believe people actually *lived* like this.

"How much effort does it take to pick up the trash in front of your house?" she muttered. She carefully climbed the crumbling stone steps, opened a screen door that had more holes than screen, and knocked three times on a weather-beaten front door that, like the neighborhood, had seen more than its share of hard times.

Margaret waited. She shooed a fly away from her ear and knocked again.

"She ain't home."

Margaret turned toward the gruff and scraggly voice. When she didn't see anyone, she leaned back a bit, then looked to her left and to her right. Across the street, a couple of old men sat on a front porch playing checkers. Neither of them had spoken, though; the voice had been close by, very close by.

"Hello? Who said that?"

"I did," came the reply, then the sound of spittle hitting a tin can. Margaret flinched.

Ragged coughing followed, the kind of sound that made it seem as if all the inside parts—guts, intestines, and bowels—were all coming up at the same time.

Margaret whirled around and peered to the left. There, sitting on the porch of the house next door, sat a wrinkled old man. Peering closer, she corrected herself. It was a woman. She looked about eighty, had her hair plaited in rows that stuck out all over, and was as dark as night.

Fearing infectious disease from the coughing and spitting, Margaret took a step back. "Did you say Glenna isn't home?"

"Nope," the hag said. "Dey up and took her to da hospital the other night. Bunch of folks did. Heard tell she ain't doing too good."

"Oh," Margaret said. Then, "Do you know which hospital?"

"Prob'ly Riverside. Dat's da one closest."

"Thank you," Margaret said.

The woman coughed again. The rattled hacking prompted Margaret to move. Quickly.

"You from Social Services?" the woman asked. "If'n you is, I ain't seen my check yet. When it be coming?"

Margaret didn't answer as she hastened down the steps and to the safety of her car.

That night after opening prayer, Roger told the Voices of Triumphant Praise about Glenna's condition.

"I went by to see her today," he said. "The doctors are doing some tests."

Krista spoke up. "Maybe we can all go see her after rehearsal."

Dwayne's arm had long since healed. He'd shed his bandage as well as his inhibitions about keeping his relationship with Krista on the down-low. "That's a good idea," he said as he patted her shoulder.

"Maybe not," Roger said. "She's in ICU."

"That's not good," Calvin piped up from his spot next to Reverend Vince. "My mama was in the ICU right before she went up to be with Jesus. I think that's the waiting room for heaven. You know, like Jesus is saying I-C-U there waiting for me. I'm calling you up next."

Krista winced.

Roger and Reverend Vince shared a glance. A couple of people said, "Calvin, please."

Margaret's full attention, however, was on the pretty woman who sat on the other side of Reverend Vince. She definitely wasn't Sister Hedgepeth. And at about twenty-five or twenty-six, she was about the right age to be their daughter. But the Hedgepeths didn't have any children. That fact registered on Margaret's subconscious, even before she slowly put the crooked pieces together. She'd seen this woman before. And the way the woman seemed to hang on Roger's every word didn't bode well.

Margaret's eyes narrowed.

"Let's all stand and have a word with the Lord to lift up Sister Glenna," Reverend Vince told the group.

"Aren't you going to introduce us to your guest?" Margaret said.

A couple of people looked at her, notably Tyrone and Roger. Margaret had to admit, she'd blurted the question out without the least bit of style and probably at the wrong time, but her curiosity was about to cause a stroke.

Roger smiled at the woman. Light and love passed between them. Margaret missed not a millisecond of the small exchange. She gasped, suddenly feeling as if someone had punched her in the stomach.

"You all right, Margaret?" Krista said. "We don't need to have two choir members sitting up in the hospital."

One of the guys—maybe Quent or Lamont—chuckled at that. Margaret just nodded, though, her voice too caught in her throat to get any words out of a mouth ready to deny what her eyes told her was the truth.

"This is Camille," Roger said. "She's a friend of mine who is in town for a few days and wanted to see how we practice for our concerts. Camille, this is the choir, The Voices of Triumphant Praise."

"Minus a few sleepyheads and Glenna," Dwayne said.

The woman stood up and expressed her pleasure at being able to see the choir in action, blah, blah, blah. Margaret tuned out the woman's words, focusing instead on the body language between this Camille and her Roger, homing in on the soft glances they seemed to share. That intimacy was something Margaret had never experienced with Roger.

Roger and this Camille woman—they were more than mere "friends." Of that, Margaret was certain.

She took a deep breath, trying to calm her suddenly racing pulse.

Surely Roger wouldn't disrespect her by bringing another woman into the fold, strutting her around like his trophy.

A red haze filled Margaret's head and her vision. In the background, she heard Reverend Vince begin a prayer, but her mind was somewhere else. In another time and place, the minute details etched themselves onto her brain like a continuous-feed video. Margaret remembered the night when she'd offered herself to Roger, completely. Totally in love, she'd offered herself in friendship and with the sweet promise of all their tomorrows stretched in front of them. . . .

The red teddy had black lace trim. The black fishnet hose had the sexy seam running down the back of the leg. The black garter belt would be his memento of the night.

Margaret had carefully shaved and showered. Her arms and legs were smooth as silk. The scented shower gel was a subtle form of the perfume she now dabbed between her breasts, behind her ears, at her wrists, at the backs of her knees. Her makeup was flawless.

She felt as pampered as a princess, and that was good. Because tonight, she would give herself to Roger McKenzie, the man she'd fallen madly, passionately, and completely in love with.

Their times together always lifted Margaret's spirits. Roger could make her laugh—at life, at herself, at just about everything. He was kind and considerate and he loved the Lord.

Margaret winced.

Thinking about God wasn't exactly where she wanted to be right now. Not when she was planning a seduction, planning to lose her virginity. But they loved each other. Their future together seemed certain. Besides, she reasoned to the small voice that nagged at her, love is always right.

Love conquers all.

"Love is a many-splendored thing," she sang. Then she smiled.

Her stomach did a little flutter. Margaret was nervous. She'd never done anything like this before. But the surety of her love for Roger and his reciprocal feelings calmed any fears she had.

Humming a hymn, Margaret applied her lipstick. Then, pretending that Roger stood in front of her, she blew a kiss to him.

Giggling, she picked up her trench coat and carefully buttoned and belted the coat over her near-naked body.

Checking the full-length mirror on the back of her dorm room door, she made sure no part of her sexy underthings peeked out. Since lots of girls on campus wore fishnet hose all the time—thanks to the influence of pop music stars—she didn't worry that her legs or high heels would draw any undue notice as she walked to the lot where she'd parked her car.

The drive from her dorm to Roger's off-campus apartment took less than fifteen minutes. But the wait was interminable. She'd timed her departure so she would arrive at the same time he got home, but her calculations had been off. His car wasn't parked out front. So she sat in her Cadillac for almost forty minutes. Right when she was ready to count the evening and her seduction plan a total loss, the beams of headlights turned onto the street.

Margaret blinked, then shielded her eyes from the bright lights of the approaching car. It was moving slowly, maybe five or ten miles per hour. She adjusted the volume on her radio and was about to start the engine of her car when the lights blinked off and the car stopped in front of her.

A moment later, the door opened and she saw Roger.

Her heart bloomed with the love she felt for him. Tonight would be their night. Tonight would be the beginning of their shared future.

She ran to him, called out his name.

Roger stumbled. "Huh? Who is that?"

"It's me, Margaret." She wrenched up her nose when the strong odor of alcohol hit her.

He lifted his face up. In the moonlight, Margaret could see that something was terribly wrong. His face was wet, and streaked with red. Concerned, she stepped closer, opening her arms to give him a hug.

His steps faltered again, and he grunted. Then he threw up all over her feet and shoes.

REVEREND VINCE

19

The Reverend Vincent Hedgepeth watched the choir members during rehearsal. There was tension in the room tonight, even more so than usual. And he sensed that it wasn't just concern about Glenna Anderson that had the choir on edge.

Things were different. They had been since the Washington, D.C., trip that had been fraught with so many problems. Roger had sent half of the group home. He'd kept the choir's contractual commitments with a handful of people and begged off and out of their other engagements.

From a purely business standpoint, it wasn't the right thing to do. No-show artists were long remembered and despised by the public.

"So are ineffective ones," Vincent had said that night when Roger told him what he planned to do. The "ineffective witness" line seemed to echo loud and long, and Vincent was sorry he'd used it.

But all these weeks later, the choir was still ineffective. It was as if they'd lost their purpose and drive.

Reverend Vince wondered if he'd counseled them in the right way. He, after all, had encouraged throwing in the towel on that trip. Tonight's rehearsal seemed as if they hadn't recovered from the decision to call a halt to the tour.

The joy and the spirit—the annointing that usually filled the place wherever they were—was missing.

Vince wondered if he was the only one who noticed.

But a glance at Marcus told him otherwise. The man's attention was on Margaret. Vincent wondered if Margaret knew the extent of the sound technician's feelings for her.

Probably not, Vince thought. She was too wrapped up in Roger, though she would have denied it to anyone who dared tease or approach her about it. Margaret Hall-Stuart was not, however, the type of person whom any of the choir members ever teased or approached.

With Glenna gone, Krista was the life of this party. And Tyrone Thomas could usually be counted on to soothe ruffled feathers, to offer a helping hand or a quick joke. Tonight, though, Tyrone sat in front of his keyboard. He hadn't said all of five words so far.

Roger finished his announcements and his update about Glenna and turned to Vince, who was ready to lead the group in a five-minute devotional period.

Reverend Vince had already decided that he would take more than his allotted time tonight. The Lord was sending a word, one the Voices of Triumphant Praise desperately needed.

"Open your Bibles to Romans eight," he told the group. "I want to focus on a passage found there. It'll be familiar to you. Roger and Tyrone wrote a song from that chapter of the New Testament."

Picking up his own Bible, Vincent glanced at the fifteen assembled choir members and musicians. "Sister Krista sings the song 'The Spirit is Life,' which is taken from the tenth verse. I know that song is a favorite with you. But have you thought about, and I mean really thought about, just what that means?"

A couple of people nodded.

"If the spirit is life, what's death?"

"Sin," Calvin called out.

The preacher nodded. "Yes. If the spirit doesn't dwell in you, there's a hole there. A gap. We talk about people filling in the gap, but you can't look to man to feed your spiritual needs. You have to look to the one who provides the life."

Reverend Vince wasn't sure just who this message was meant for specifically, but he trusted that God would deliver it to open and willing ears.

"I have a question," Marcus said.

The deep voice startled Vince. For a moment, he wasn't sure it was Marcus who'd actually said something. The sound technician was good at his job, but he looked and acted more like a hit man. Rarely, if ever, did he actively participate in group discussions. Instead, he was just there physically. In many ways he was like Margaret, except that while her standoffishness seemed to stem from a haughty spirit, Marcus seemed to be more brooding and assessing.

"What's that?"

"It's my recollection that that particular chapter also talks about some other kinds of sin, the sins of the flesh. Things like sleeping around and gambling and lying on folks."

A few people squirmed in their seats and suddenly developed an intense interest in the tile pattern on the floor. The room's tension level seemed to jump a few notches.

"Yes, it does," Vince said, wondering where the question was leading. "The examples you mention aren't necessarily mentioned by name in the Scripture."

"Yeah, I know," Marcus said. "But when that kind of sh—" He caught himself. "When that kind of stuff is going on *in* the church and with the so-called people of God, doesn't that mean that there are a whole bunch of church people going straight to hell?"

"Why don't you get off my case, man?" Scottie growled under his breath.

Marcus sent a distracted glance in Scottie's direction. His gaze flickered over the younger man's. "I didn't name any names, my brother. But, since you're putting your business in the street, your little game is likely to land you in some serious trouble with the law. You think you're smart," he said, tapping his head with a finger. "But there's always somebody smarter. There's always somebody quicker."

"You'd be wise to shut up."

Marcus folded his arms. "I think it's time to bust your cover, Scottie. Why don't you tell everybody who doesn't already know just what you do when these folks are out singing about Jesus."

Scottie jumped up, knocking his chair over in the process. "I don't have to take this."

"What is this?" Roger asked, looking between the two men.

Scottie stepped to Marcus, who didn't flinch or move. The smaller man glanced around. No one met his eye. "I'm outta here. Forget you, Marcus."

"If you show your face here again," Marcus said, "it'll be the last time. And that's not a threat, Scottie, it's a promise."

Scottie snorted. Looking around, though, he didn't see any backup. "Forget all of you," he said, false bravado accenting his words.

A couple of people exchanged knowing glances but kept quiet. Calvin glanced from Scottie to Marcus, then from Marcus to Scottie. "I heard you say bad things about Miss Glenna and Miss Krista, Scottie. That wasn't very nice."

"Shut up, you retard."

"You leave him alone," Krista said, jumping up to defend Calvin. "Why don't you leave? We'd all be better off without you."

Scottie made a step as if to confront Krista, but suddenly Marcus was there. Then Dwayne got up and stood beside Marcus.

Scottie jerked his head. Then, with a finger to Marcus, he huffed out of the fellowship hall.

No one said anything until the door closed behind him. Marcus and Dwayne exchanged a glance and then tapped fists in a gesture of solidarity.

"What was that all about?" Roger asked.

Murmuring filled the room. Krista glanced at Dwayne, who shrugged as he took his seat again. Krista leaned close to Roger and whispered in his ear.

"What?!"

Roger's stunned expression encompassed the entire group, then narrowed in on Krista, Dwayne, and Marcus.

"Is what she said true?"

Marcus didn't say anything.

Dwayne shifted in his seat. "Well, I don't know what she said. But if it's what I think it is, yeah, I suspect it's true."

Roger held his head in his hands, closed his eyes, and expelled a long breath. "How long has this been going on?"

"Excuse me, Roger," Reverend Vince said. "Some of us don't know what all the whispering is about."

"I know, Reverend Vince," Calvin piped up.

"Shh, Cal," Krista said. "Not now."

Calvin looked at her and smiled. "Okay, Sister Krista. But I'll tell him later. Reverend Vince, too."

Looking out at his choir, Roger sighed. "Marcus, you were asking a question," he prompted.

Marcus eyed Roger. "My point was made. Part of it, at least."

With that cryptic comment, Marcus settled back in his seat.

"Reverend Vince," Roger said.

Nodding, Vince picked up the lesson in the eighth chapter of Romans, reminding the choir members that they should let nothing separate them from God's love. When he finished, he asked if there were any questions. When none came, he turned the floor back to Roger.

"All right," Roger said. "Let's run through a couple of numbers, then I'll teach you a new song."

Groans echoed through the choir room.

"Roger, what's the point?" Mary asked.

"Yeah," Quent added. "We're never going to be big-time. We all want it, but look at what happened on the tour. We couldn't even get through a week without falling apart."

Roger's face mottled. Vincent hoped the choir director remembered the relaxation techniques Vince had been sharing with him. Roger wasn't popping the antacids in his mouth, but whatever had just happened with Marcus, Scottie, and Dwayne, coupled with Quent's challenge, was likely to send him over the edge.

Vince steepled his hands and waited to see how Roger would handle the situation—explosion or explanation.

Roger bit his lower lip in what looked like a blatant attempt not to lose his cool.

"I don't share your opinion, Quent," he said. "As a matter of fact, I think God is about to move in a big way with this choir."

"We walked away from commitments," Mary said quietly. "That's not good."

"The Voices of Triumphant Praise met its commitments," Roger said. "Enough of us went on and performed the remaining engagements in Maryland and Philly."

"Yeah, well, I took a week off work for that so-called tour," Quent said. "I couldn't get that time back, even though I was one of the ones you sent home."

Listening to this new exchange, Vincent wondered if Quent had just crossed Roger's tolerance line, particularly since they'd all had this very same conversation a week or so after the aborted large group tour.

Roger's face pinched up. "Look," he said, "Scottie just walked out of here. If anybody else feels the Lord doesn't have them here for a specific, ordained ministry, you can leave now, too."

"Well, I've been thinking about just that," Quent said. "Minister Fred Alston invited me to join his group."

Roger held his arm out toward the door.

"Fine," Quent said. "My sister's coming with me, too. Ti'Nisha, let's go."

Folding her arms, the young woman pouted. "Just because you—"

"I said let's go."

Ti'Nisha cast a worried glance at Roger. The alto was one of the strongest voices in the choir. As Quent's younger sister, though, she mostly did what she was told.

With an apologetic look at Roger, she ducked her head. "I gotta go, Roger." She shrugged. "I'll call you, okay?"

The choir director's gaze was stony, unyielding.

When the door slammed behind them, Roger faced the group. "Anybody else?"

Krista and Dwayne glanced at each other. They clasped hands and faced Roger. "I don't know about anybody else, Raj," Dwayne said, "but me and Krista, we're here to stay."

"Thank you," Roger said. He looked at the remaining members. No one said anything and no one else left. "All right, then," Roger said after a long, awkward moment. "We have work to do."

Vincent eyed Margaret, who'd been quiet throughout the defections. But Margaret seemed to be lost in her own world. The same was true of Tyrone.

As for Roger, the weight of the world seemed to rest on his shoulders as he moved to his keyboard. "This is a variation of 'Just As I Am,'" he said. He played the song through, then divided up the parts for the remaining choir members.

Reverend Vince closed his Bible. On one level, he shared some of the choir director's obvious frustration. There was so much potential here, so much talent. Yet the choir, pregnant with possibilities, seemed to self-destruct at every turn. Maybe, Vincent thought, God was culling them down to be the choir He wanted, rather than the choir Roger or anyone else wanted.

From conversations with a few of the members, Vincent had been able to piece together the tangled history of the Voices of Triumphant Praise. This was the third or fourth version of the choir that Roger had founded with the help of his cousin and best friend, Tyrone. The two had coaxed several local singers to join them in a small ensemble that eventually grew to a twenty-two-voice choir. Infighting over who would sing solos and what the choir should wear for engagements had led to a split. When the fray ended, Roger and Tyrone and five of the original singers remained.

Twice now the choir had grown and apparently thrived before falling apart, ripped to pieces by dissension and jealousy.

The pattern, apparently, had three common denominators: Roger, Tyrone, and the soprano Margaret, who'd apparently always been singing with Roger in one group or another. Margaret was quiet and efficient, even if she was a bit standoffish.

Reverend Vince thought about the kiss he'd seen between Margaret and Marcus. If there ever was one, *that* was an unlikely pairing.

Eliminating Margaret, that left the two cousins to consider.

Was Roger, like Moses, forbidden to enter the Promised Land? The goal of national recognition that Roger so cherished always seemed just outside his reach. Vince's gaze shifted to Tyrone. He sat there looking glum, so unlike the usual exuberance emanating from the talented musician and singer.

Maintaining the biblical parallel, Vince wondered if Roger's cousin Tyrone was Joshua. Joshua had gone into the land and brought back a good report. It was Joshua who had eventually led the people into the land of milk and honey. Was *that* the source of the tension in the group? It didn't seem likely.

His gaze went back to Roger. The puzzle started and ended there.

The pager at his waist vibrated, cutting off the intriguing thought process. Vince recognized the number and waited for the written message from his wife to scroll across: "Call home. 911."

"Excuse me," he said reaching for his Bible and his suit jacket.

In the hall, he quickly dialed home on his cell phone.

"It's Glenna Anderson, from the choir," his wife said without preamble. "The hospital called for you. She'd apparently put our name and number as next of kin on the forms."

20

In a lot of ways, Elaine Hedgepeth resembled her husband. They were both short, on the stout side with oval faces and benevolent eyes. Elaine Hedgepeth looked as if she could be her husband's sister. She still wore her white dress, hose, and shoes. The women's prayer circle at their church had had its monthly meeting that night. Before she had time to change, the call had come in about Glenna Anderson.

On the drive to the hospital, Reverend Vince had slipped on a cleric's collar.

Together, looking like missionaries in the field, they rushed to the ICU.

"Do you think she's all right?"

"I don't know," Vince said. His Bible was clutched in his hand. His wife carried a small Bible and a large white-lace handkerchief.

At a nurses' station, they stopped to ask for directions and were pointed toward the right wing and hall.

At another station they asked after Glenna. Glancing at a clipboard, the nurse told them that Glenna was about to be transferred to another room. Her condition was still serious, but had been upgraded from critical.

The Hedgepeths waited. They spent the time, almost an hour, visiting with other patients, some they knew and others they didn't. In the years they'd ministered together, they'd discovered that just the presence of clergy helped many sick and shut-ins. A prayer here, a soft or gentle word there, and a calming spirit went a long way toward healing and recuperation.

About an hour later, they found Glenna's room, a place shared with two other patients. They pulled the privacy curtain around and sat close. Swathed in tubes, Glenna looked lost in the hospital bed. Her boldly colored hair no longer had its luster. The smile she usually bestowed on every person she encountered was a thin line marred by pain, a gross caricature of her normal self.

At times, Glenna seemed to fade in and out, sometimes aware of their presence, and at other times oblivious. But they sat with her, reading Scripture, praying and humming the songs of Zion.

After a while, Elaine Hedgepeth patted Glenna's hand. "I'm going to go find some coffee for the reverend," she said. "Is there anything I can get for you, sister? A magazine from the gift shop, maybe?"

Glenna shook her head. The edges of her mouth turned up in a small smile. "Thank you, though."

With another comforting gesture and a squeeze to her husband's shoulder, Elaine slipped from the room to give the two some privacy.

"Nice lady," Glenna said.

"That she is," Vince agreed. "I've been wondering something, Glenna."

She waited for his question.

"Why me?"

She closed her eyes for a moment, then took a deep steadying breathe. "I don't really know my pastor. The church is so big. You, though," she said. "You and Roger. Y'all be my preachers."

Vincent smiled.

"You should rest," he said.

Glenna shook her head. "I need to tell you a story."

"A story?"

"Maybe you can fix things. Make it right."

She closed her eyes for a moment. Vincent sat there, curious but unwilling to rush or disturb her.

A moment later, she struggled to sit up. He helped her by tucking an extra pillow behind her. He found the bed control and levered the top up. When she was comfortable, she smiled.

"Thank you, Reverend Vince."

He pushed her glass of water and straw within reach on the bed table. When she shook her head, he moved it away.

"Did you know Roger met me in an alley?"

"Yes," he said. "Roger told me you were in pretty bad shape then," he said.

Glenna nodded. She closed her eyes and leaned her head back a bit. "I'd given up," she said. "I wanted to die."

"When was this?"

"About two years ago. Almost three, maybe, by now."

She opened her eyes and met his gaze. "I turned tricks," she said. "I turned tricks to pay for food and a habit."

Vince was surprised, but he didn't show any of it. He'd known, of course, that Glenna had a bad background. That much Roger had told him. But he'd had no idea of the depth.

"I've been clean since that night. It was a long, hard trip," she said. "Roger was there every step of the way. He was my rock."

"Why are you telling me this?"

"Cause somebody's trying to hurt him. I can feel it, Reverend Vince. I can feel it in my spirit." She reached for his hand. He was surprised at how cold she was. Her hand felt like an ice cube on his.

"Roger hasn't mentioned anything about anyone trying to harm him."

"It's the devil," Glenna said. "The devil comes sneaking in all over the place." She paused, taking a deep breath. "I saw something," she said. "It still don't make a lot of sense to me. But I wanted to tell somebody—you know, in case I don't make it out of here."

"Sister Glenna, don't talk that way."

She shook her head. "Don't get all weird on me like Roger does. The doctors said my pressure is so high it's a wonder I ain't already gone. That plus the other stuff." She shrugged. "You know, years of hard livin'. It's all caught up with me."

"What?"

"The tricks. The needles. I'm HIV-positive."

"I didn't know," he said, reaching for her hand. He gave her a gentle, encouraging squeeze.

"Not something you broadcast all over. But it's not that. The cancer'll kill me long before AIDS or pressure does."

"Is there anything I can do?"

She shook her head. "The cancer, it's eating me up. It's related, yeah, but different."

"We each have to walk through the valley experiences," he said. "The valleys and the wilderness teach us just how much we need the Lord. When we come out, we come out shining as pure gold."

Glenna chuckled, a sound that turned into a cough. When she leaned back again, a smile was at her mouth. "Well, I came out, all right," she said. "But I was a bit tarnished."

"'You're a strong woman, Sister Glenna."

She held up a hand. "I need to tell you what I saw."

He waited.

"I been praying about this thing," she said. "I just didn't wanna believe it, so I gave it to the Lord."

And then she told him. And then Reverend Vince knew why Marcus had run Scottie out of the choir.

Like Glenna, Vincent wasn't sure what to make of the situation. The next night he still considered what he knew about the players and ultimately decided that what he knew wasn't enough. He filled his wife in on the disruption that had happened during rehearsal.

"Apparently, everybody in the choir knew Scottie was running numbers and a gambling operation except Roger and me. A gospel choir was a good front for him."

"Running numbers?" Elaine Hedgepeth looked up. They were in the kitchen putting the finishing touches on dinner.

"Honey," she said. "Are you sure you should be associated with that group?"

Vince pinched a carrot from the salad. Smiling, she slapped his hand away. "I think I'm supposed to," he said, leaning against the counter as they talked. "I mean, look at how it all came about. I met Roger and Tyrone at that ministerial conference, and then we were paired up in the counseling pastoral sessions. Then, when I turn around, who's there staring me in the face in a prayer line?"

"Coincidence."

He patted her on the behind, then picked up the salad bowl and carried it to the dining room table. "You know better than that," he said. "There's no such thing as a coincidence. Everything in this world happens for a reason."

"Well, I don't want the reason to be so you can find out what it's like to be arrested and go to jail."

"I'm not going to be arrested."

"Why didn't Roger know what was going on right under his nose? I thought you said he was pretty sharp."

Thinking, Vincent paused for a moment. "Usually he is. He's been distracted lately. I think canceling the full-choir performances up in D.C. took something out of him."

"Maybe something else is wrong."

He mulled that over as he picked up a bottle of ginger ale. "I don't know. Could be. There's always been an undercurrent between him and the guy who works the group's sound system. I've never really been able to pinpoint what's up between them. Every time I ask Roger he just shrugs it off. And the sound guy—Marcus is his name— he's like a stone wall."

Following with a casserole and string beans, Elaine glanced at the table to see if anything was missing. "Ice."

A few minutes later, with soda poured in tall glasses filled with crushed ice, the couple said grace, then picked up the conversation.

"The few times I've been with them," Elaine said, "things always seem to be in such turmoil. Don't get me wrong; they can sing. There's some serious talent in that choir."

"But something's missing."

She nodded.

"I've been trying to figure out what it is," he said. "Roger and his cousin, the one with the fancy suits, were at it for a little while. But tonight they seemed okay."

Elaine served her husband a double helping of the beef-and-potato casserole, then served herself. "I forgot the rolls." She got up, went to the kitchen, and came back with steaming yeast rolls from the oven. "You know," she said, "the problem might be more basic than you think."

"What do you mean?"

She looked at him. "They all know the words, the music. They sound good together. But sounding good and going through the motions isn't the same thing as having a one-on-one relationship with Jesus. Singing the words to gospel music and having an annointing to sing gospel are two completely different things."

Vince looked thoughtful. He mulled over all that Glenna had told him from her hospital bed. "You may be right."

"I know I'm right," Elaine said. "I'm the wife and the wife is—"

"Always right," he said, finishing the long-standing joke between them.

Elaine smiled at her husband. They'd been together for twenty-three years now. The time had passed quickly. Married in their late twenties, children had never come. The stray souls they took in, the young people they mentored and ministered to, and the volunteer time they each put in with groups like the Voices of Triumphant Praise filled the gap in their lives that a lack of children might have left.

For a few minutes they ate in companionable silence. Then, Elaine remembered something.

"Didn't you tell me Roger was planning some sort of testimony project?"

Vincent's brow furrowed. "Yes. He was, come to think of it. As a matter of fact, the three of us talked about it. Me, Roger, and Tyrone. It probably got dropped through the cracks somewhere."

"Well," Elaine said, buttering a piece of a roll, "maybe a good old-fashioned testimony-and-prayer meeting is what they all need."

Vincent looked up from his meal. He put his fork down and regarded his wife. "You know, I think you're onto something."

"Besides," Elaine said, "if somebody was running numbers, everybody in that group ain't saved."

ROGER

21

"I've made a mess of things," Roger told Tyrone.

The two men were sitting in Denny's, eating breakfast for dinner.

"What do you mean?" Tyrone reached for the syrup, then waved at their server. "Some more napkins, please."

"I've handled some stuff badly."

Tyrone glanced up from pouring syrup over a stack of steaming pancakes. "Uh-huh. That, cousin, would be what they call life."

Roger shook his head. "I mean really messed up. Everything."

"You're gonna have to be a little more specific if you're looking for help from me. And keep in mind, I ain't exactly the best source for sidewalk psychology these days. My own house is in turmoil."

Knowing what he meant, Roger told his cousin, "Georgie called."

Tyrone attacked the stack of pancakes with more force than necessary. "I know. She's been paging me all day. I finally just turned off the pager. But we've been down this road. It's your turn on the shrink's couch."

Roger hadn't touched his omelette. He reached into his jacket pocket and pulled out some papers. Staring at them for a bit, he finally handed them to Tyrone.

"What's this?" Tyrone shoved a piece of sausage in his mouth, accepted the napkins from the waitress with a mumbled "Thanks," and wiped off his hands before he took the proffered items.

"My life lately," Roger said.

Tyrone smoothed out the crumpled edges and glanced down to read. A frown curved his mouth at the first note. He looked at Roger as he shifted to the second and the third. Then, "What the devil? Is this a joke?"

"I wish it were. Somebody is either trying to scare me or blackmail me."

Tyrone sat back. "Blackmail?" Tyrone glanced around the restaurant. "Cuz, this ain't TV. This is real life we're talking. Have you been to the police?"

Closing his eyes, Roger shook his head. "To say what? 'Officer, I've gotten a couple of threatening notes'?"

"This is more than a threat," Tyrone said, flipping through them again. "'You can run but you can't hide,'" he read from one, and "'Time's running out.'"

The two men looked at the sheets of paper. The notes, all four of them, were typed on standard white typing paper, the kind available at any office supply store.

"How many of these have you gotten and when did they start?"

"Just those," Roger said. "Well, the first one I got I ripped up. It came at that motel in D.C. The next one," he said, leaning forward to point out which, "also came on the road, demanding five hundred dollars."

Tyrone's eyes widened. "Get out. What'd you do?"

Roger sighed. "I took some of the choir's money and made the payoff."

Tyrone didn't say anything for a long time. Then he asked, "Is that why you wanted to end the tour?"

Roger exhaled heavily. "That and everything else that was going wrong. The second one was delivered during that concert we did right after we got to Baltimore. The third one was in my music at the church one Sunday, and that one," he said, pointing to the message that said *Tick tock Roger dodger. Better check your brakes,* "that one came today. It was clipped to my newspaper when I picked it up from the porch today."

Tyrone pushed his plate away. "This is serious, Raj. You've got to go to the police."

Roger shook his head. Tyrone was about to protest when a realization dawned. "You said blackmail. That means something went down that somebody knows you don't want people to know about." He let the question hang.

For a long time Roger just sat there. A thousand emotions crossed his face. He wanted this nightmare to go away. To be over. If somebody truly wanted him dead, wouldn't they have done it by now? At least there had been no additional demands for money. That was a good sign. Since he didn't have any to begin with, the idea of somebody actually blackmailing him for cash seemed ludicrous. That left him with nothing: no ideas, no clue to who might know his terrible secret.

"There's something I need to tell you," he told Tyrone. "Maybe if I'd said something a long time ago, this wouldn't be happening now."

"What?"

And Roger told him. Told him how he'd lost the talent shows, how his music was stagnant, how bitterly depressed and angry he'd been at the world, at God. Then came the gin. The anguish. The accident. Roger told his cousin all of it.

When Roger finally stopped talking, Tyrone just stared. They sat there, both men breathing hard, one from panic and the other from disbelief.

When words finally came to Tyrone, they were monosyllabic. "When? Where? Who?"

"A long time ago is the when," Roger said. "As for the who, her name was Janice Lydell. She was a wife, mother of two kids. The newspapers wrote lots of stories about the hit-and-run. Because they could never find the vehicle and there weren't any witnesses, everybody assumed it was somebody from the Navy base who shipped out right after the accident."

"You just drove away?"

Roger hung his head. "I have a box with all the newspaper clips in it. I don't know why I've kept them all these years. Guilt maybe."

Tyrone shook his head, still trying to take it all in. Then he thought of something. "Remember when we shared that apartment in the East End, you used to have nightmares. You'd wake up screaming 'I'm sorry. I'm sorry.' Is that what that was all about?"

Roger nodded. "I still have them. Worse now."

Tyrone sat back and folded his arms. "Well, you need to go to the police."

"And say what exactly?" he said, his voice rising. "About ten years ago I hit—"

"*Shh* . . ." Tyrone said, glancing around. Luckily, except for a couple snuggled together in a booth and a guy drinking coffee at the counter, the restaurant was empty.

Leaning forward, Roger whispered. "What am I supposed to say if I go to the police? I hit some lady twelve years ago and left the scene of the accident? It was a hit and run and I was drunk at the time?"

"I don't believe we're having this conversation."

Roger snatched up his notes and stuffed them in his pants pocket. "I never should have said anything."

He threw a ten-dollar bill on the table to cover his uneaten meal and slid from the table, grabbing his jacket as he left.

"Aw, man, Raj. Hold up, cuz. Hold up."

With a forlorn look at his pancakes, Tyrone dug around and came up with enough cash to pay for his food. He snatched the bacon and sausage from his plate and hurried after Roger.

"It's on the table. Keep the change," he called out to the server, who was standing at the register.

Tyrone followed Roger to his car. They both stopped and stood there looking at it. "Uh," Tyrone said.

Roger mumbled something under his breath. It distinctly sounded like profanity, but the moment itself was profane.

"I'm not getting back in that car," Tyrone said. "You saw what that note said. Man, have you been driving this all day? Are you crazy?"

Roger kicked the passenger door, then yelped as pain shot up his foot and leg.

"Well, that looked productive."

Glowering at Tyrone, Roger leaned against the car and stared out at the shopping center beyond the restaurant's parking lot.

"Now what?" Tyrone asked.

Roger slid down the side of the car until he sat on the ground. Tears were falling from his eyes.

"Oh, man," Tyrone said. "Roger. Come on, cousin. We're gonna work this thing out."

Two hours later, after waiting more than forty minutes for a tow truck to show up at Denny's, then schlepping to a mechanic's shop, and another thirty minutes for a cab to pick them up there, Tyrone and Roger sat in Vincent Hedgepeth's study.

Sister Hedgepeth brought them crumb cake and coffee, then excused herself, saying, "There's more coffee brewing if you want it. I'll be upstairs." She kissed Vincent, then left the men to their talk.

"We've got a problem," Tyrone said. "A big one."

Roger shook his head. "No. *I've* got a problem."

Tyrone opened his mouth to refute his cousin, but Roger held up a hand.

"Reverend Vince, I just told Ty about this tonight. It's been . . ." He glanced at Tyrone. "Well, it's been going on for a while."

Vincent waited.

Roger looked at the pattern on the rug, then at photos on the mantel. He took a deep breath and then started talking. "You know what happened in D.C., right?"

Vincent nodded.

"What?" Tyrone asked.

Figuring that Tyrone would catch on, Roger didn't answer. "Whenever I get really stressed, the dreams start up again. That was the worst they've ever been. I think you were right, Reverend Vince. You, too, Ty. Organizing that tour was a mistake—for a lot of reasons. The main one being that it wasn't the time. *I* want to get there," he said pointing his finger in the air. "To the big time. To the stage at the Dove and Grammy awards."

He stood up, paced to the mantle and then back to the sofa. "But where is *there?* It's wherever I'm not." He shook his head. "It's a heck of a way to live. I want to marry Camille. She's very special to me. And we're compatible. I also know that to make it in this business, having the quote-unquote 'lovely wife' to share in the ministry adds brownie points. Otherwise, there's the gay stigma."

Tyrone frowned. "That's—"

Reverend Vince held up a hand to halt Tyrone.

Pausing for a moment in his pacing of the living room, Roger faced them. "In reality, instead of running toward my goals, I've been running away *from* my past." He pulled the crumpled papers from the pocket of his slacks. "It's caught up with me, though, and now it's time to pay for the sin."

He handed the notes over to the minister, who read them and then looked first at Tyrone and then Roger. "How can I help you?"

Roger turned around. "What?"

"How can I help you?" Vincent repeated.

"You want to help me? There's really nothing to do. I need to go to the police."

"Roger . . ." Tyrone said.

But Roger shook his head. "In the Bible, all the men of God sinned against God. Look at David: he chased women. Moses was a murderer. They all, one way or another, had to pay." He shrugged. "For me, going to the police means maybe my dream gets deferred for a while. But at least I'll have a clean conscience. And I'll be able to sleep without demons chasing me. And maybe I'll be able to tell Janice Lydell's family that I'm sorry." He shrugged. "I'll be able to start over. Washed clean."

He sang a line from John P. Kee's "Wash Me," then grinned at the small joke. Neither Tyrone nor Vincent smiled back. Roger sighed.

"I have a couple of friends you can talk to," Vincent said. "One is a police detective who is also a minister. The other is a counselor that I think you might benefit from talking with."

Roger laughed. "I don't need another shrink," he said. "I already have you two."

The three talked a little while longer. Then, with the understanding that they'd meet at the police station downtown at ten the next morning so Roger could turn himself in, the three men prayed together.

Brrrinnngg.

Brrrinnngg.

"Wha . . . ? Huh? Who is it? Georgie, get the phone," Tyrone mumbled. He turned over and promptly jammed his side into the metal frame poking up on the edge of Roger's pullout sofa.

"Oww."

Brrrinnngg.

Blinking his eyes, Tyrone got his bearings. He wasn't at home with Georgie. He was camped out on Roger's sofa. He crawled over to the offending alarm clock propped on a stack of magazines on a box filled with sheet music. He slammed it off and sat back.

"Raj? Man, what kind of clock is that?"

When he got no answer, he called out again, louder. "Raj?"

Tyrone slowly got up, rubbing the kinks out of his back. He padded to Roger's bedroom. The bed was made, but there was no sign of Roger.

"Roger?"

Shaking his head, he went to the bathroom. After relieving himself, he saw the note taped to the bathroom mirror. *Errands to run. Meet you downtown at 10.*

Roger's scrawl included, at the bottom of the piece of notebook paper, a big *R*.

It was eight-thirty. Tyrone had planned to be at the studio at ten today, but Roger's crisis took precedence. Tyrone called in, said he'd be in late, then showered, dressed, and scrambled some eggs for breakfast.

At five minutes to ten, he pulled into the police station parking lot and met Reverend Hedgepeth, who was already there.

At twenty after the hour, Tyrone paged Roger. He paged him again ten minutes later.

At a quarter to eleven, Reverend Vince turned to him. "I don't think he's coming."

"But he left a note," Tyrone pointed out. "Said he'd meet us here. Maybe he got tied up at the mechanic's shop. He wanted to get the car looked over, you know. After that threat, he wanted to make sure no one had been messing with the brake line or anything. He'll show. Just give him a little more time."

The two men waited another half an hour. Roger never put in an appearance.

Tyrone's defeated sigh said he knew Roger wasn't just late; Roger wasn't going to show.

Reverend Vince clapped Tyrone on the back. "I have some rounds to make at the hospital." He pulled a business card from his wallet, wrote a name and number on the back, and handed it to Tyrone. "Give this to him when you see him, all right? And call me if anything's up. Anytime, day or night, understand? Roger's state of mind right now is . . . well, with everything on him, he might think there's no way out of this."

Tyrone looked at the minister, at the concern in his eyes. Did he think Roger would try to kill himself over this? Yeah, things were bad, but they weren't *that* bad. He shook his head. "Roger wouldn't do anything like that. I know him. He's my blood, Reverend Vince. He'll do the right thing. I know it. He just got delayed."

The preacher nodded. "God's peace to you, my brother."

Tyrone watched Reverend Vince head to his car. He slapped the card against his hand, then looked around the parking lot as if Roger might be pulling in any moment. "Roger, where are you, man? Where are you?"

PART
THREE

ODEUM

22

God resisteth the proud, and giveth grace to the humble.

—1 Peter 5:5

Usually Margaret enjoyed choir rehearsal. Margaret loved singing. She always had. Tonight, though, as Roger and Tyrone ran them through some of the songs they already knew, Margaret's mind wandered.

She thought about Glenna. She thought about her job at the Brinker Foundation and she calculated how much longer she thought she might be able to put up with her boss, Nate Hawthorne. She thought about the position in Charlottesville and what it might mean to pick up and start over again in a new place.

But mostly Margaret thought about what it might be like to be married to Roger McKenzie.

She'd loved him forever—even when, in her first and last act of defiance against her parents, she'd run off and married a joker who could talk a good game but was merely after the financial gain Margaret brought to the union. Roger was different, though. He was her friend first, and that was important in a relationship. Roger loved her, down deep. That's what she kept telling herself.

Choir rehearsal had been strange. First that business with Scottie and Marcus, then Reverend Hedgepeth leaving in the middle of his sermonette. Margaret had tried to get Roger to open up about what was on his mind, but he patted her hand and told her not to worry her pretty head.

At the time, she'd preened at the compliment.

Now, she bristled at the patronizing platitude.

In her king-size bed, special ordered with thoughts of sleeping double in mind, she tossed and turned.

Margaret didn't sleep that night. Her mind kept racing, turning over all the things that had transpired recently. She kept thinking about the offer from Rondell Isaacs. She kept thinking about *everything* he was offering her: a dream job, a dream relationship, a new place, and a new beginning. So far, despite all of her efforts, fair and foul, to persuade Roger otherwise, he still didn't seem to look at her as anything more than a friend.

She'd sent him a couple of notes, little things that might make him smile. She really hoped the little jokes would spur his memory about all they meant to each other. So far, he hadn't responded to a single one of them. Not even to acknowledge he'd gotten them. She worked with words all the time, and maybe her plays on words had been too subtle for him.

She'd spent a lot of time crafting the last one: *Tick tock Roger dodger. Better check your brakes.*

How many clues did a woman have to give a man to let him know her old biological clock was ticking? He'd been dodging her for years and it was time, way past time, for him to slow down that fast drive and make her his bride. She'd been waiting long enough. They'd been friends long enough.

That part frustrated Margaret. The whole forever friends thing. She wasn't a particularly patient woman, but she'd been more than patient with Roger. She'd done all she knew to do. She'd tried to seduce him years ago, and her effort was rebuffed. The sting of that humiliating night still rankled.

Margaret went into her closet. Meticulously organized, the room was as large as most people's bedrooms. In the back, in a box she hadn't looked in in years, were the reminders of that night. The sexy teddy and the black garter belt she'd planned to leave with him as a memento of their night of passion. She thought about the shoes he'd ruined and how she'd just dumped them and her fishnet hose rather than soil her car.

In the middle of her closet, she sat on the floor, fingering the garments, remembering her pain, wanting to die from the shame of it.

* * *

She'd arrived at his apartment ready to throw herself on him. Instead, reeking of alcohol, he'd thrown up all over her.

Half dragging him, Margaret got Roger to his apartment door. They fell in a heap over the threshold, Roger moaning and talking gibberish the entire time.

She managed to get him to the shower, where he slid to the floor. She turned the water on full blast. It sprayed all over him and he floundered, sputtering and swallowing water.

Margaret surveyed her ruined shoes. They'd cost her two hundred dollars and were brand-new, purchased just for this evening of enchantment.

"I didn't mean to do it," Roger cried.

Disgusted at him and at herself, Margaret snapped. "Well, you did." Counting the shoes a total loss, Margaret held her coat ends up and lifted a foot and let the shower water run over her leg. She did the other one, then snatched a towel from the rack.

"Is this clean?"

"It was an accident," Roger wailed. "I'm so sorry. So sorry."

Margaret glanced back at him in disgust. She took off her coat, then shed her shoes and the fishnet hose. She dumped both in the trash can under the sink.

"Do you think you can stand up?"

Roger was sitting in the shower stall, water pouring over his head and chest. His face was all scrunched up as if he was crying.

The very sheltered Margaret had never experienced anything like this before. Totally out of her element, she surveyed the bathroom, trying to figure out what to do next.

"Dry clothes, coffee, and then I'm out of here."

Rummaging in his drawers, she found a clean T-shirt and shorts. Several minutes later, a stumbling and still stammering Roger, with the less-than-willing support of Margaret Hall-Stuart, made it to his unmade double bed. A trail of water attested to the struggle it was to get him from the bathroom to the bed. She pushed and Roger tumbled face-first onto the bed.

Arms akimbo, Margaret stared down at the sorry sight.

"Some seduction this was."

But he looked so pathetic that her heart twisted. He'd profusely apologized about throwing up on her feet. Something bad had obviously happened to him tonight. Despite her earlier pique, Margaret knew she'd do what she could for him.

He was still mumbling. "Car. Didn't see. So sorry. So sorry."

"It's all right, Roger. I'm here. Let me just get your shoes off."

She managed to untie his shoes then wrench the soaked shirt from him. Most of the buttons popped off in the process, but it didn't really matter. When it came to his wet pants, Margaret paused.

She bit her lip. "I'm going to need some help here, Roger. Roger?"

He didn't answer.

She kneeled on the bed and peeked over his head. "Roger?"

He was out cold.

Margaret plopped down on the bed, stretching out beside him. They lay there face to face.

With a finger, she traced his jawline, then his eyebrows. A smile curved her mouth as she fingered his. Then, she leaned closer and kissed him.

Their first kiss.

Margaret exhaled a dreamy sigh. She kissed him again.

He didn't stir.

She enjoyed the quiet time with him for a few more minutes, contentedly watching him sleep. Then, she tugged the sheet up over him and slipped from the bed. Barefoot, she let herself out of the apartment.

Now, sitting on her closet floor, Margaret sighed. It had all happened so long ago. She'd been a child then.

She'd never mentioned that night to Roger, and he hadn't said a peep about it either—even after all these years.

Maybe he didn't remember it.

Margaret Hall-Stuart considered that. It had never really crossed her mind before.

"Oh . . . my . . . God."

The realization shook her foundation: If Roger didn't remember that night, maybe he didn't really know how she felt about him. She'd based her entire relationship with him on the fact that he knew how she felt because of the bond they'd forged so long ago, first in the chapel at school, and later as their friendship developed.

Margaret stared at the black-and-red lingerie.

Was it possible he didn't know?

"We have to talk about this sooner or later," Georgie said.

"So you pick church, twenty minutes before service is supposed to start?" Tyrone wanted to hug her, but he was still angry.

"I knew you'd be here."

She looked great. Georgie Thomas wore a gold suit with elaborate embroidered appliqué trim. Her hair, piled high on her head in a twist, was in his favorite style. The earrings he'd given her for her last birthday dangled at her ears.

"You look good, Ty," she said.

Tyrone had on a white Nehru-cut long jacket with white slacks and Stacy Adams shoes.

He wanted to compliment her as well, but the kind words stuck in his throat. "Georgie, you know I'm supposed to be in the choir room right now."

She reached for his hand. "Ty, promise me. After service. Just the two of us. We'll go somewhere and talk."

Tyrone sighed. Then he nodded. "Yeah, Georgie. Sure. After church. Meet me in the back parking lot."

She smiled, tentative, unsure. "All right." She turned away, then faced him again. "You'll be there?"

Tyrone huffed. "I *said* I'd meet you after church, all right?"

Georgie nodded. Then, quickly, before he could react, she came up and kissed him on the lips. "I love you, Ty."

A group of children dashed by. "Hey, hey, stop that running," Tyrone called out.

"Hi, Minister Thomas," they chimed.

When Tyrone looked up again, the door leading to the sanctuary was closing behind Georgie.

All throughout the service, Tyrone's attention was on Georgie. She sat on the left side of the church, at an angle so she could always see him at the organ.

The church's mass choir had rehearsed twice that week. It was a good group, people Tyrone liked working with. Sometimes he liked his church choir more than he liked the Voices of Triumphant Praise. And sometimes he liked the church choir even more than he liked his own group, Blackstone. But right now, his mind wasn't on any choir. He'd missed cuing two soloists so far today. He was distracted. And the distraction was wearing a bright gold suit and a too-bright smile.

As the service leader led the responsive reading, Tyrone realized that if he and Georgie were going to work out their problems, there would have to be compromise on both sides. Georgie already seemed more than willing to meet him halfway.

The problem now was forgiveness. Could he forgive her for lying to him? It *was*, after all, something that happened before they met and got together.

Tyrone glanced back at her. Her head was down as she recited the words from the back of the Baptist hymnal. The Scripture was about stewardship, but Tyrone's mind was on the virtuous woman.

He'd found one. Or so he thought. Was it possible for anyone to be truly virtuous?

He knew the answer to that: No.

And you're not even close to being Mr. Perfection, he reminded himself.

Was it possible for them to move beyond this difficult road in their relationship?

All marriages went through rocky patches. Right?

He watched her. At one point, she glanced up and saw him watching her. His first reaction was to look away, but instead, he smiled at her. Georgie's face lit up with pleasure. Her answering smile radiated with the warmth that had first attracted him to her. Georgie's smile filled him with . . . well, with a sense of rightness. He loved her so much.

After the responsive reading, the choir was supposed to chant and then sing "Oh, the Blood." But Tyrone flipped the script. After the chant, he played the intro to another song, another old hymn of the church. He had a message he wanted to send, one he hoped Georgie would recognize and accept as his way of offering an olive branch.

They had a "date" to talk after church. Tyrone decided right then and there that he'd make the most of that meeting. He didn't like sleeping on Roger's lumpy sofa bed. He wanted to be with his wife. They could work this thing out.

The mass choir waited for his direction. Instead of cuing a soloist, though, Tyrone adjusted a headset microphone and began singing, "All to Jesus, I surrender. All to thee I freely give."

The hymn "I Surrender All" was Georgie's absolute favorite. It had been sung at their wedding, and Georgie even had a little poster with the lyrics at her work station at the bank.

With the church's mass choir singing the chorus, Tyrone looked back at the congregation. Scores of people were on their feet, arms raised in praise. Georgie, too, stood. Her hands clutched the back of the pew in front of her and she leaned forward, as if trying to get closer to him.

Tyrone held his hand out to her. Her eyebrows rose. He nodded and she rose. Georgie made her way forward to an area near the altar. A deacon handed her a cordless microphone.

With a cue to one of the musicians, who picked up on the electric piano, Tyrone slipped from the organ and joined Georgie. Together they sang the last verse of the song, her soprano melding with his rich tenor.

When they finished, hallelujahs rang out through the sanctuary.

Tyrone wrapped his arm around Georgie's waist and pulled her close for a hug.

In that moment, with the spirit floating all around them, Tyrone knew that they'd find a way to work through their problems.

The dreams were worse than ever. Roger knew that the solution to his nightmares lay in absolution. But fear of what might happen to him kept him in abeyance. It had been two weeks since he'd stood up Tyrone and Reverend Hedgepeth at the police station. He'd been there, though, watching from across the street. The right thing to do would have been to get out of the cab and walk straight into that police station, confessing all and taking his punishment like a man.

But Roger felt much less than a man.

He hadn't been able to make that long walk toward freedom. It didn't seem like freedom that he'd get; though on some level, he knew that the cause of all his anxiety, the nightmares, and the sick feeling he carried in his stomach each day had more to do with the guilt he felt about what had happened so very long ago.

Roger often wondered about the woman he'd killed that night.

Was she missed by her husband and children?

There were gaps in his memory, too. To this day, he didn't know how he got the woman's shoes or her stockings. But they'd been there in the trash can in his bathroom. Had he talked to her?

Sometimes in his dreams, he was gagged by those black stockings. At other times, when the demons really chased him, his arms and legs were bound by the hose while he sank deeper and deeper into the murky depths of a vermin-filled lake. Drowning. In guilt. In shame. In the misery that he'd created and run from.

But the running was wearing on him. His music was no longer a shelter. He couldn't write or create the songs that at one time in his life had come so effortlessly. He couldn't because the guilt and his conscience ate at him: *How dare you sing of righteousness when you fall so short of the mark? Who do you think you are, spouting pretty words about grace when you've been granted more than you ever deserved, more than you merit? How much longer are you going to pretend that you are a minister of the gospel when below the skin, you're just another common criminal, a would-be convict who managed to escape the justice he so rightly deserves?*

Liar.

Thief.

Sinner.

More than a decade of running hadn't built up his spiritual muscles. A decade of running had merely worn him down and out until he was frazzled and fried, in the brain, in the gut and in the spirit.

Roger twisted and turned on the bed. He lashed out, crying, moaning, hoping for relief while knowing it would never be his—not as long as he continued to run from the crime he'd committed.

As if his body could no longer take the abuse of his pain, he wrenched from the bed, fell to the floor on his knees, and cried out.

"Lord, I'm sorry. I'm sorry. I'm sorry."

He rocked on his knees, his hands steepled in prayer. He rocked and prayed, swayed and moaned. Cried out to the heavens for justice and mercy and grace and favor.

And then, finally, spent and overcome, Roger collapsed across the bed. His sobs echoed through the bedroom, his pajamas soaked through with the sweat of his surrender.

Many minutes later, he pushed himself up. He slumped to the floor, his back propped against the edge of the bed. It was time, way and long past time. His running days had to be over.

23

Let patience have her perfect work.

—James 1:4

Glenna Anderson walked slowly. This was her first day out of the nursing center. She'd been kept in palliative care for a week after being released from the hospital. Then she'd spent another week in the nursing home, surrounded by the old and the dying.

Glenna wasn't old, but she was dying. She knew that. She accepted that as part of the price she had to pay for living the life she'd lived. In her short twenty-some years, Glenna had packed more hard living and physical abuse onto her body than most people did in a lifetime.

Today though, she was clean. Clean and sober, just as she'd been for the past eighteen months. She had Roger McKenzie and Jesus to thank for that. Roger had saved her from the rats that were trying to feed on her beaten and abused body. Jesus had saved her from an eternity of hellfire and damnation.

Until she'd met Jesus that night in the alley, Glenna was sure that she'd already been to hell. Every day of her life, turning tricks on the street corners, mainlining heroin, and being slapped around by a no-good pimp had been living life in hell.

But all of that was behind her, almost as if it had happened to another person entirely.

The needle marks on her arms had finally faded away. She'd put on a little weight and she'd opened her mouth to sing about the goodness of the Lord.

Roger knew her story, and so did Reverend Vince. She'd told him that night he'd come to visit her in the hospital. She'd also told him that she'd seen Scottie doing some things that put them all in jeopardy, things way too much like her old life to give her any peace of mind. That situation had to be put to rights, and she could trust Reverend Vince to handle it.

She didn't, however, trust enough to let her friends know just how sick she was. She'd had enough pity, was tired of being the one with all the problems.

So Glenna had let on to a couple of people in the choir that her pressure was really high, that the doctors said she could die from the hypertension. But the high blood pressure didn't matter very much. The cancer was killing her faster than that ever would.

It was too far gone to do anything about it, the doctors said. The best they could do was make her comfortable. Give her drugs for the pain that would wrack her slender frame.

Glenna didn't want to take the medicine, though. It reminded her too much of when she'd taken other drugs to ease the pain in her life. But she took this medication; she took it because she knew her time was short and she had two things she wanted to do before she died. The first would be easy. She wanted to get her testimony recorded. The second would be all but impossible.

She sat in the hard seat in the concert hall, waiting for the choir to finish up. She couldn't sing now. She didn't always have breath for talking long stretches and she was tired a lot. But she wanted to be here, for this.

When they finished rehearsing a song about the unconditional love of Jesus, Roger made his way to her.

"You're looking as tired as I feel, Roger," she said.

His smile was sad. Glenna didn't know if he was sad for her or about something else going on in his life. She'd gotten a hint from Krista that Roger and the choir had been going through some changes. But Krista told her not to worry about anything.

"Just a lot on my mind," he answered.

"I like that song," she told him. "It's been a long time since anyone loved me unconditionally. All my life I've had people lie to me, steal from me, anything to take another piece of me." She shrugged, her shoulders thin under the green cotton jersey of her shirt. "Not much left to take now."

"Don't talk like that," Roger said. "God can . . ."

He nodded. "He can. But he won't. It's too late," Glenna said. "I'm all right with that, too. There's just a coupla more things I want to do, and then I'll be ready."

"Glenna . . ."

She glanced at him. Her morbid talk was apparently getting to him. Glenna didn't always remember that not everyone was comfortable talking about death and dying. She'd come to grips with it, though. Actually, she was surprised she'd lived as long as she had. When she first hit the streets at twelve years old, she didn't think she'd make it to sixteen. But she had, and she'd given birth to two kids by then.

That was one of the things she wanted to do, if she could. She wanted to see her babies. She didn't want to talk to them or interfere in the lives they had; she just wanted to see that they'd grown up okay. Any kind of life without her in it would have been good for them. And she'd wanted the best for her babies. Always had. That was why she'd given them up. She'd named them Ricki and Monet, two girls, but she was sure they had other names now.

Roger took her hand. "Are you all right? You look so . . ." He searched for a word. "Lonely."

Glenna's smile was sad. She took a breath, then squeezed his hand. "I'm not lonely. It's just me and Jesus, and good friends like you."

"I haven't been a very good friend lately," he said.

"No, you haven't."

He frowned. "You didn't have to agree so quick."

A flash of her old smile appeared. "It's the truth. Sickness scares people. And when it's terminal, well, I think a lot of folks think it's contagious or something. It's not. Don't worry."

"That's not what—"

"Let it go, Roger. Tell me some more about this testimony project of yours I heard about. You know I can't sing."

Roger leaned forward. "You don't have to," he said. "All I want to do is record your testimony. That's the idea. I'm going to get the choir members to talk their testimonies into a tape and we'll use those in between the tracks on the new CD."

She nodded. "Nice. I like that. And boy, you know *I've* got a testimony."

"Yeah, I know."

"I'll do it. Just tell me when."

"Marcus or Tyrone can get you whenever you're free. It'll take as long as you want it to take. He just turns the machine on and"—he snapped his fingers—"you're rolling."

"All right."

Roger moved to leave. She reached for his arm. "Roger."

He raised an eyebrow.

"I hear you've been having a rough time."

He huffed up. "I don't see—"

"Hold up," she said. "This is something I've been meaning to say for a while. Then I got sick. This might be my last chance."

Roger winced at that, but he settled back into the seat.

"You've been asking and wondering why the Lord hasn't moved in your music the way you want. Sometimes, as Patti LaBelle told us, we block our own blessings."

"Glenna, I really . . ."

"Hear me out," she said. "I've been there, so I know what it's like to be running. Running from or running to, it don't make a difference. But running all the time, afraid to face the reality of the day, of the moment." She shook her head. "Roger, that ain't no way to live. God wants us to live what Pastor says is abundantly. In his richness and his glory. Pastor preached about that not too long ago. But you can't live abundantly if you're always afraid of what's around the next corner or if you don't allow God to make his own moves in your life."

Roger slumped back with a weary exhale. "Your discernment is always startling."

"Look at me, Roger."

Reluctantly he turned toward her. Glenna edged up in her seat and took both of his hands in hers. "Look at me," she said again.

His gaze connected with hers. She stared into his eyes for a long, quiet time. Then, "Let it go, Roger. Let it go."

He snatched his hands away and stood up. "You know, some people say you're psychic."

"Been talking to Margaret again, huh? She's the only one who thinks that. Funny, though," she said. "Just a second ago you were calling it discernment."

Roger shifted from one foot to the other. "Well, whatever. I have some work to do."

Glenna reached for the cane that aided her steps. Roger leaned forward and assisted her up.

"I know you don't want to hear what I'm saying," she told him. "But it's time, Roger. It's time for you to let God move. He'll make it all right."

Roger didn't forcibly yank his hand from her arm, but his quick movement unsteadied her. She bowed her head and got a grip on the support of the walking stick. "The Scripture says whatever you ask for in His name, he'll give it to you. I'm asking for peace for your spirit, Roger. What do *you* want from the Lord?"

With that question hanging in the air, she carefully made her way across the front row of seats and up the side aisle of the auditorium.

Noises and laughter from backstage filtered through to Roger's consciousness. Soon, the stage hands would be putting the risers together for the concert that evening. Roger stared at Glenna's slowly retreating back. He watched until she made it to the door, then pushed it open. Daylight spilled into the dim depths of the auditorium.

Roger sat down and put his head in his hands. His world had completely fallen apart. The worst part of it was that Glenna, in her usual way, had been right on the money. That anyone could know the breadth and depth of his despair frightened Roger. But then, he realized, if there was anyone he knew who could really claim to have been at just about the lowest point a human could be, it was Glenna Anderson.

Roger wasn't at all sure that he had the patience to deal with Margaret right now. Although the rehearsal for their concert tonight had gone well, the conversation with Glenna lingered in his head, bothering him. Margaret, though a dear friend, could sometimes drive him crazy with her intensity. Everything had to be perfect for her. Always.

She'd asked if they could have dinner together before the concert. Roger hadn't been keen on the idea, but he didn't have a good enough excuse to get out of it . . . or the accompanying expense. Besides, she'd been inviting him to dinner at her place for a while now. Unable to go those times, this was as good a time as any to try to make amends. So he tucked his Mastercard in his wallet and prayed that he had enough open on the account to pay for their meals at one of the city's upscale eateries. They were Margaret's favorites.

But her choice of restaurant surprised him. Big time.

They sat at a booth at a steak house that catered to hungry working-class families, oblivious to the noise of bantering waitresses, orders being called up by a cantankerous cook, and the many conversations flowing around them from other tables.

After placing their orders, Margaret stirred her coffee, avoiding Roger's gaze. She'd always known they'd have this conversation. Her hope, though, had been that it would be safely within the confines of a strong marriage—not like this, with her very future on the line.

"Roger," she began. "You know I've always been there for you."

"Of course," he said easily. "We go back a lot of years."

She nodded. "This thing between us . . . our relationship. It doesn't seem to be . . ." She sighed.

"Margaret, whatever it is you're trying to say, just say it. It's me. Your boy."

"Man," she corrected. "You're a man."

He frowned. "It's just a saying, Margaret. You don't have to take everything so literally."

Deciding to change her tack, she let that slide. For now. "That woman. The one who was with you at rehearsal that night. Didn't I see her when we were in Washington?"

"You mean Camille? Yeah. She lives up there. What about her?"

"She's your . . . ?" Margaret leaned forward, silently urging him to fill in the blank.

He didn't take the opening. "Margaret, you know we sing tonight. I agreed to dinner because you said you wanted to talk about something important. What is it?"

"I want to talk about us, Roger. You and me. Our relationship."

His brows drew together and he sat back. "What, exactly, do you mean?"

She leaned forward. "You do know, don't you?"

"Know what?"

She pushed her coffee cup out of the way and placed her clasped hands on the table. "I love you, Roger. I've always loved you."

"I love you, too," he said. "That's what friends—"

"I don't mean *that* kind of love, a friendship love. I mean *in* love."

"Uh." He looked at the sugar, fiddled with his spoon, glanced at the booth across from theirs. He did everything but meet her earnest gaze.

Her eyes widened. Her mouth dropped open; then she quickly snapped it shut. "Surely you knew that. Roger, I've loved you since we were in college."

His expression clearly said he'd neither known nor suspected anything of the sort.

Stunned, hurt, and confused, Margaret sat back. "I don't know what to say."

"You've said a lot," he mumbled. Then, louder, "Margaret, I'm sorry. I didn't know you felt that way. I . . . we're just friends. Good friends who love the Lord and love singing gospel music. Camille and I . . ."

Margaret shook her head. "How could you not know? I offered myself to you. I've given you gifts through the years. I've followed you to every little backwater town and country church to sing with you."

"But that was because you sang in the choir."

"It was because I loved you."

"Margaret, this is, well, first a surprise and a shock. If I've unintentionally led you on, I apologize about that."

"It's her, isn't it?" she butted in. "That Camille woman."

"Margaret, there's no need to . . ."

She snatched up her purse. "I've been a fool. But not anymore, Roger McKenzie. Not anymore."

Before he could do or say anything, she dashed from the booth and was bursting out the restaurant door.

Incredulous, Roger sat there. Could this day get any weirder?

"Here you go, sir," a waitress said as she placed their orders on the table, a salad for Margaret and a steak, medium-well-done for Roger.

He looked up at the woman. "Have you ever had one of those days?"

"Honey," she said with a glance around the place, "I work here. Every day is one of those days."

24

Roger wasn't at all surprised when Margaret failed to show up for the concert. It was the first performance she'd ever missed in all their years singing together. That she thought she was in love with him still messed with his mind. She was trim, pretty, and rich, and she had a voice like an angel's. But . . . He couldn't even think of a but—just that she wasn't his type, had never been. And he couldn't imagine why or how she'd got into her head that they were anything more than friends.

"Where's Margaret?" Tyrone asked. "We're short on sopranos."

With Glenna out as well as Ti'Nisha, they were down strong altos, too.

The good thing about an all-volunteer community choir was that when everyone was there, the sound was fabulous. The bad thing was that you never really knew until a program began just how many voices you were dealing with—particularly for engagements when they weren't doing a full concert.

"She's not coming," Roger told him. "We had a . . . something of a disagreement."

Tyrone looked curious, but not curious enough to follow up with a comment fifteen minutes before the show was to start. "They just pulled the order. We're on second."

"I'll tell Krista that she needs to push for the high notes," Roger said.

"Raj, I have a suggestion."

The unusual hesitancy in Tyrone's voice made Roger look up. "What?"

"Georgie can sing with us."

That earned a raised brow. "And you two are . . . ?" Roger wagged a finger.

Tyrone grinned. "Working things out."

"Does that mean I get my spare room back?"

"Yeah," Tyrone said. "Yeah. It does."

"I'm glad for you two," Roger said.

Tyrone slapped his cousin on the back, then went off to round up the musicians.

That night fifteen groups queued up to sing at the city-wide Singspiration, an annual event hosted by the Interdenominational Ministers' Association. Because they were on early, the Voices of Triumphant Praise were poised to enjoy most of the program.

The trouble started backstage just as the first group, an a cappella men's ensemble, finished their last song.

The musicians, already in place behind a curtain that would soon go up, joked among themselves. Only Marcus seemed to take the night's work seriously, and he'd been in a foul mood most of the evening. He double-checked the cables that ran the length of the stage, and counted the microphones.

"For a ministry, you all have some mighty cavalier attitudes."

"Why don't you lay off, man," Lamont said. "You done already run Scottie and Quent out of here. Your job is to check the sound system."

Marcus got in Lamont's face. "That a fact? Well, why don't you go—"

"Hey, hey, hey," Tyrone said, jumping in between the men. "It's about the gospel. Not being at each other's throats."

Marcus backed off.

"What is his problem?" Lamont said.

"I don't know. You all cool?"

The singers, all twelve of them, filed out and took their places. The MC, a local gospel radio station announcer, was introducing them; then Reverend Vince said a few words.

"And now, ladies and gentleman, show some Christian love for the Voices of Triumphant Praise."

Marcus deliberately stepped in Roger's way as Roger moved forward to go on stage. The two eyed each other, circling and almost growling like two lions ready to fight over territory.

"Come on, Raj," Tyrone said. "Marcus, chill, brother."

Roger switched on the cordless microphone. Marcus glared at him. "Has God been good to you tonight?" Roger called out to the audience as he walked on stage.

The crowd amened.

"Well, tonight," Roger said, "the Voices of Triumphant Praise are gonna sing about the goodness of the Lord."

Tyrone and the musicians kicked up with the song Roger had written about unconditional love. They sang three other tunes, then made their way off stage as the MC told the audience to give it up again for the Voices of Triumphant Praise. He made an announcement about the group's latest CD, *Spread the Word,* then introduced the next act.

Roger got in Marcus's face just as soon as he saw him backstage. "What was that all about?"

"What?"

"Slamming into me right when I'm headed out to minister."

"I didn't slam into you."

"Yeah, Marcus. You did. And I'm pretty fed up with whatever it is that's been up your butt for the last two months. You've been giving me nothing but grief."

"Ha!" Marcus said, practically spitting in Roger's face. "Grief, what do you know about grief? All you know how to do is take. Well, let me tell you this, Roger McKenzie. I've been biding my time. Waiting. Just waiting. Margaret told me to be cool. That you'd come around. But you know what? I'm sick of waiting."

Marcus shoved Roger. The assault took Roger by surprise. He stumbled back, fell into Dwayne who steadied him, then stepped to Marcus.

"Brother, what is your problem?" Dwayne asked.

Marcus pushed him aside and then went after Roger. "How could you treat her like that?"

Before anyone knew it, fists were flying. Marcus's solid right connected with Roger's jaw. The choir director landed in a sprawl, knocking down music stands as he crashed to the floor.

Heads turned. A couple of the women screamed.

"Good God almighty!" the MC said as he headed backstage and saw the fight. He jumped into the fray, grabbing Marcus's arm.

It took Dwayne, Calvin, and the MC to pull Marcus off of Roger.

Lamont and a couple of musicians from the next choir scheduled to go on helped Roger up. Krista and Danita were there with tissues for his bloody nose.

"That was for Margaret," Marcus hollered as he was dragged down the hall.

Reverend Vince quickly checked on Roger, then hustled after the crew taking Marcus somewhere to cool off.

The flare-up apparently over, choir members in a variety of robes and outfits began straightening up the backstage area.

"I tell you," one said, shaking her head, "it ain't even safe around church folk anymore."

Reverend Vince checked the dressing room that had been assigned to the Voices of Triumphant Praise. No sign of Marcus. He knocked on a few other doors, then saw an exit door. He pushed it open and there, in the back of the auditorium on the loading dock, stood the three men.

"Uh, I'm gonna go back inside to listen to the groups," Calvin said. "Is that all right?" He looked between Marcus and Dwayne.

Reverend Vince strode up. He patted Calvin on the back. "That's a good idea, Brother Calvin. You go enjoy the show."

"Okay," Calvin said. Then he looked at Marcus and shook a finger. "It's not nice to hit people."

Marcus ran a hand over his dreads. "Yeah, I know, Cal. I know. You go get yourself a good seat."

Calvin grinned. "You coming, Dwayne?"

Dwayne looked from the minister to the soundman. Reverend Vince nodded. After another look at Marcus, Dwayne took his leave. "God don't like ugly."

Marcus jerked his arm. Reverend Vince stepped between the two. "Go on."

"Come on, Dwayne," Calvin said from the door. "We're gonna miss the Angelic Gospelaires."

With another tentative glance at the two men on the loading dock, Dwayne left. The back door clanged shut and Vince was left alone with Marcus.

"You want to tell me what that was all about?" the minister asked.

"Not particularly."

"Why don't you tell me anyway?"

"It's between me and Roger."

Reverend Vince shook his head. "It's between you and Roger when two grown men sit down and talk about their difficulties. When fists start flying, in the middle of a program that's supposed to be about celebrating the gospel in song, it's something else entirely. You've been picking a fight with Roger for weeks now. Who are you, Marcus?"

Marcus cut an eye at the preacher. "What kind of question is that?"

Vincent blocked the escape. "One I'd like to know the answer to. I see a lot, you know. I saw you and Margaret kiss one day. And just now," he said, aiming his head back toward the hall, "you were talking like you're avenging her. I notice she wasn't here tonight."

"She's gone."

"Where?"

"Ask Roger."

"Marcus, we're both grown men. Let's cut the games."

The younger man stared at the preacher. Then he turned away, staring out into the night. "I worked for the dealership a long time ago," he said. "I did some work for Margaret's father. Made myself useful."

"You were a bodyguard?"

Marcus turned and smirked at Reverend Vince. "Nothing so fancy as that. I just took care of stuff that needed taking care of, all right? And boy did I have a thing for Margaret. Of course, she didn't give me the time of day. Not that I asked. Her head was always someplace else. She probably doesn't even realize I worked for her daddy. She didn't pay much attention to the employees unless she needed something. She had a crazy ex though."

"Boyfriend?"

"Husband."

"Margaret was married?"

Marcus shrugged. "Not a lot of people know. He came around once or twice and I . . . I handled the situation."

"Did she know? That you were, er, handling things."

Marcus shook his head. "Didn't need to. I eventually went on to some other things."

"But you never forgot Margaret," Reverend Vince said. "Because you love her."

Marcus scowled. "I need to go."

Vincent stopped him with a hand on the younger man's shoulder. "You fell in love with her, but Margaret . . ." He paused, trying to figure out how such a scenario may have played out. "But Margaret wasn't interested in you," he said. "She's been interested in Roger."

"Roger dumped her tonight. I ran into her in the parking lot at a place where she was having dinner with him. She was upset, crying."

"And so you took it out on Roger. Physical violence doesn't solve problems. It just creates new ones."

"I don't need a sermon, preacher man." Marcus stalked away.

"Maybe you think you don't. But you could use some—"

Marcus yanked the door open and it slammed behind him, cutting off Vincent's words.

"You could use some Jesus," Vincent finished.

But there was no one on the loading dock to hear him.

No amount of chanting or candle burning helped Margaret that night. She pulled out her tarot cards, quickly laying them out on her dresser top. She cried out in frustration, not at all liking what she saw.

On some level, she'd always known that Roger didn't share her feelings. Every reading of the cards told her, but she'd refused to believe, instead following the beating of her heart and the dreams she'd harbored.

But the dream had ended tonight. Abruptly. Painfully.

The only nice thing about this horrid day had been running into Marcus. He seemed to show up in the oddest places, but Margaret had grown to enjoy his quiet company. She opened her jewelry box and pulled out the little tack pin he'd given her. Her guardian angel he'd called it.

Marcus was all right.

There was another man whose company she enjoyed. Rondell Isaacs was waiting for her in Charlottesville. He'd offered her a new chance, a new lease on life, a new job in a new city.

Margaret decided to jump at the chance.

She looked at the tarot cards, at that blasted Wheel of Fortune card. If it hadn't been coupled with The Tower of Destruction card, she'd have been able to glean a positive interpretation. But the cards, laid out in a ten-card spread, as well as her repeatedly battered and bruised heart, told her there was nothing here for her anymore. No reason to stay.

Angry, she swept the cards from the dresser and stomped to her closet. She pulled out her bags, a large duffel and a garment bag. She stuffed dresses, blouses, and skirts into the garment bag, then snatched up shoes and lingerie and dumped them into the duffel.

She could be in Charlottesville in less than three hours. The drive would do her good, she figured. Except she couldn't stop crying. She snatched up a remote control and powered on the sound system for a little music. Music always calmed her, always soothed her spirits.

Except this time, it wasn't a soothing tune she heard. The local gospel station was playing a cut from the Voices of Triumphant Praise *Spread the Word* CD.

"Araggh!" She cried in angry frustration. Margaret snatched a shoe from her duffel and threw a Prada at the system.

Sparks flew and glass crashed.

Then she got an idea.

She ran to the kitchen and pulled a tall kitchen bag from under the sink. Then, she went through her house grabbing every gospel music CD and cassette tape she owned. When she finished, the plastic bag was nearly full.

Margaret marched outside to her garbage can and dumped the bag in the trash. Then she spit on the bag.

"Good riddance."

Feeling inordinately pleased all of a sudden, she marched back into the house, calmly packed some additional items, and then tossed the bags in the trunk of her car. She locked the house and got on the road. Somewhere between the stop sign at the corner of her street and the exit for Interstate 64, she started crying again.

But by the time she hit the outskirts of Richmond, her tears had subsided. Throwing out every gospel music CD and cassette she owned had been cathartic. She tossed them out just as she'd toss Roger from her heart.

She drove the big Cadillac DeVille with an easy skill that had been honed since she was sixteen and got her first Caddy. When she arrived in Charlottesville, she'd start over. She'd make a happy life with Rondell Isaacs. She'd start fresh without any reminders of Roger McKenzie or gospel music.

Rondell would make her happy. He'd promised.

PART
FOUR

REQUIEM

25

Consider it pure joy, my brothers, whenever you face trials of many kinds, because you know that the testing of your faith develops perseverance.
—James 1:2-3

The lawyer recommended a bench trial for Roger.

"The fact that you waited twelve years to come forward with this, and then only because you were being blackmailed, is not going to endear you to a jury."

"Or to a judge," Roger said.

He and the Reverend Vincent Hedgepeth sat in the lawyer's downtown office.

"And I want to set the record straight," Roger said. "I didn't just spend the last decade of my life hiding from this. This has been on me all my adult life. It's always been on me. I've had nightmares . . ."

The attorney shook her head. "A jury—and a judge, for that matter—is going to want to know why you waited. If, as you say, it's been on your mind all this time, why didn't you turn yourself in the next day, or the next week, or the next year?"

"I thought you were going to defend me," Roger snapped.

"I am," she said. "But this is what you have to look forward to, particularly if you face a jury. That's why I recommend a trial by judge."

"Mrs. Davis," Vincent said, "isn't there a statute of limitations on these sorts of things?"

"Not manslaughter," she said. "And not if a case file remains open. A hit-and-run homicide would be on the books as an unsolved crime."

"So I'm going to jail?"

"Maybe," the attorney said. "You need to be prepared for that. We can go in and show your community work. Your church and ministry," she said with a nod toward Reverend Vince, "will be something in your favor. Your youth and state of mind at the time, well, that could go either way. Do you still drink?"

"I didn't 'drink' then, Mrs. Davis. I'd had a really, really rough period. I did something stupid and got drunk. Then I did something even more stupid by getting in a car to drive home. To tell you the truth, there's not a lot I remember about that night. Mostly it's just the images in the dreams."

He shook his head just recalling the recurring nightmares.

"But you're sure you hit someone? A person, not a deer or some other animal?"

Roger glanced at Reverend Vince before answering. The minister nodded, encouraging him to speak freely.

"I'm sure," he said after a moment. Then he pulled out a shoe box. Inside were all the newspaper clips about Janice Lydell's hit-and-run death. "And somebody knows. They know and they've been holding the information all this time, waiting to taunt me. To send me down, right when I'm . . ."

"Roger," Reverend Vince cautioned.

The attorney looked first at the minister and then at Roger. "Mr. McKenzie, if I'm going to represent you, I need to know everything."

Roger didn't say anything. It was Vincent who entered the breach. "A few weeks ago, there was some trouble within the choir. There were harsh words and hurt feelings."

"And?" she prompted, her gaze not leaving Roger's face.

"And I wouldn't put much stock in those notes," Vincent said.

"You think . . ." Roger started.

"I believe they were sent either by a woman who wanted to have a relationship with Roger or by a man in the choir who didn't like Roger."

Roger shook his head. "That makes no sense. If Margaret was supposedly in love with me, she wouldn't threaten me like that." He grimaced. "Now Marcus, on the other hand. Or Scottie?"

The lawyer scribbled something on her note pad. "Who are these people? Start with Margaret."

"She's a member—a former member, of my choir. We've been friends since college."

Mrs. Davis looked up. "So this is someone who may have known about the accident?"

"That's impossible," Roger answered.

"It's not only possible, it's probable," Vincent said. "You yourself told me she was always around."

Roger shook his head. "But that night, that particular night . . . I don't think so."

"Well, what is Margaret's last name and what's her address and number? I'd like to have that just in case we need her as a witness."

Roger passed along the information but added, "No one's seen her in days. Marcus is gone, too."

The minister shook his head. "I don't think that's relevant."

"I'll be the judge of what's relevant," the lawyer said.

So Reverend Vince told them what he knew, including what Glenna Anderson saw and had accurately suspected about Scottie.

"But Marcus," Roger said. "Margaret is what all his attitude was about?"

Vincent shrugged. "Apparently. Love will make people do things."

"Yeah, things that they know are wrong," Roger said.

The three looked at one another for a moment. Then, sighing, Roger leaned forward, his hands clasped together on the table.

"All right, Mrs. Davis. Tell me what I'm facing, the minimum and the maximum."

She consulted her clipboard, reviewing her notes for a moment. "Well, there are quite a few variables at work here. And each case is different."

Roger waved his hand in a forward motion. "I mean the law. What's the worst that could happen to me?"

"What you've described is what the law calls aggravated involuntary manslaughter," she said. "The minimum is a year in prison."

Roger winced. "And the maximum?"

"Twenty years."

Roger's mouth dropped open. "Twenty years? In prison?"

Mrs. Davis nodded. "That's a worst-case scenario."

Roger hung his head. Twenty years in prison for one night of stupidity. It hardly seemed fair.

"Of course," she added, "a judge could also find you not guilty. Or he, or she, could sentence you to some time and suspend most of it."

"What is that?" Reverend Vince asked.

"A suspended sentence is like time waived. If, for example, someone got a five-year sentence with four years suspended, he'd serve just a year." She shrugged. "And probably not even that with good behavior. But before we get to all of that, you have to decide how you want to proceed, Mr. McKenzie."

She told him her fees and gave him an estimate of how long it might take to resolve the case.

"And until then," Roger said, "I can just go about my business? Go to work, work with the choir?"

She nodded. "Everything we've said today is covered under attorney-client privilege."

Roger took a sudden and thorough look at his fingernails. "So," he slowly said, "I could decide to do nothing? I could go about my business with no one the wiser?"

The lawyer folded her arms, sat back in her chair, and studied him. "You could," she said with as much deliberation as Roger used asking the question. "But I'd like to think you won't."

Roger didn't meet her gaze.

She stared out the passenger-door window into the schoolyard. The nondescript white sedan they sat in blended into the atmosphere of the quiet tree-lined street. Young people milled about; a few sat in the grass talking as they ate lunch from sacks. The day was warm and sunny, perfect for the occasion.

It had taken a lot of begging and pleading—a lot of letters, phone calls, and faxes from doctors and social workers. But the day had finally come.

Glenna's gaze darted back and forth among the kids. "Where are they?"

"Right there," the woman at the wheel said. "The tall one in the blue jumpsuit talking to the girl with gold and blue ribbons in her hair."

Glenna glanced back at the social worker. "The one with the cheerleader outfit on?"

The woman nodded.

Glenna's gaze again took in the two girls. She held her hand to the window, her eyes wide.

"They're beautiful."

Tears formed at her eyes. "I . . . I just don't know what to say. They're beautiful."

She sat watching for a long time. The shorter girl turned, and Glenna gasped. "She looks just like my mama. That's my baby, Monet. I saw this picture once, in a book. It was drawn by a guy named Monet. Even though that's a man, I thought it sounded pretty. So I named my baby that. Monet. She's . . ." Glenna thought about it and looked back at the social worker. "Lord, I was just a little bit older than they are now when I had them. Ricki came first."

"They're twelve and eleven," the woman said.

Glenna nodded.

"Can I get out?"

"Ms. Anderson, you can't approach the girls. This visit is, itself, highly unusual. But . . ."

Tears filled Glenna's eyes. "I understand." She turned back and stared out the car window at the daughters she'd given up so long ago.

They were much better off now. They had happy lives. They looked healthy. They were enrolled in a private school. The social worker said a teacher and a doctor had adopted her babies. They probably went on vacations to places like Disney World, and took dance and music lessons. All the things Glenna never had and never would have been able to offer them.

Glenna was glad the doctor and his wife were raising her children. "They done good by my girls," she whispered. "They done good."

A bell rang and the students started gathering their lunch bags and backpacks.

Glenna twisted in the seat, watching as Ricki and Monet, laughing, skipped back into the school with their friends.

"Bye, babies. Mama loves you so much."

The choir and musicians of the Voices of Triumphant Praise stood at the rear doors of the church where the Reverend Vincent Hedgepeth was an associate pastor. They'd just had a fellowship dinner in honor of Glenna. She'd officially turned in her resignation from the choir.

She didn't want long or mushy goodbyes and had told the group as much. So they'd all eaten, laughed, and, of course, sung.

Now it was time.

"I don't know what the next part of this journey will be about," Glenna told them all. "But I'm glad to have been in communion with you all. Y'all been the family I always wanted. The friends I never had. Thank you for your love and for your fellowship."

"Where are you gonna go?" Lamont asked.

"Home," she said.

"Glenna," Roger whined.

She grinned at him. "For real," she said. "I'm going to swing by my house and see if there's anything I need to take care of. Then . . ." She shrugged.

"What about your daughters?" Krista asked.

Glenna's smile widened, transforming her thin face into a radiant vision that had the other choir members smiling in return.

"I saw them," she said, almost in awe.

"Where?"

"At their school. The agency I placed them with, they okay'd me seeing them, given that I'm . . ." She paused at Roger's pained expression. "They said they thought it would be all right. They were in the school yard, talking to each other at lunch. I was outside the gate and the lady pointed them out. They're in a good home, getting love and nurturing and toys for Christmas and dental checkups."

Glenna brought a thin hand to her chest and held it there as if trying to hold the emotions inside. "It was wonderful. They're all grown up."

Krista hugged Glenna. That hug was followed by ones from Calvin, Dwayne, and Mary, and then everybody was hugging everybody and tears flowed freely.

Outside, a car horn sounded.

Glenna wiped her eyes on her sleeve. "That's my taxi. You all come see me off. And quit all that crying. I'm trusting in God. You all should, too."

Everyone filed outside. Glenna turned and hugged Reverend Vince and then Elaine Hedgepeth. "Thank you, pastor. For everything."

The last hug went to Roger. "You be strong in the Lord, Roger."

He nodded. "Glenna . . ."

"Shh," she said. "All the words are over with now."

She faced the group, everyone was sort of drifting toward the cab at the curb. But Glenna held up a hand to stop them. "I can see my way to the door. You all stop looking so sad. Y'all acting like I'm dead already."

That brought a hesitant smile to a couple of faces.

The cab driver, seeing her struggle with the cane, got out and opened the door for her. Glenna put first her purse, then her cane inside.

"Remember now," she called back to her friends as she settled onto the backseat of the taxi. "God won't take you anywhere his mercy won't keep you."

Glenna Anderson died three weeks later.

The Voices of Triumphant Praise sang at her funeral.

EPILOGUE

Margaret Hall-Stuart stood in the faculty house, sipping a bit of cider from a delicate china cup. She admired the fine detail of the cup, and the rim outlined in twenty-four-karat gold. The warm cider felt good on the cool fall night. She'd spent the afternoon talking with her colleagues, enjoying her stature, basking in the glow of her newly launched office. She was an up-and-comer on campus, having used all of her energy and talent in establishing her directorship and showcasing her skills.

All the hires had been made. She'd bought and settled into a house, a lovely Tudor tucked in a quiet cul-de-sac in an established and affluent neighborhood in Charlottesville. The University of Virginia area with its pastoral surroundings was just what she'd needed to renew her mind and spirit.

She and Rondell were happy. Just last night they'd celebrated their six-month anniversary of exclusive dating. Margaret was sure that he'd propose soon. He'd hinted as much.

The life she lived these days proved that the tarot wasn't always right. Just today, for example, her reading warned of impending disaster. But the only trouble she could see on the horizon would be if she didn't get another of the delicious shrimp hors d'oeuvres. She snagged one from a passing waiter, nibbled it and then took another sip of cider.

Margaret smiled. All was right in her world. Finally. She'd even heard from Marcus. He'd left Roger and those hypocrites in that choir shortly after Margaret had.

The melodic tinkling of a silver spoon on a crystal goblet drew everyone's attention to the front of the room. Near a roaring fireplace, the president of the university asked everyone to gather around.

"We have a special surprise tonight," he said. "In addition to celebrating the terrific work of our newest director, Margaret Hall-Stuart . . ."

Heads turned toward her and glasses were raised in salute. Margaret beamed at the compliment and the attention and gave a slight nod of her head acknowledging the recognition from the top man.

". . . We have a family member to welcome home," the president said. He held out a hand, and a stunning woman stepped forward. A murmur of surprise and delight filled the room.

"Where'd he go?" the university president said as he looked around him in the crowd. His smile was bright when he spotted the person he was looking for. "There you are. Come on up here."

With an arm around the waist of the woman and the man, the president continued his speech. "I'd like to introduce to some of you Dr. Nicole Sheppard-Isaacs. She's just returned to us after a six-month sabbatical to Oxford, where I'm told she acquitted herself and the university very well with her research. Rondell, I know you're as proud of your wife as we are."

The sound of loud cheers and applause concealed the crash of bone china shattering on the hardwood floor.

Roger folded his hands under his head and stretched out, getting comfortable. The song on the radio made him smile every time he heard it. The first track on the *Testing of Your Faith* CD was Roger's favorite. It opened with Glenna's husky voice giving part of her testimony.

"Cue music," he said as Glenna's voice faded and the introductory chords to the song started just as they had after the final recording and studio work on the CD.

Roger closed his eyes as the sopranos and altos started to hum the melody. And then came the words that he had written over the course of a weekend that seemed so long ago.

"Consider it joy, my brother, when the world has got you down. Consider it joy, my sister, when the storm clouds make you frown. Count it all joy, my people, when the trials they seem so long. For the trial is but a test. And the test will measure your faith. But when the storm is finally over, and that rainbow shines again, you'll consider it joy. You'll consider it joy. And you'll have a test-ti-mony. Test-ti-mony. So count it all joy."

The music faded, the humming started again, and then Roger heard his own voice giving testimony.

"A long time ago, I did I something. I sinned in the eyes of God and man. But I'm here to tell you tonight, that God is a forgiving God. The price we pay for our sin is nothing compared to the ultimate price that Jesus paid for you and for me."

Roger didn't have to listen to the rest; his mind wandered back to that night when the choir performed "Testimony" for the first time. It was several months after Glenna's death. The choir members had all recorded their testimonies in the studio, but no one except Roger and Tyrone had heard the final cuts.

The church was packed for the live recording of the CD. And the spirit had moved the entire night.

The "Testimony" track was getting a lot of air time all over the country, and there was talk of a possible Grammy nomination.

Roger smiled. All of his dreams for the choir were coming true. And his nightmares had long since faded into distant memories. All but one, that is.

A loud buzzer sounded and the clang of metal slamming onto metal echoed all around him.

"Lights out!" a guard barked. The lights throughout the cell block shut off, casting the prisoners in darkness for the night.

Roger turned down the volume on his small radio. He had the upper bunk in the cell, his home for the next eight years. He pulled his thin gray blanket up over his body and crossed his hands on his chest. He said his prayers, then turned over and went to sleep.

TESTIMONY

FELICIA MASON

This Reader's Guide and Discussion Questions section is designed to assist discussion in and among reader groups. The first eight questions relate to characters in the novel TESTIMONY. The next group, questions nine to twelve, are about the story, and the remaining ones are designed to get you talking about some of the contemporary issues in gospel music and the church.

DISCUSSION QUESTIONS

1. Which character in *Testimony* did you feel the most empathy with? Why and how did that character speak to you?

2. Who do you think is the strongest character? Why? How did that person's strength reflect on the other characters?

3. Roger McKenzie, the choir director, wanted to wield a lot of influence in the gospel music industry. Some would argue that strong leadership and vision is healthy. Others would say it's a built-in recipe for ego-tripping and disaster. What do you think?

4. Did you expect Roger's dilemma to be the one it was? Roger obviously had a difficult choice to make. Did he choose the right path? Given the same circumstances in your own life, what would you have done?

5. Tyrone and Georgie's marriage was a source of pride and turmoil. To what degree do you think American marriages are unions of love? Unions of convenience? How would your relationship with your significant other have been affected if given the same circumstances as Tyrone and Georgie's?

6. What did you think about Glenna?

7. Is too much expected of pastors and spiritual leaders today? If you'd been placed in the Reverend Vincent Hedgepeth's shoes, how would you deal with the myriad problems and issues?

8. Have you ever met anyone like Margaret? Did you find yourself feeling sorry for her or being angry with her?

9. The choir adopted as its motto: "Christians aren't perfect, just forgiven." Given what you now know about the choir members in *Testimony*, what do you think their motto should have been? Do they owe their listeners and fans true testimony, or does the concept of "saved by grace" exonerate them?

10. To what extent, if any, do you think church people rely on psychics, clairvoyants, and tarot readings?

11. What is the significance of the names of the four parts of *Testimony:* ensemble, solo, odeum, requiem?

12. Have you ever been a part of a church, community, or school choir? In what ways did your experiences mirror or differ from the ones in *Testimony?*

13. Why are choirs and creative groups so prone to self-defeating behaviors?

14. How does it make you feel about organized religion when you see church people doing the same things as the unchurched?

15. What is your testimony?

An Exclusive Interview with the Author of *Testimony,*
Felicia Mason

Felicia Mason is a motivational speaker and award-winning author. She took time from her schedule to answer some questions about her new novel, *Testimony.*

1. This book and its story line are a departure for you. Why this type of book, and why now?

I've wanted to do this story for a while. If by departure you mean it's not romance, well, it's not. I've been writing all my life, and I write some of everything. When I got serious about writing books, the first story idea I reached for was a romantic one. Two characters and their love story called to me the most, so I sat down and wrote it. That story became *For the Love of You.*

As time passed, I became known for writing romance, and it was difficult either to find the time to write the other stories I was interested in or to have them accepted by publishers. Karen Thomas, my editor at Kensington, is very open to new ideas, and for that I'm very grateful. I struggled with which story idea to develop for her for this project, and *Testimony* kept bubbling to the top.

2. You refer to story ideas as if there's a store or fountain you go to.

That's funny. It's more of a file than a store, and I like the fountain analogy. When an idea for a short story or novel or play comes to me, I write it down. I date it and stick it in a file. When I write short stories I usually go to the file to see what looks like a good idea for whatever I'm in the mood for.

When it comes to the novels, though, I let the characters speak to me. They tell me which story comes next.

Usually, the ideas for books have been knocking around in my head for a few years before I actually write them. By the time I sit down to write, the characters are so real to me they are like people I've come to know and love—or hate, as the case may be. The book ideas that don't have that percolating time are the ones that I don't seem connected to. They never work out right and I always end up returning to something that's stronger, more real to me.

3. Are any of the characters in *Testimony* based on real people?

No. I don't do that. I know there are authors who base their fiction on real people. That's just not something I'm comfortable with.

I hope that as people read *Testimony,* they will see in the characters traits of people they know.

One of the biggest compliments I get from readers is when they tell me that a specific character in one of my books was "just like my . . ." (and here fill in the blank—sister, mother, cousin, brother, minister, etc.) When people tell me that, I know I've hit just the right universal theme.

I've been in and around church all my life. My father is a minister, so is a cousin. And an uncle was the long-time pastor of the family church back home. I've been singing and traveling with choirs since I was in junior high school. I even had the misfortune of having to play piano for a church choir when I was a teenager. I hated it so much, I didn't even want the money. I'm a terrible piano player and haven't touched the keys in years.

What I'm saying is that in *Testimony,* this was territory I knew well.

4. So you follow the "write what you know" philosophy?

Not exactly. I'm a journalist by profession. I started off as a reporter in Pittsburgh. I've been a reporter, a copy editor, an editorial writer, an editor, a columnist, and I even taught journalism as a college professor. One thing that journalists excel at is knowing a little about a lot. They have to in order to do their jobs. So while in this case, *Testimony* is a book about a subject that I'm well acquainted with, as a rule I say instead of writing what you know, write what you don't know and learn something.

I've had a terrific time learning about all sorts of things I had little or no knowledge about before I started writing fiction.

5. What are some examples?

Oh, goodness. Let's see. Well, in *Testimony* it was tarot. I knew nothing at all about that. Researching other stories, I've learned about the U.S. Marshals Service, court stenographers, truck driving, pop music producers, art history. It really depends on the story. I also keep clip files on topics that interest me. And I have a pretty extensive collection of research books on everything from religion to relationships.

6. What, if anything, surprised you about this book?

The biggest surprise was Reverend Vince. He was supposed to be a minor character, just someone I tossed in to give the main characters a sounding board when they were at one another's throats. By midway through the book, though, Reverend Vince emerged as a leader. I just let it roll to see what might happen. It worked, so I left it and him alone.

7. Where did the idea for *Testimony* come from?

It was a couple of things. Several years ago I was at a friend's house in Pennsylvania. Her mother had a video of a gospel choir concert on, and it opened with a couple of singers saying why they like singing. That was the first bit of inspiration.

The second came while I was at a gospel concert. I love watching choir directors work. The best ones really get into it. At this concert, my seat was at an odd angle, so instead of watching the directors, I got to see a lot of the backstage stuff: what was going on as the choirs and groups were preparing to go onstage. The sound system at the hall was horrible, so my mind really drifted into the "What if?" state. I jotted down some notes and stuck them in my story idea file.

8. You've written connected books. Is there a sequel in the works for this story?

The connected books and stories have come about as a result of a secondary character in a story being so intriguing that even as I was writing the first book, I began taking notes on the secondary character.

But no, there is no sequel in the works to *Testimony*. But who knows what may be down the line.

9. If you were to write another book with these characters, which character would intrigue you the most?

You won't let this one go, huh? Well, actually, there were two characters in *Testimony* who really intrigued me. The first was Glenna. The second was Margaret. Glenna obviously isn't going to have any other story. As for Margaret, she intrigued me because she was so conflicted. But she had her closure in this book.

10. You divided the book into four parts. Why?

This is actually something I did toward the end of the writing. I realized that there were some definite departure points for the story and for the characters. The names, of course, are all music-related and directly correspond with what's going on in the story. In Ensemble, the first part, the entire choir is together. In Part Two, Solo, I addressed the individual story lines. Since there are basically four separate story lines going on, I thought concentrating on each one exclusively—or solo—would be a good approach.

Part Three, Odeum, takes its name from the musical term for a concert hall. And that's the major focus of the section after the choir members get themselves together to some degree.

As for the last part, Requiem, well, that pretty much explains itself. As music for the dead, Mozart's "Requiem in D Minor" comes to mind as a haunting example. In the case of the characters in *Testimony,* the death is not just a single physical one. Glenna has what some might call the easiest death because she's secure about her future in the afterlife. She's tied up all of her loose ends and can die in relative peace. Roger and Margaret, however, their "deaths" are symbolic and not at all easy, emotionally or intellectually.

11. What other books have you written?

Testimony is my eighth published novel. The first six were romances published by the groundbreaking Arabesque line of African-American romance. Those books included two that won awards and one that was made into a television movie. My seventh novel is one you can't get. It was a serial novel I wrote with reader input for the *Daily Press,* the newspaper I worked for for twelve years. It was published two chapters a week for a little more than a year; at the end of every chapter readers were invited to determine where the story went next.

I've also written eight novellas, which have won some awards, and I've had poetry and short stories published. For information on my books, check my Web site by logging on to www.geocities.com/Paris/Gallery/9250/

12. What comes next?

Vacation. I love to travel and I'm overdue for a trip.

Oh, you mean what book? Well, I'll just have to see which characters leap forward saying "Me next!"